VANQUISH

THE XANDER KING SERIES

XK2

The Xander King Series
by Bradley Wright

WHISKEY & ROSES
VANQUISH

VANQUISH

Bradley Wright/King's Ransom Books
www.bradleywrightauthor.com

Vanquish/ Bradley Wright. -- 1st ed.
ISBN **978-0997392616**

For Danica
Three 2.

"People are like stained glass windows; they sparkle and shine when the sun is out, but when the darkness sets in, their true beauty is revealed only if there is light within."

-Elizabeth Kubler-Ross

"If you prick us do we not bleed? If you tickle us do we not laugh? If you poison us do we not die? And if you wrong us shall we not revenge?"

-William Shakespeare

VANQUISH

Life-Threatening News Travels Fast

"Xander killed the wrong man."

Sam's blood ran cold. Her iPhone dropped into her lap. Her body was too paralyzed by shock to pick it up and respond.

"Hello? Sam? Sam, are you there?" Special Agent Sarah Gilbright called to her from the other end of the line. She knew this information would be devastating to Sam, so she gave it a moment to sink in as she mashed the gas pedal to the floor. Her rented Ford Taurus screamed at her as she swerved onto Versailles Road in Lexington, Kentucky, her heart thudding in her chest.

Sam could hear muffled noises coming from the phone, but her mind followed the memory of killing Sanharib Khatib with her own bare hands, no more than a week ago. Though it caught her off guard, she wasn't completely surprised by the news. She told Xander before they ever flew to Syria that it was possible that Khatib wasn't the right target. Her shock stemmed from the immediate reality that this would devastate Xander. She had no idea how she would tell him that his parents' killer was still alive. No clue how she would reveal that his friend Sean, even though he died valiantly while destroying a terrorist cell, he didn't die helping to avenge Xander's mortal enemy as they had thought.

"Sam. Sam, I know this is terrible news, but unfortunately, it's not the worst of it. I need you to talk to me. Sam!"

Sam finally broke her trance from the yellow-orange flames that crackled in the fireplace in front of her. She picked up the phone while she steadied her nerves.

"Did you say that wasn't the worst of it? How could—"

"Sam, Xander is in danger."

"Danger? Xander is fine. He's playing on a yacht in the Virgin Islands with Kyle and a few young ladies they picked up along the way."

"I've been trying to contact him for the last half hour, and he hasn't answered. That's the reason I'm talking to you. They know where he is, Sam. And my team that I left in Moscow last week, while you all were in Syria hunting Khatib, has information that a jet full of ex-KGB, sent by Vitalii Dragov, is on its way to the Virgin Islands right now as we speak."

"Vitalii Dragov? The Russian mafia? Why would they—"

"It's a preemptive strike. Someone in the CIA leaked information to Dragov that Xander King was looking for his parents' murderer. They are going to the Virgin Islands to kill Xander. I can explain everything on our way."

"On our way? I don't—"

"Sam! We don't have time for this. You're at Xander's mansion, right?"

2

"R-right . . . in Lexington," Sam said in a daze, her mind running into overdrive as she tried to wrap her head around all that was happening.

Sarah swerved in and out of traffic as she barreled toward Xander's horse farm.

"Then I'm assuming you have access to your choice of weapons? Grab everything we'll need to thwart an attack on a yacht. We don't have a minute to spare. Dragov's plane is scheduled to land in St. Thomas in just three hours and twenty minutes. If we're incredibly lucky, that will give us enough time to get there before it's too late."

"But Xander's plane isn't here. We have no way of getting there—"

"I have a jet waiting at the Bluegrass Airport. A local businessman, Tom Wright, happened to be in town and he is letting us use it. Sam, just do what I ask and do it now if you ever want to see Xander alive again. I'll be there in ten minutes."

Before Sam could respond—not that she could have anyway—she heard the line click off. Her emotions had gotten the better of her during that call. She swallowed hard and brought them under control. She kicked back her chair, dialed Xander's cell phone, and made her way to the weapon room. The quiver in her lip stopped and the steel returned to her nerves. No one was going to kill Xander King tonight.

Not on her watch.

Another Day in Paradise

The sun began to settle on top of the water, hovering, ready to dip its fiery toe. The evening sky's orange light cast over the crystal blue waters fifteen miles off the coast of Virgin Gorda, British Virgin Islands. Seagulls cooed to each other as they floated in front of the fiery ball of life, and the warm breeze said hello in the gentlest of ways. The local fishermen had already called it a day and the other leisure boats had done the same. That is why the two-hundred-foot, three-story yacht, anchored in the middle of the ocean, had the most unobstructed view of that sinking sun in all of the Caribbean.

At least Xander King thought so. And let's be honest, that's all that really mattered to him.

The girls were dancing to some completely annoying electronic dance song, by one of those talentless hacks of a DJ on the top deck. Kyle Hamilton—Xander's oldest friend in the world—took a break to walk over to Xander, who was perched on an oversized half-moon lounge chair on the raised deck that overlooked the girls having a blast in front of that beautiful sunset. Sweat-drenched from dance, Kyle plopped down beside Xander, put his arm around him, and gave his glass of King's Ransom bourbon a clink.

"I don't know what's more beautiful, that sunset or those five gorgeous young ladies dancing in those bikinis." Kyle pointed casually in the direction of the beautiful butterflies fluttering about on the back of the yacht.

Xander smiled and raised his glass, his dark hair blowing in the warm and salty breeze.

"Yes, you do."

"You're right, I do." Kyle winked. "I'll tell you what isn't beautiful, this god-awful music. If you can even call it music. You'd have to be on drugs to like listening to this shit . . . Got any to put me out of my misery?"

"I know, it just drones on and on, doesn't it? No heart, no soul." Xander sipped his drink and took a pull from his Davidoff Oro Blanco cigar. Ah, now there was some soul. He puffed the sweet cigar smoke out through a relaxed, half-open mouth and watched it plume out against the tangerine skyline.

"Can I plug your phone in? I know you have better music than this."

"I do, but it's dead."

"Dead? Xander King with a dead cell phone? I never thought I'd see the day."

Kyle took the back of Xander's neck in his hand, squeezed it, and gave it a loving pat.

"I'm loving the new X."

"New X? What do you mean?"

"I don't know, ever since we took out Khatib, you've just been, well, relaxed."

"Yeah?"

"Yeah." Kyle sighed, relaxed. His six-foot-three-inch frame sprawled out across the lounge chair. He and Xander were similar in height, but Xander had a good fifteen pounds of muscle on his fit and trim friend.

"I must say, I do feel like a weight has been lifted."

Xander was speaking of the now dead, 160-pound boulder of cutthroat, murderous terrorist, to be exact.

Xander sat his cigar on the edge of the heavy glass ashtray, ran a hand through his hair, and let out a sigh. Kyle removed his grip from Xander's neck and turned to face him.

"Uh, oh. What is it?" Kyle asked, sensing something weighing on Xander's mind.

"Nothing."

"Come on, X. Let me guess . . . Natalie?"

Kyle was of course referring to Hollywood sweetheart Natalie Rockwell. He could tell the wounds from Xander's fling with her were still fresh; he just hadn't wanted to say anything. Before Xander was forced to answer yes and give some sappy spiel about how he couldn't get Natalie off his mind even though he knew they couldn't be together, the ladies had finished dancing and were walking over to see what the two of them were up to.

Saved by the bell. Or *belles*, as it were.

"Ladies." Xander scooted away from Kyle and made room for all five of the gorgeous women, whom they had met at the roulette table in the pool casino at Caesars Palace in Las Vegas just a few hours ago. Xander took Kyle there as he had promised a few days ago when they were in the plane on their way to Syria. Xander was drawn by the promise of high stakes poker while Kyle's interests never reached far beyond the ladies. The two of them were on a good run at the pool casino under the waterfall when they noticed a group of the sexiest five women they had ever laid their eyes on, who were playing blackjack at the table next to them. After a couple of mutual admiring glances shared between the two groups, Xander leaned back and spoke to the perfectly tanned, long-legged blonde in the emerald-green bikini with the matching, and sparkling, emerald-green eyes. One perfectly braided strip of hair stood out playfully among the rest of her stick-straight strands.

"Quick," Xander said, "what's your name, where are you from, and what is your favorite number?" Xander gave his most sultry smile. A smile most naturally brought on by a never-ending river of bourbon.

The blonde tucked her hair back behind her ear, gave a mind-melting smile of her own, and answered as the dealer started the little white ball around the roulette wheel. "Kelly, Newport Beach, twenty-one."

Xander gave her a wink, leaned back to his table, and pushed a tall stack of chips over to the red number-twenty-one square in the middle of the table. Kelly's jaw dropped and she stood up to get a better look.

"Whoa, how much money is that?"

The dealer centered the chips on the number and politely answered for Xander.

"Table maximum."

Kelly's eyes, which matched the green felt of the roulette table, went from the stack of chips to the little black sign that stated the minimum and maximum bets for the table, then back to Xander.

"Five-thousand dollars? Are you crazy?"

If she only knew.

Kyle smiled and jumped up to his feet as well, and the waist-high pool water swirled all around them in his wake. Kelly's four friends gathered around her when they heard the outrageous amount that Xander had bet. They were intrigued by the fact that he bet it just because it was the favorite number of a woman he had never even met before. As the ball danced around the roulette wheel, Kelly's dark-haired friend asked for clarification.

"Holy shit, how much will he win if it lands on twenty-one?"

"The odds are thirty-five to one on any single number, ma'am," the dealer answered. When he saw only a blank look on the pretty brunette's face staring back at him, he finished the math for her. "That's $175,000."

The waterfall that separated the casino pool from the Garden of the Gods Oasis continued to rush, and gasps from the girls filled the rest of the air around them. The ball clinked a couple more times along the raised slats of the wheel that separated the numbers, teetered like it was going to stop on six, then made one final jump into the number-twenty-one slot.

The roar from the seven of them and the twenty some-odd people looking on from the bar filled the entire outdoor pool area at Caesars. Kyle and Xander jumped up from the table splashing wildly, shared celebratory hugs with the girls, and ordered shots of Don Julio Tequila Blanco for everyone around them to celebrate.

Needless to say, Xander King was a hit at Caesars.

The shots arrived and a celebratory toast was offered. Another crowd roar of appreciation rattled the entire hotel casino. Kelly pulled Xander aside and asked him just how he intended to reward her for the big win. And just like that, Xander called Bob and told him to fire up the jet. One hour later they left McCarron International Airport on Xander's Gulfstream G650 luxury private jet, and that's how they all ended up on Xander's humble *little* yacht in the middle of a gorgeous Virgin Island sunset. All that whirlwind of the day could now be seen in Kelly's weary eyes as she took a seat in Xander's lap.

"Wow. I swear, Xander, I've never had so much fun in my entire life. When I woke up this morning in Las Vegas, I never in my wildest dreams would have thought that I would end the day on the lap of a gorgeous man, on a gorgeous yacht, anchored in the middle of the turquoise waters of the Caribbean. Crazy."

Xander admired the twinkle in her eyes as the sun disappeared behind her. Kelly was as beautiful a woman as he had ever seen. And while staring into her eyes, it became apparent that the steady flow of liquor hadn't done a thing to damper the usefulness of his equipment. This fact became evident to her as well after a long, passionate kiss. When she felt him bulge against her bottom, she backed away with a wry smile, then quickly straddled him, pressing her warmth against him. The weariness in her eyes turned to a bright shade of wild.

"Now this . . . is my kind of party!" Kyle shouted as he pulled the brunette—Angie—onto his lap. The soft yellow lights lit up the large deck area, casting a dream-like glow over the seven of them.

Amidst another shot of bourbon for everyone in the group, a man came out from the interior cabin dressed in his yacht whites.

"Xander?"

"Hey Tony, what's up?"

"Dinner is ready. Would you like to enjoy it on the outdoor dining table or at the dining room table inside?"

Xander looked from Tony to Kelly and found her biting her lip in anticipation, looking a lot more like she'd rather have him for dinner. Then he looked over at the others and found they had zero interest in dinner themselves.

"What are we having tonight?"

"Your favorite of course, pizza."

Xander nodded and turned to Kyle and the girls. "You all okay with cold pizza later?" The answer was a resounding yes. He turned back to Tony, "Just put it in the fridge if you don't mind. We'll come down and heat it up later. We're having a little too much fun right now."

"Of course. Cold pizza is better anyway."

"Thanks, Tony. We're good up here if you want to give everyone the rest of the night off."

"Thank you, sir. I'll do that. Don't do anything I wouldn't do."

"Can't make any promises."

Tony laughed, gave Xander a fist bump, and walked back inside. Kelly leaned over, kissed Xander on the neck, and whispered in his ear.

"There anywhere more private we can go?"

She ended the question with a nibble at the bottom of his earlobe. He felt her breasts pressing against his chest and her hand gently caressing him. The almost shy, "aw-shucks" woman he first spoke to in Vegas was currently nowhere to be found. Thank God. Xander wrapped his hands around her, picking her up as he stood from the lounge chair.

"You all gonna be okay up here for a while?" Xander asked the group.

Kyle leaned back in his seat, spread his arms out wide, and worked up the biggest shit-eatin' grin he could muster.

"I got everything I could ever want right here, brother."

Xander knew just how much his friend meant that and couldn't help but laugh to himself. He smiled and made eyes back and forth between Kyle and the girls.

"Perfect. You girls okay?"

They said they were perfect. Xander dipped Kelly over, and as if she could read his mind, she grabbed the bottle of King's Ransom.

"Perfect. There is plenty more to drink behind the bar, and the bedrooms are down the hall on the left and the right. We'll see you in the morning." Xander gave them a wink, and Kelly raised her arms in the air as he carried her inside the cabin, headed straight for the master suite.

This is going to be one hell of a night, he thought to himself as he laid her on the bed and she undid her top.

If only Xander had turned on his cell phone and checked his messages. Then he would have seen just how right he was about what kind of night it was going to be.

Hell.

Paradise Lost

A couple of hours, half a bottle of bourbon, and two magical
sexual encounters with the scintillating Kelly later, Xander was
awoken by a weighted pressure in his bladder. A fog hung over
his brain and he rubbed his eyes to try to clear it.

Still drunk.

The curtain that covered a rather amazing view of the ocean
from the bed had separated from where it met the wall, and a
strong ray of moonlight poured in, uncovering yet another
amazing view. Kelly. The beam of yellow-white light lay
perfectly across Kelly's bare torso. She was lying on her back,
the sheet just high enough to cover her most private area, one
arm across her stomach and the other resting back behind her
head. If he were in charge of a sexy photo shoot, he wouldn't
have changed a damn thing. Her head was turned toward his,
and even as she slept, she looked flawless. He became lost in
her beauty until his bladder reminded him of the reason he had

awoken. He really had to go. Before he got up, however, he couldn't help but lean over and run his lips along the outside of her breast, the softest and most supple skin on a woman's body. Kelly opened her eyes, smiled, and ran her hand through his hair, tracing her thumb over his permanent five o'clock shadow, then up along his razor-sharp cheekbone.

"I'll be right back, beautiful. You need some water?"

She nodded her head and mouthed the words "thank you." He kissed her forehead and swung himself up and out of bed. It wasn't until the first step that his body reminded him just how drunk he still was. He wobbled twice, staggered once, and then proceeded more cautiously toward the bathroom. After he finished in the restroom, he staggered back to bed, water in hand.

Kelly sat up, took a big swig of water, and let out a sigh.

"It's crazy how delicious something plain like water can be when you really need it, isn't it?"

Xander laughed.

"It is. And it's startling how fantastic you look in the light of the moon."

Xander took her water and set it on the nightstand, then took her once again in his arms. His appetite for her body was insatiable. All he could think about, drunken haze and all, was being with her again. Just as the heat began to rise between them, Xander heard something in the distance. He leaned back from on top of her and cocked his head toward the ceiling. Though it had to be more than a mile away, it wasn't a sound that Xander, after years as a Navy SEAL, could ever mistake.

"A helicopter," he said aloud, to no one in particular.

Kelly pulled him back toward her, but Xander's mind had already made the leap. He didn't know who it was or what they wanted, but he knew it wasn't good. Fortunately for everyone on the boat, Xander had prepared for this moment, and he had prepared his yacht and crew as well.

"Xander? What's wrong? Are you okay?"

A flashback ripped through his mind. What he was about to tell Kelly, he had told Natalie almost the very same thing before his home in Lexington had been invaded in the middle of the night.

"Kelly." He took her face gently between his hands. "I need you to listen to me now, and I need you to do exactly what I say. Okay?"

He looked up to the ceiling again as the helicopter was right above them now. He didn't have time to wonder who it was. He only had time to get everyone to safety. It sure would help if he wasn't still hammered drunk.

"Xander, you're scaring me."

"Good. Now, I'm about to hit a button that will let the crew know that there is danger. They will be ready for you and your friends in a secured room at the bottom of the boat. Go right now and get them down there. I don't care if you have to carry them."

"Secured room? Xand—"

"Kelly, this is not a game."

Either it was the tone of his voice or the depth of seriousness on his face that made the difference, but she got the picture and bolted out of bed. She grabbed a robe from the chair in the corner and started down the stairs. She stopped just before disappearing.

"You're coming, right?"

"Yes, I'll be there in a minute," Xander answered as he hit a button on the wall beside the headboard. It lit up red and a loud, continuous alarm—*MOCK! MOCK! MOCK!*—began to blare throughout the entire yacht. Between each siren blare he could hear the thumping of the helicopter rotors directly above them.

This was about to get ugly.

Xander knew as soon as Kyle heard the alarm he would get the ladies where they needed to be. They had been over this every time they boarded the boat. Xander's only concern, as was his concern for himself, is that Kyle might be too drunk. Just as that thought hit him he heard the distinct sound of boots hitting the top of the boat above him, and he knew they had been boarded. He moved quickly down to the floor and pulled a long, hard-leather case out from under the bed. He almost face-planted as he hit his knees, the liquor still heavy in his bloodstream. This was the worst-case scenario. Innocent people on his yacht and he wasn't even properly sober to defend himself, or them.

"Pull it together, X," he said to the empty room. He then gave his head a shake, hauled the case on top of the bed, and pulled on his white linen pants. He opened the case, grabbed the sawed-off shotgun with a pistol grip, strapped Rambo—his trusty knife—to his leg, and, as best he could, readied himself for a fight.

"Xander still hasn't answered his cell," Sam announced to Sarah. The look of worry on Sarah's face matched the feeling deep in the pit of Sam's gut. When they landed the jet at Cyril E. King Airport on the island of St. Thomas, they immediately jumped on a waiting helicopter. The pilot informed her that another helicopter had left there no more than five minutes before them. Nine men dressed in tactical gear, carrying several large cases. He had no idea where they were headed.

Sam did.

Fortunately, Sam kept a tracking device on each of Xander's toys, so she gave the pilot the yacht's exact coordinates. While Sarah strapped on her bulletproof vest, Sam readied the rope for a quick rappel down to the boat.

"How far out are we, Sam?" Sarah asked over the thump of the chopper's rotors.

"Three minutes."

"Nine men did he say? Oh God. Sam, will we be too late?"

Sam grabbed Sarah's worried eyes with a hard gaze.

"If he's sober? He'll have already taken them out. If he's drunk—"

She left it at that. Sarah gave a worried nod. Every indication had been that Xander and Kyle had been celebrating all day. Sam had mentioned that the last time she spoke with him, he had just boarded the jet in Las Vegas. Sarah tried not to let it show that she was bothered when Sam had mentioned the group of women tagging along. She tried, but she didn't think she had succeeded. Sam had just shaken her head with a laugh. "Boys will be boys," she said. Sarah knew she had no right to be jealous. Hell, she hadn't even spoken more than a few sentences to him. But the last six months of her life in the CIA had been dedicated solely to Xander.

"Have you had a lot of field training, Sarah?" Sam asked as she clipped the rappel rope to her harness.

Sarah shook out of her daze.

"I know how to put a bullet in someone's head, if that's what you mean."

"That's exactly what I mean." Sam turned her head toward the window and noticed a faint glow rising from the dark ocean off in the distance. Sam loaded her sniper rifle. "There it is. You ready?"

Sarah cocked the hammer back on her nine-millimeter and clipped the rappel rope to her harness.

"Let's get these assholes."

Xander had stumbled his way down to the main level of the yacht. There were two entrances from that level, the sliding doors leading out to the deck at the back end of the yacht, and the service entrance on the starboard side that led into the kitchen. Xander knew that if it were him, he would enter through the kitchen. That is why he went directly to the oven, turned it on broil, and stuffed it with as many paper towels and napkins his blurred vision could find. The smoke would give him an advantage. He would need every single one he could get.

He was now posted by the large sliding glass doors that led from a large living room out to the deck. The sheer white curtains were closed so he knew no one could see in, but the yellow lights still glowing on the deck would enable him to see shadows as they passed. Listening for the men would be futile with the alarm continuing to blast. He positioned himself where he could see someone entering either from outside or from the kitchen where a steady rise of smoke now emerged. He also could keep an eye on the stairway that led down to the service quarters and to the secured room. The only light where he stood was the red alarm light flashing on and off, momentarily turning everything red, then everything black. It was playing tricks on his inebriated eyes, further compounding his condition.

At that moment a shadow passed outside along the deck, causing a flicker in the yellow lights beyond the curtains. Then another shadow, then another and another. Four men. So far. Xander slowly opened the sliding door and slinked out onto the deck, the shotgun extended in front of him. The sound of the alarm wasn't as loud outside, so he could hear the helicopter had moved on. He could, however, still hear it out in the distance. If he wasn't mistaken, it was getting closer again.

Weird.

He checked the stairs that went up toward the wheelhouse, where the men had come from, and when he moved his shotgun around, it felt like slow motion. Xander knew his reaction time wasn't up to his standard, and it was at that moment that he decided waiting for them to make a move would be a massive mistake.

He needed to go on the offensive.

Just as that revelation washed over him, a man walked around the corner and Xander blasted him with twelve-gauge power. The jolt of the slug against the man's protective vest was so hard it blew him off the side of the boat. A moment later, Xander heard his splash.

A full half-second slow. Xander internally assessed his reaction time of that shot. He knew that much delay could be just long enough to get himself killed.

"Put gun down, Xander King!"

Xander couldn't see anyone, but he certainly heard the Russian in the man's accent. Xander racked the slide on his shotgun and moved toward the long walkway down the side of the yacht where the first man had come from.

"Put gun down now! Or friend dies!" a man's voice shouted from above Xander.

They have Kyle.

Just then two more men came out from the living room and pointed their Uzis at Xander. Pops from their guns clamored through the night air, and Xander dove for the walkway around the corner. On his way down to the ground, he felt a burning pain sear through his left calf muscle, and he fired his shotgun at the man who had been waiting for him on that side of the yacht. The dark-haired man's head disappeared in a pink mist. At least he thought it was dark hair. He didn't have long enough to take it in before the man's head blew off in pieces on the walkway behind his now headless body. The two men behind Xander continued to fire as Xander checked for a hole in his leg. His left hand found it, and the blood on his fingertips offered a sobering moment.

Two dead, two firing at me, and at least one more holding Kyle—or someone they shouted as my friend—at gunpoint.

The gunfire stopped, but the thumping of helicopter rotors grew louder and louder. If there were more coming, he had to get rid of the men already on the yacht.

Right now.

"All right! All right, I give!" Xander shouted, giving him a moment to pull two spare shotgun shells from his pocket and load his gun. He then rounded the corner and shot both gunmen dead where they stood on the back deck. Xander heard Kyle scream his name; then three pops from a pistol come from the direction of the sliding doors.

It was too late.

A bullet ripped through Xander's stomach and blew him back against the half-moon lounge chair he'd been partying on a few short hours ago. He managed to hold on to his shotgun, and through the pain he pointed it at the man holding a gun to Kyle's head. Hot blood leaked from his stomach, and sharp, burning pain singed all the way to his back.

At least his leg didn't hurt anymore. Silver linings.

With everything he had, he forced himself up and over the back of the chair and took cover behind it. He maintained his shotgun point toward the man holding Kyle.

"Let him go!" Xander shouted. His voice didn't carry the weight he would have liked it to. It's difficult with a hole in your belly.

The man walked Kyle forward into the yellow light. He was about the same height as Kyle, but unlike Kyle he was wearing more than board shorts. He was in full military gear, all the way up to his hideous buzz cut. Xander wasn't sure if God made a mistake and put his legs where his arms were supposed to be. Or they could have been tree trunks.

"I make demands now. You are in no position."

"Who sent you?"

"Still with the questions. You don't listen so good."

Clearly he was Russian, but what the hell were Russians doing invading his yacht in the middle of the night, in the middle of the ocean? Four more men walked out onto the deck and spread out, two to the left and two to the right. Xander never would have guessed nine men. And in a matter of seconds, God only knew how many more might be coming out of that second helicopter. Xander could feel himself becoming weak. He glanced down and couldn't believe the amount of blood that had pooled beneath him.

"W-what do you want?" Xander managed. His voice was losing steam fast, as was the rest of him. He could feel a wave of blackness coming over him.

He was going to pass out.

"You. My boss would like word with you."

Xander tried to ask who his boss was, but it wouldn't come out. The men moved in closer. He took a deep breath and a long blink. The helicopter hovered above them now. He had failed. The Russian started to say something else, but all Xander could hear was a very distinct and unmistakable voice.

"WHOOP WHOOP!"

Sam.

Xander looked back up at the Russian just before a bullet blasted through the side of the bull of a man's head. Everything moved in slow motion as Xander lost his grip on his shotgun. He fell onto his side and could only watch what was happening in front of him. The man who had been shouting at Xander and holding a gun on Kyle collapsed, and Kyle fell with him, the man's blood splattered all over him. It looked like Kyle was screaming, but Xander could no longer hear.

He was going into shock.

The four remaining gunmen turned their attention to the helicopter when a flash bomb popped in the middle of them. As they shielded their eyes, Xander watched as a figure dressed in all black, complete with long blonde hair, rappelled down and landed on one of the gunmen, putting a bullet in his head. Immediately after that a brunette hit the deck, did a front roll, and shot the gunman crawling toward Xander. Blood sprayed like an open fire hydrant from his throat. Xander blinked again and saw the brunette bend down over Kyle as the blonde shot the other two—still stunned—gunmen in the head.

As the blonde walked toward him, he could swear he had seen her somewhere before.

Then everything went black.

Is This a Bad Time?

"Sam?"

The only thing in front of Xander was darkness. Pure black. Had he actually said her name out loud? And what was that beeping noise? Xander tried to clear the darkness, but it was like his mind was hunting for the light switch. Unsuccessfully. The last thing he remembered was being on the yacht, watching Sam and some blonde-haired woman take out the Russians who had—for whatever reason—invaded his yacht.

Sarah Gilbright.

He remembered the blonde's identity. What in the hell were Sarah and Sam doing together? How had they known to come to the yacht? Wait, was he still on the yacht? Are they still fighting the Russians?

They need me.

Xander tried to use the muscles that it took to get up from the ground—specifically what it took to get up from the deck of a yacht with a hole in your stomach. However, nothing changed. He tried again, his mind willing his body to move. What if Sam, Sarah, and Kyle needed him? He remembered dropping his shotgun just before he fell. It must be close. He reached out. He felt something—definitely something—but not a shotgun.

A hand?

It was definitely a hand, and he felt it squeeze around his.

"Xander?" he heard from some far-off place. "Xander, it's all right." The voice closer—British.

"Sam?"

"Xander?"

Xander's eyes opened and found Sam's face staring back at him, surrounded by a hospital room. The look on her face was different. Happy.

"What's with the look of love, Sam? It looks good on you." Xander didn't miss a beat.

"You sarcastic son of a bitch. You scared the hell out of me. Out of all of us." Sam held her smile.

"All of us?" Xander sat up. Surrounding him were all-white walls, an out-of-date television hanging in the corner, and a steady beeping coming from his hospital monitor. At the back of the hospital room, in two separate chairs, a beautiful blonde was asleep in each one.

"Yes, all of us. Seems you make quite an impression on hopeless romantic—well, hopeless—young women. It's been quite a contentious week, neither one of them wanting to leave your side in fear you'll see the other first."

"You know you're the only girl for me, Sam."

"Right. I'm just glad you're all right." Sam rubbed his hand.

Affection? From Sam? Vegas Kelly was asleep in one chair and Special Agent Sarah Gilbright asleep in the other. Both looking like angels. It must have been pretty bad. How did—

"Wait!" Xander shot up in bed, almost ripping the tubes from his arm and the stitches in his stomach. An awful pain drove through his belly like a train through a tunnel. "Did you say contentious *week*? I've been here for a week?"

"I'm afraid so. You lost a lot of blood. It was touch and go for a while."

Xander began to rustle in the bed. So much so that Sam had to hold him down.

"What are you doing? You're in no condition—"

"Let go of me, Sam. I've got to get out of here."

"Xander, sit back, the Preakness Stakes is already over. I'm sorry, but you've missed it." Sam already knew Xander's concern.

In front of him, Kelly and Sarah were awakened by his panic. But the only thing Xander could think of was his horse. He had missed the second leg of the Triple Crown. He missed King's Ransom's big day. The Preakness was always the second weekend after the Kentucky Derby. This year, it came after the Kentucky Derby that his big black thoroughbred had won just two weeks earlier. He was supposed to go straight from the yacht in St. Thomas to watch him win in Baltimore. And he missed it? He looked at the ladies who were now standing at the foot of the bed, and then to Sam; she could see the question in his eyes.

Sam delivered the good news. "He won, Xander. King's Ransom won the race."

Xander didn't know why, but hard emotion ran through him. Unexpected emotion. Tears welled in his eyes. He knew that horse meant a lot to him, but it wasn't until that very moment that he understood just how much. It was—horse racing—his last ongoing connection to his lost father. Hearing the news that Ransom had won made him so proud, and he knew it made his late father proud as well.

"There he is!" Kyle shouted as soon as he walked through the door and saw Xander sitting up. He noticed the emotion on his friend's face. "Everything okay?"

"He won?"

"Who—oh, Ransom? Of course he did!" Kyle set a couple of coffees down on the bedside table and walked over to Xander, giving him a hug. "Don't ever do that to me again. I don't know what I'd do if I lost you."

Xander, either high on the news of his horse winning or high on morphine, felt a rush of adrenaline from the surrounding love.

"Looks like you've got a lot of people who love you, Xander. You are a lucky man." Kelly rubbed his foot. Her smile still had the ability to melt steel.

"Yeah, maybe too many people." Sarah shot Kelly a look. She may as well have urinated on Xander; it wouldn't have been any less subtle a way to mark her territory. Kelly returned Sarah's look of disdain with one of disgust.

Sarah walked around the bed, and Sam let her pass. She took Xander's hand in one of hers and began to stroke his hair with the other.

"I'm glad you're okay, Xander. We almost didn't make it to the yacht in time."

Xander took her hand.

"But you did. Thank you. You saved my drunk ass, and Kyle's and Kelly's too. I'll never be able to repay you what you deserve."

"It was nothing." She smiled at him. Then she turned that smile into a boasting sneer as she looked back at Kelly.

Kelly rolled her eyes and walked over to the other side of the bed, bumping Kyle out of the way. She put her hand on Xander's cheek, stroked it, and leaned in for a long, passionate kiss. She pulled her head back and gave him the most sincere look.

"I'm so glad you're all right. I was so worried about you. You saved my life, and my friends' lives, by getting us down to the bottom of the boat."

Kelly gave him another open-mouthed kiss, and as she rose, she gave Sarah a "take that" sneer in return.

"Raeer!" Kyle gave a cat growl from behind them, mocking the two women vying for Xander's attention.

Sam was utterly revolted. "Okay, ladies, get a fucking grip. Jesus," she snapped at them. "The man's been awake for all of two minutes and you are already smothering him. You think that's gonna keep a man like Xander?"

"All right, all right." Xander lay back down in the cramped hospital bed. "Sarah, thank you so much, but I'm sure you have some *special agenting* to do. And Kelly, don't you have to get back to California?"

"We *are* in California, baby."

Xander shot a look at Sam.

"I thought it best to get you out of Lexington. Horse country is abuzz about what happened to Xander King, the owner of their beloved King's Ransom. We are at Scripps

Mercy Hospital in San Diego. We've all been taking turns at the beach house until you came 'round."

"Oh, that makes sense." Xander could only imagine the buzz in the racing world. A scintillating scandal with the owner of the horse going for the Triple Crown. The stories practically wrote themselves.

Wait, the stories . . .

"What did you tell the press? What do they know?" A worried look came over Xander.

"Sarah did a great job helping us spin this. She released a statement that the government was investigating an attempted robbery and murder. Fortunately, it's not much of a stretch to believe that people would want to steal from a billionaire," Sam explained.

"Is that what happened?"

Sam saw the confusion on Xander's face.

"Oh . . . right. We have a lot to discuss, Xander, but now is not the time." She glanced over to Kelly.

"What? Now is *exactly* the time, Sam. What the hell were Russians doing coming after me in the middle of the Virgin Islands?"

"Not right now, Xander. You're not well."

The heart-rate monitor beside Xander's bed began to pick up speed.

"Don't bullshit me, Sam! Tell me what's going on!"

At that moment, the hospital door opened and in walked Natalie Rockwell.

"Is this a bad time?"

An Explosive Conversation

"I flew in from Paris as soon as I heard."

Kyle cleared everyone from the room and pulled a chair over beside Xander before he left the room with them. Kelly, at first in awe that Natalie Rockwell was in the room, quickly came back down to earth when she realized she was there for *her* man—Xander. Kyle promised to explain while they were on their way out. After glancing at Kelly and Sarah, Natalie gave Xander a brief "I see how it is" look, then sat down and took his hand. For Xander, it was like seeing the sun itself. Her beautiful face was cast aglow in the harsh florescent light that hung above them. He had missed her so much.

"My news made it all the way to Paris?"

"Well, there is this new thing called the Internet," she teased. Her smile did more to take his pain away than any medicine ever could.

"Right. So you were checking up on me?" He flashed a wry smile.

"Not a chance. I was checking up on my four-legged friend, King's Ransom. And of course, when I went to see if he'd won the Preakness, all the stories were more about his owner. Xander . . . what is going on? Is this really how you want to live your life?"

"So much for pleasantries."

"I'm sorry. It's just that . . ."

Natalie trailed off. A look of pain held tight on her face. She was hurting, and it was his fault. All of a sudden the pain from the wound in his stomach came back in a rush to say hello. Or maybe it was heartache.

"No, I'm sorry, Natalie. I should have never dragged you into this . . . into my life."

"Which, still, I clearly know nothing about."

"You do. You know *me*. The rest of this, well, it's a mess. My mess."

"Talk to me. Let me in. I can help you—"

"Natalie, thank you for coming, but I'm sure you are needed back in Paris." His own words sounding like someone else's.

The hurt on Natalie's face thickened.

"So, that's it?"

"I'm no good for you, and you know—"

"I know what?" Natalie's face hardened, her jaw set. "I don't know anything except for the way you make me feel. *No one* has *ever* made me . . . You know what? You are just scared."

"Scared?" Xander looked confused.

30

"That's right. That's why you are pushing me away. I'm not like whoever hurt you in your past. I'm not them."

"Natalie, you are the one who said you needed time. And I'm not some psychology patient. No one ever hurt me."

Natalie saw right through that statement. It was as if she knew Xander better than he knew himself, and *that* scared him. She let him know this with a look.

"Fine, you don't want to open up to me? You don't want me in your life, Alexander King? Then stop leaving me messages saying otherwise."

"Messages? I haven't contacted you, not once. Messages," he scoffed.

"Yeah, Xander, messages."

She was so sexy when she was angry.

"Like?" He did his best to look clueless.

"Like whiskey and roses on my balcony in Paris?"

Xander couldn't help but smile. Clearly his message had been received.

"Whiskey and roses?" He played dumb.

"Don't. And don't do it again." Natalie stood up. He had hurt her feelings. "If you don't want me, I've got plenty of other things going on in my life. I'm sorry I ever came here!"

Natalie turned and huffed toward the door. Before she could make it there, and before Xander could stop her and try to explain, the entire east wing of the hospital exploded and burst into a fiery flame. The blast was so strong it knocked Natalie to the floor; the flames could be seen from Xander's hospital window, lighting up the otherwise black night. His IV stand was knocked over, and the entire structure shook beneath them. The lights flickered on and off as a rumble settled in around them.

31

Sam blasted through the door, helped Natalie back to her feet, and went straight to Xander.

"We've got to get out of here, now."

Natalie was visibly shaking. "What's going on?"

"Not now, Natalie. Just help me get him up." Sam looked at Xander. "Can you walk?"

The two of them pulled Xander to a sitting position. His stomach wailed in pain.

"Guess we'll find out. And Sam?"

"Yes, Xander?"

"Don't look at my equipment. It will ruin every other man for you from here on out."

"You're insufferable." Sam rolled her eyes as she helped him out of the bed.

"You know what this is about, Sam?"

"It's about you and your need for revenge," Sam snapped at him.

Natalie helped steady Xander on his feet, wearing fear and confusion on her face.

"This explosion has to do with you? What the hell?"

Xander looked dead into her eyes.

"I told you I was no good for you." He turned to Sam. "Do you have another gun?"

"Of course I do." She walked over to her black leather jacket, pulled out a nine-millimeter, cocked it, and handed it to Xander. "How's your equilibrium?"

"I'm fine," he answered.

Natalie watched in horror. "Who the fuck *are* you two?"

Sam ignored Natalie's question, and while Xander pulled on a pair of black joggers, she checked the "In Case of Emergency" map on the wall beside the door. Sarah ushered

Kyle and Kelly back into the hospital room with a pistol in her hand and a battle-ready expression on her face. It occurred to Xander at that moment that Sarah Gilbright just might be a badass.

"Okay, spill it right now. What are we dealing with here, Sam?" Xander was through with being kept in the dark.

Sam tore the emergency map off the wall, walked back over to Xander, and motioned for Sarah to join them. Apparently, Sam considered Sarah a badass as well. Otherwise, she would have *never* let her in the huddle. Before a strategy could be fleshed out, gunshots rang out from a distance followed by screams from the last few of the staff trying to exit the hospital. Sam looked up at Xander, stone-faced.

"I'll explain when we get out of here. Just know these are high-level Russian ex-military, same that invaded your yacht. We'll need some of that X-man magic right about now."

"Okay, so what do we know?" Xander asked rhetorically. Shots continued from a distance and commotion in the hallway was constant. "Obviously, they are after me. Judging from the playdate on the yacht, they aren't fucking around. But we have to assume that they have been following reports of my condition this week, and we must also assume they have someone on the inside. Someone on the nursing staff. So they still think I'm in a coma. Blowing up the opposite wing is a distraction—"

"If they have an insider, they would know where you are. Why not just blow this room and leave?" Sarah asked.

"Because if they are willing to go to these lengths to kill me, they have to make sure that I'm dead. The only way to do that is to personally see to it that I am gone. They won't chance it on a blast. Hence, the distraction. Someone—probably their best assassin—is on his way to this room right now to finish me. You all must leave, right now."

Sam put her hands on her hips.

"Leave? We're not going anywhere."

"Let's give them what they are expecting."

"What, you lying here on this bed? No way, they'll kill you."

"I hate to break this huddle, Sam," Kyle said from the door as he peered out the small window that looked out into the hall, "but the hallway is clear. They must be getting close."

"Sam, get everyone out of here now. Use the map to find the best route."

Sarah stepped forward and pulled out her cell phone.

"We're not leaving you, Xander. Let me call this in, I can have a CIA chopper—"

"We don't have time for this! They won't get here in time and I *will not* be owing the CIA any favors." Xander walked over to the hospital bed and laid the gun on the table. "The police will be here any second and they will be focused where the explosion occurred. It will just be me and my assassin. I like those odds. Sam, leave me a cell phone and I'll call you when I am finished here. Do not let Sarah call this in."

Sarah folded her arms while Sam nodded her head toward him. Natalie couldn't help but make a plea.

"But Xander, this isn't a joke, they've blown up half the hospital already. They'll kill you!"

Xander walked over to Natalie and took her by the shoulders.

"Sweetheart, this is what I do. You are in the best of hands with Sam. She will get you out of here. Just do *everything* she says and you'll be fine. I promise."

"Sweetheart?" Kelly stepped toward them, a jealous scowl on her face.

Sam stepped in and exchanged looks with Kelly and Natalie. "Can we please sort this out after we survive the professional killers and gunmen with all the explosives?" She then looked at Xander. "You really know how to bloody complicate things don't you?" Then back to the women. "If you want to survive this mess, follow me. Romeo here is quite good at handling himself. We'll see him soon, *if* you all can do without him for even a few moments."

Sam's sarcasm lay thick on all of them. After another loud explosion—this one even closer—they focused their attention on following her.

"Xander, do not underestimate what is coming, and I will do the same as I take them out of here. My phone is there on the bedside table. Call Kyle if you need me. I will come back and let Sarah handle getting them out."

"I'll be fine, Sam. Just make sure you get them out safe. If you run into trouble, call me. Now go!"

Xander took in the concerned look on everyone's face as they stared back at him.

"I said go!"

Kyle nodded to him and then ushered them behind Sam out into the hallway. Natalie gave one last worried glance before turning the corner of the wall. The hospital had become eerily silent now. The door closed behind them, and Xander walked over to the window to see if he could get an idea of just what they were dealing with. The sun had yet to rise. He was thankful that it was a time of night where there might not be as many family and friends around visiting patients. He couldn't believe what he was doing had brought all of this on so many innocent people.

Things had to change.

His life had to change.

Sam's phone chirped from beside his hospital bed. He walked over to see if it was for him.

A text from Kyle's phone: "X, you were wrong. Not just 1 assassin. 4 men are heading your way, heavily armed. Sam is headed toward you. I promise, Sarah and I will get Natalie and Kelly out of here. See you in a bit. BE CAREFUL."

As If I Haven't Had a Bad Enough Week, Now I'm Seeing Ghosts

Those four men didn't stand a chance. Xander wished that Sam would have just stayed with the others until they were safe. He figured she thought he was weak, just being out of a coma and all. Remarkably, he felt good considering. He slid the phone into the pocket of his joggers, reached across the bed for his gun, and just as he almost had his fingers on it, a bullet ricocheted off the table and hit the wall. Xander saw a gun pointed at him through the small, square door window as he dove behind one of the lounge chairs someone had pulled up to the foot of the bed. Two more shots fired, and one bullet skipped through the window behind him. He would have just made his exit that way, but he didn't want to leave Sam alone with the four other gunmen.

Women.

The hospital room door flew open, and he stood to face the four men, using the chair as a shield. To his surprise only one man walked in. A surprisingly unassuming man, not very tall, not very well built, but a very familiar face.

Nicoli Pavlovich.

Number-one assassin for Mafia boss, Vitalii Dragov.

At one time the most wanted man in the world. Xander remembered this when his Special Operations unit was studying for a possible mission. A mission that never deployed because Nicoli Pavlovich was found dead. Xander let out a sigh and rolled his eyes.

"As if I haven't had a bad enough week, now I'm seeing ghosts?"

"You know me, I see."

"I know you died."

"Much easier to walk in shadows if you no longer exist."

Xander could appreciate that sentiment. If people thought him dead, no one would be trying to kill him right now. Nicoli trained his gun on Xander's chest. His face was hard. A large scar under his right eye, further menacing his permanent scowl.

"So, what is it that you want with a measly whiskey entrepreneur like me?"

"Boss says you are dangerous. Me? I think . . . not so much."

"Dragov? If he wants some free bottles of whiskey, tell him there are easier ways."

"Cut shit, King. I am not in mood. You killed three of my best men."

"On my yacht? Your best men? Really?" Xander looked genuinely surprised. "Why, Nicoli, I'm disappointed. They were taken out by a couple of girls. I didn't have to lift a finger. What's that say about you?"

As Xander spoke, his eyes were trained on Nicoli's trigger finger. As soon as he saw it twitch, he tossed the chair at him, sending the bullet that had been meant for Xander's heart up into the ceiling tile. Before Nicoli could adjust, Xander front kicked the side of the second chair, sending it sliding into Nicoli's groin. In the hallway, he could hear gunshots.

Sam.

Xander knew she could handle herself, but she clearly didn't know all that was going on if she thought more than one man was coming for him. Kyle could have been wrong. What if there were more than four?

Just as Nicoli repositioned his pistol, Xander hit his hand with a perfectly placed spinning wheel-kick and sent the gun flying against the far wall of the hospital room. He followed that with a straight right-hand, but Nicoli weaved to his left and countered with a left hook to Xander's stomach. A direct hit to his nearly but not completely healed stitches. As Nicoli brought a right hook toward him, Xander managed to step in, the right side of his hip to the right side of Nicoli's, and with a sweep of his right arm and a twist, Xander threw him onto the floor, judo-style. He landed in a thud but let the momentum send him into a back somersault, landing him next to his pistol, which he picked up, aimed at Xander, and fired a shot that just missed because Xander had simultaneously thrown himself into the hallway.

Xander heard gunshots coming from the exit at the end of the hall, so he grabbed a nearby metal bedpan and immediately ran in that direction.

Better than nothing.

He figured at this point it was either Sam or the rest of his group taking gunfire, and regardless, he was a sitting duck in that hallway, so he had to move. Just as he shut the door to a stairwell, a bullet whizzed through its square window and nearly smacked him in the side of the head.

He glared through the now glassless window and locked eyes with Nicoli back in the hallway just outside his hospital room. He wanted nothing more than to stay and fight this notorious assassin—to make him dead for real this time—but he heard a scream one floor below, followed by a string of gunfire. Nicoli shot his gun once again, but Xander was already halfway down the stairs. For the first time a shot of pain screamed through his calf muscle that had taken a bullet on the yacht. It was Sam's scream he had heard; she must have been ambushed. He blasted through the door that led to the second-floor hallway and slung his bedpan like a Frisbee, hitting the man who held a gun on Sam in the head. As if she knew he was coming, she shot to her feet and dove at the other man who had swung his gun toward Xander, her momentum carrying them both through the open door of the first patient room on the floor. They disappeared from Xander's view and he jumped to his feet. As he jogged to the man he had just struck with the bedpan, he noticed a red spot growing on his white hospital gown. He lifted the gown and saw that blood ran steadily down into his joggers. Nicoli's right hook had popped his stitches. There was nothing he could do about the open wound, so he bent down, wrenched the gunman's neck until it gave a loud pop, picked up his bedpan, and ran to the room Sam had tackled the man into. Just before he made it inside, he heard gunshots behind him—Nicoli—and a burst from an Uzi from the other end of the hall. As soon as he got inside the room, Sam was

40

putting the finishing touches on her offender with a skull-crushing boot to the head.

"Just like old times, huh?"

"Are you all right, Xander? You're bleeding."

He put his finger to his lips, pointed in the direction of Nicoli, and then signaled that there was someone else, the other man who shot at him from the other end of the hall. He and Sam would have made excellent charades partners.

"Do you have a gun?" he asked her.

"No, lost mine in a skirmish and his gun is empty."

"Skirmish?" He took the time to smile.

"Xander King, we have you surrounded now! Put hands up and come out slow!" Nicoli shouted from the hallway.

"No thanks," Xander told him.

"You are trapped. Don't be stupid. You probably don't even have weapon."

"I didn't need a weapon upstairs, did I? You hack!"

"Hack? You think you are better assassin than Nicoli Pavlovich? Ha!"

Sam shot Xander a "please don't antagonize him" look. Xander shrugged his shoulders and raised his bedpan for Sam to see. Her eyes closed and her shoulders slumped. They could hear multiple sets of boots walking toward the door from both sides. They had nothing to defend themselves with. Sam unscrewed the metal rod that held together a nearby IV stand, and Xander readied his bedpan. Though they knew their "weapons" couldn't beat actual guns, they weren't about to go down without a fight. But they could see in each other's eyes that they both knew this was it.

They were trapped.

"There are four of us out here now. I suppose you are going to kill us all?" Nicoli's thick accent echoed in the hallway.

Before Xander could answer Nicoli, a woman shouted his name.

"Xander?"

"Run! There are too many of them, run!" Xander shouted back.

As the words left his lips, bullets began to fly. The hallway filled with blasts and pops, ricocheting bullets and breaking glass. Xander moved to the doorway, but Sam pulled him back in. The bullets stopped and Xander ripped away from Sam's grip. Just when he got to the doorway, a gun pointed down the hallway emerged into view. Xander instinctively swung at it with the bedpan, knocking it from someone's hands. Shots fired immediately from the other end of the hall, and whoever was holding the gun bolted back in the direction of the exit. Xander peeked around the doorway, down the hall, and there stood Sarah Gilbright.

Badass.

"Sarah?"

"Xander! I thought you were dead!" She ran toward him.

"Sam?"

"She's fine."

"Who was that man?

"Nicoli Pavlovich"

"Pavlovich? Dragov's former assassin? That's impossible, he's been dead for years."

"Call it in. Give the police a description, maybe they can pick him up before he gets to his extraction point. Are the others okay?"

"They're fine. I came back for you as soon as I knew they were safe. Kyle is with them. He said he knew how to use a gun, so I left him with my spare."

Xander was really beginning to like Sarah Gilbright. CIA connections be damned.

Sam emerged from the room.

"You came back for us?"

"Of course. I couldn't leave the two of you here to fight alone."

"Thank you," Xander told her just before his knees buckled. Sam and Sarah moved in simultaneously to keep him upright. "You know, normally, I am much better with two women."

"Jesus, Xander, you're a bloody mess." Sam looked down at the blood-stained gown. "Are you all right?"

"I'll be fine, just as soon as you tell me why I am being targeted by a ghost assassin, sent by the biggest Mafia boss on the planet."

Sam looked at Sarah.

"Let's get him to the Escalade. It's not far."

They started walking him toward the exit. Xander stopped and turned toward Sam.

"Sam, did Vitalii Dragov murder my parents?"

No More Secrets

For the second time that day, Xander woke up, foggy, with a beautiful woman staring back at him.

"Don't pinch me if I'm dreaming."

Natalie gave him a soft smile and continued to dab his forehead with a cool, wet towel. She had her hair pulled back into a ponytail, and for the first time Xander got a glimpse of her adorable little ears.

Delicate.

"Are you all right? Do we need to take you to another hospital?"

Xander sat up.

"Please, I think I've had enough hospitals for one day." He looked around and everyone was there with him; they were in the living room of his beach house on Coronado Island. His home in San Diego was much different from his home in Lexington. On purpose. His home in Kentucky was much more traditional; it kept to the wonderful and rich history of where he grew up. He wanted something different when he was in California. His mansion on the small island, which on one side looked out to San Diego Bay and on the other, the Pacific Ocean, was much more modern. More squared lines and marble floors rather than crown molding and hardwood. The living room where he sat up on the couch was almost entirely white. White marble floors paired with white walls that reached all the way up to the white twenty-five-foot ceiling. The three-piece couch brought in a little color, light gray, but most of the pop in the room came from a few bright paintings on the wall. They were modern abstract paintings. Xander actually hated them. They filled the room with absolutely no feeling of home; instead they made it feel more like a hotel. However, his interior designer had been a real tigress in the sack, and just as every other man before him, that fact forced him to make some bad decisions. And whatever; the towering wall-length windows forever filled with beach and ocean made up for anything that lacked in the rest of the grand room. He looked over to Sam.

"Did Kelly finally have enough?"

Sam walked over, Kyle and Sarah followed, all of them taking a seat on the couch opposite of him and Natalie.

Sam gave a smirk. "I believe so. We just sent her back to Orange County. I think she had some episodes of *The Real Housewives* to catch up on."

Natalie patted Xander on the leg. "She your girlfriend?"

"Please. I'm not like you and Pepé Le Pew. I didn't move on quite so fast."

"Like me? Do you mean the costar of my movie, Jean? Please. Is that why you just left something on my balcony in Paris and ran away? Alexander King, a jealous man?"

Xander rolled his eyes. "Sam, I think it's about time you catch me up on just what in the hell is going on."

"I intend to. Natalie, do you mind? Maybe take a shower or check out the beach?"

"No, no. She needs to hear this. She said she wants me to let her in. Well, let's let her in. Hold nothing back." Xander shifted on the couch to give his midsection a break.

Sarah shifted as well, but her discomfort came more from the realization of just how much Natalie meant to Xander. She wasn't aware of the feelings he had for her. Apparently, Xander wasn't the only one with a jealous streak. This was making Sarah uncomfortable.

"Are you sure that's a good idea, X? You can't unsay it, once you say it." Kyle leaned against the couch.

"I agree with Kyle," said Sam.

"Yes, this isn't for civilian ears. I'm not even sure Kyle should be here for this," Sarah added.

Before Kyle could take offense, Xander addressed Sarah. "Listen, anything you have to say to me, you can say to Kyle."

"But, Xander, this is government business."

Xander's blood began to boil, and everyone in the room felt the temperature change.

"This is *my* business, and if you don't like it, maybe you should get back to CIA headquarters and leave this to us."

That cut straight through.

"There would be no *us* here"—Sarah made a circular motion with her finger encompassing everyone—"if it wasn't for *me*. Don't forget that."

Sarah was right. In the last week she had saved his ass twice, and Sam's once. That was enough to make her one of *us*, if anything was. He took a deep breath and brought his eyes back to her, contrite.

"You're right. I'm sorry."

She nodded.

"Please, fill everyone in on what is going on. Natalie is a big girl, she can make up her mind what she wants to do after that." Xander took Natalie's hand. She squeezed it in return.

Sam spoke up first.

"All right then, I'll start so everyone is on the same page. Natalie, Xander's parents were murdered right in front of him when he was just a boy."

Natalie shot a look at Xander. Her eyes filled with emotion. For Xander, the fear of Natalie knowing had given way to relief.

No more secrets.

"Ever since that day, every decision he has made has been in the vein of avenging their murder. As soon as high school ended, he joined the navy. As soon as he was eligible he then became a Navy SEAL. For years he has been with Special Ops, carrying out top secret black-ops missions all over the world—honing his skills so that one day he could use those skills for revenge. Correct me if I'm wrong, Xander, but along the way Xander could no longer stomach the innocent casualties and the recklessness of the United States government. That is when he dragged me into all of this."

"Sorry to interrupt, but how did you two meet exactly?" Natalie asked.

"Another story for another day. Let's just say that Xander made quite the impression."

"As did you." Xander smiled. Okay, maybe not all the secrets had to come out. What's wrong with a little mystery?

"Anyway, I followed Xander and we've been administering private justice these last few years while searching for who could be responsible for his parents' murder."

"Private justice?" Natalie asked. "Do I even want to know?"

"Let's just say that the bad guys haven't had a lot of good luck the last few years." Sam smiled.

"I see." Natalie went along with it, not letting the need for details ruin the moment. "So, I'm assuming you now know who killed your parents? Is that who came after you while we were in your bed in Lexington?"

Sarah adjusted the fold in her blouse. Trying not to let on. She didn't even realize how strong her feelings were for Xander. Not until she saw Kelly kiss him, and not until Natalie's words. Sam interjected before Xander could answer.

"If I may?"

Xander nodded for Sam to continue. "We thought that those men were sent by Xander's parents' killer. They were, but we were wrong about just who that man was."

There it was. Finally, confirmation. In that moment, Sean's face flashed in front of his eyes. His friend who died because of Xander's haste in Syria. Sadness fell over his chest like a weighted vest.

Sam continued. "Last week—I'm sure you heard about it while you were in Paris—we attempted to avenge their murders, and while we were successful in our mission, we took out the wrong monster."

"Why would I have heard about this while I was in Paris?"

"It was all over the news," Xander said. "The terrorist cell that got taken out in Syria?"

Natalie's face went white.

"That was you? But . . . the report said fifty-some terrorists died in that attack. You did all that?"

"Me, Sam, Kyle, and one other friend who didn't make it."

Natalie stood and began to pace the room.

Sarah spoke up. "I told you we shouldn't have told her. This is government business, Xander. You are out of line."

Natalie stopped in her tracks and laid a laser stare, set on incinerate, into Sarah's eyes. "I am fine. It's just a lot to take in. What the hell do you have to do with any of this anyway?"

Sarah stood up and took a step toward Natalie. Natalie held her ground. "I, *Hollywood,* am the reason Xander is alive on that couch right now. I broke rank and protocol to make that happen."

Natalie's face softened. "I'm sorry." She went back over to Xander and sat down. "Thank you. I didn't mean to imply—"

"It's fine," Sarah cut her off. "Real-life drama is a lot different from the movies, honey." Natalie took that jab and held her smile. "I'll take it from here if that's okay, Sam?"

"By all means, Sarah, this is your part of the show."

"Thank you."

Kyle shot Xander a look. Xander knew exactly what Kyle's raised eyebrow was about, Natalie versus Sarah, and it said, *watch out.* Xander paid it no mind, however, because this information from Sarah was the part he was interested in. He gave Sarah his full attention.

Sarah proceeded to explain how she came about the information that, in fact, it was Vitalii Dragov who was responsible for the murder of Xander's parents. The part that Xander wasn't prepared for is the reason why. He had no idea that his father had dealings with the Russian Mafia. Why would he? Xander was just a teenager when his father's business was at the height of its profitability. And even though Sarah didn't know why his father got involved in the first place, he knew that it would have to have been because that low-life Dragov threatened him and forced him in. His father was a good man. No one would ever be able to convince Xander otherwise, and God help anyone who tried. He had a lot of questions for Vitalii Dragov, and he had every intention of getting every single one of them answered. No matter what that took. Dragov had not only killed his parents, but he also put all of Xander's loved ones' lives in danger in the last few weeks.

"I'm sorry, Xander, I know that must have been hard to hear," Sarah finished.

"It's all right."

"You know your dad must have been forced to deal with this son of a bitch." Kyle echoed Xander's thoughts. Mind meld.

"I know."

Natalie shifted toward Xander.

"What are you going to do?"

"Kill him." Xander said without hesitation.

"You are going to go and try to kill a man who Sam called the biggest Mafia boss in the world? You're crazy. You have a death wish."

"What would you like me to do, Natalie? You've seen that I can't just leave it alone. You were at my house in Lexington when they raided it and you saw what they did to that hospital."

"I know, but what if you can't kill him? What then?"

"There is no what then." Sam stood up. "Xander will kill him."

"Not without the CIA you won't." Sarah knew that wouldn't be met with cheers, but it had to be said.

"It will *not* be with the CIA." Xander stood to meet her eyes. The tension in the room was as tight as a cramped hamstring.

"Xander, Director Manning has been calling me for hours. I'm not certain I still have a job. But I am certain that there is no way he will let you do this on your own. He'll ground your plane and freeze your bank accounts."

"Let him try," Xander growled, his hands instinctively formed into fists.

"She's right." Sam sighed.

"What? Not you too."

"Xander, it's the US government, for Christ's sake. They can take away everything if they want."

Xander let that statement hang in the air. The seagulls cooed just outside the open windows, and the ocean chimed in as it crashed against the shore. Xander knew she was right. Director Manning had him by the short and curlies. There is no way he could make a move without him. If he wanted to take down Dragov, he would have let the CIA in. The very thought of it made his skin crawl. There was no telling how far the consequences of working with them would ripple.

"Goddammit."

"I'm sorry, Xander." Sarah softened her stance. "It's the only way."

"But it will be on my terms."

"I'll call Manning. They may already be shutting you down after this little hospital stunt. I doubt he's in a generous mood."

"He owes me. The government owes me for all I've done for them. You tell Manning I'm coming to collect."

51

Vitalii Dragov Raises the Stakes

Forty miles south of Moscow, in the most prestigious neighborhood in Russia—Rublyovka—two doors down from Vladimir Putin, Vitalii Dragov sat behind his desk chewing on a cigar in his thirty-million-euro ultra mansion. Dragov was scowling furiously at Nicoli Pavlovich, trying to decide whether or not he would actually make him a ghost this time. His massive belly hung down over his belt, and his greasy and poorly dyed black hair reminded Nicoli of a bad Elvis impersonator. An old—shar-pei wrinkled—whale of a bad Elvis impersonator. The crater-sized pockmarks in between those wrinkles—on an already hideous face—made for one ugly-ass son of a bitch. However, Nicoli knew the true ugly in Dragov lay beneath that disgusting exterior. He also knew that he was about to get a heavy dose of it for letting Xander King get out of that hospital alive.

"I do not understand. Why he is not dead?" Dragov's voice was guttural, his accent thick.

"I told you, he had people there. Military people. I will not miss again."

Dragov was in a difficult position. For the last fifteen years, Nicoli had been his most valuable weapon. But he knew when dealing with a man like Xander King, there was no room for error. Dragov didn't make mistakes, and he didn't tolerate them either.

"I gave you entire team. Plenty of guns and explosives. Still, he walks. Tell me what I am supposed to do about this."

"Let me do my job."

"This is third time you have failed. Failure has consequences."

"This is the first time I have failed, I had nothing to do with the job in Kentucky and whatever you attempted on that boat in the Virgin Islands."

Dragov placed the gnarled cigar in the golden ashtray that sat on top of his mahogany desk, looked over to one of his men, and nodded. The man brought a briefcase over to the desk and placed it in front of Dragov.

"What is it you want most from me, Nicoli?"

"Out. You know this."

"That's right. You want out. And I have always told you that there is no way out. No?"

"Yes, no way out."

Dragov placed his two fat thumbs on the chrome buttons of the oversized brown leather briefcase, popped it open, and turned it toward Nicoli so he could see what was inside.

"This is more money than you will ever be able to spend. Thirty million euros."

Nicoli couldn't help but stand. The pile of cash in front of him would be enough to get his brother out of prison and for them to live on for the rest of their lives. Prison in Russia doesn't work like it does in America. If you had enough money, you could get anyone out, no matter the crime. His brother had been in prison for five years of his three life sentences, for murders that Nicoli himself had committed. Since everyone thought Nicoli to be dead, they pinned all of it on his brother. It had haunted Nicoli every night in his dreams since the day they put him away. Nicoli promised his brother he would get him out or die trying. Now was his chance.

"I will give you this, and your freedom from your debt to me, if you kill Xander King. But I must have proof. You must bring him to me and kill him in front of me. Nothing else will be acceptable."

Nicoli had always been the exact opposite of an emotional man. But the thought of freedom with his brother—the only family he had ever known—almost overwhelmed him. And he and his new love could live happily ever after. He would use every ounce of his twenty years of the highest levels of training to get this job done. Xander King's days were officially numbered.

Dragov took a sip of vodka.

"I see this means a lot to you."

Nicoli had no response.

"But let me tell you this. You don't succeed? I kill you, your brother, and that pretty little brunette of yours. Understand?"

Nicoli did understand. Perfectly. Nothing in his degenerate, self-serving cockroach of a life had ever, nor would ever, mean more than this . . .

Killing Xander King.

Apparently Vigilante Justice is a Team Game

During the entire flight back to Langley, Virginia—CIA headquarters—Sam had the cabin television tuned to Fox News. Xander couldn't stand Fox News. He couldn't stand CNN either, for that matter. You can't get *real* news from biased news stations. Those who formed their opinions of the world from the things they learned by watching this *slanted* programming did nothing but make themselves look ignorant— no matter their political views. Mr. Rogers knew more about what was actually going on in the world than the sheep that blindly tuned into this type of programming. Xander knew the lies firsthand from all of the black-ops missions he carried out. They always reported on the outcomes of his missions like they were stating facts, when in fact they were the furthest thing from the truth. The reports about what happened at Scripps Mercy Hospital in sunny San Diego yesterday morning were just another shining example of how gullible the American people could be. It was reported as fact that the attack on Scripps Mercy—like every other attack these days—was an act of terrorism. And it was reported as such only because some random "terrorist cell" took credit for the attack using their Twitter account.

By the mercy of God himself, the plane landed in Virginia, and they no longer had to watch any more bullshit news. Unfortunately, the next thing Xander had to do was say good-bye to Natalie. Something that only got harder to do, not easier. She wanted to stay, but she had halted filming her new movie as long as the production company would let her without throwing an absolute conniption. It would take a while before the look on her face when she said good-bye was no longer absolutely seared into Xander's mind. She was hurting. They had talked for an hour on the jet about how to proceed. They both wanted the same things, but like Natalie said, timing is everything. And this couldn't possibly be a worse time for a burgeoning romance. Natalie knew it, Xander knew it, and so they were going to do their best to leave it at that. If their paths crossed, they would cherish a moment in each other's arms. Anything more than that put Natalie in danger, and that was not something Xander was willing to risk.

Their entire conversation was of course private; however, it's impossible to keep completely private in a confined, enclosed space. Much to Sarah Gilbright's delight. She wasn't trying to listen in, but she wasn't going to put on headphones either. While it wasn't the easiest thing to hear—how much they clearly cared for each other—Sarah couldn't be happier about the decision to let *fate* bring them together if the timing ever were right. Sarah had nothing against Natalie, she seemed like a nice enough person, but as far as Xander King was concerned, she liked him uncommitted and untangled. Sarah would just wait for the right moment to show him what he really needed, and when that time was right, you'd best believe she would pounce like a kitten on a ball of yarn.

The four of them—Xander, Kyle, Sam, and Sarah—all waited impatiently outside the office of CIA Director Thomas Manning's office. Their main goal—Xander's goal—was to talk Manning into leaving them the hell alone and letting him carry on as he always had. Sarah's first goal was to make sure she still had a job. Second, she would try to go along with Xander's goal, but she knew Manning would never go for it. So anything north of grounding Xander and her not being fired would ultimately be good enough for her.

"Xander, were you able to contact your sister, Helen?" Sam broke the silence between them. All around them phones were ringing and people were buzzing. Apparently, business was good at the CIA. Or bad, depending on how you look at it. The complications that Xander's recent *stunts* caused for the CIA had only further swirled the beehive, and Sam knew this would be evident when the queen bee himself—Director Manning—began his tirade.

"Yes, I spoke with her last night. Thank you, Sam. She said the men you sent were parked out front and back of her house. She doesn't understand or like why they are there, but she said she felt safe. That's all that matters to me."

"How's Kaley doing?"

"Growing like a weed. Her favorite word is 'again.' She loves yelling it, particularly when I make the mistake of tossing her, spinning her, or holding her upside down." Xander smiled, as he always did when he thought of his niece.

"Are you talking about your niece?" Sarah asked.

"I am. She's five years of absolute adorable."

"That's sweet."

What wasn't sweet was the way the door to Manning's office flew open. All four of their smiles immediately shifted. Kyle's shifted to fear, Sam's became solemn, Sarah looked away nervously, and Xander's went to five-alarm-fury. No words were spoken and Xander was already preparing for a fight. Manning walked out. He was a bulldog of a man—short, stout, and slobbering mad, his face permanently red and his suit screaming for help as it tried desperately to stay buttoned around his ever growing—stress eater—belly.

"Well, if it isn't the biggest pain in my ass since my double hemorrhoid of 2011," Manning barked.

Xander shot to his feet. Sarah noticed that the two of them could literally not be more different. Manning looked worn, gray, stubby, soft, and completely devoid of style. Xander was fresh, tall, and hard as a rock. Xander's photograph belonged in the pages of a men's style magazine. He wore his tight-fitting navy blazer, white collared shirt, gray skinny jeans, and navy Italian loafers like an all-out stud. He combined the dapperness of a European with the sexy strength of a full-blooded American. It was the very best of both worlds. *A man built in a lab,* Sarah thought, despite the tension of the moment.

"By pain in the ass I'm assuming you mean doing your job for you. Taking out no less than seven of the FBI's ten most wanted in the last twelve months. That pain in the ass?"

"So, you're going to come in here, to a man who holds your fate in the palm of his hands, and be a smart-ass. Fuckin' prick, I oughta throw you in jail right now."

Xander took a step forward.

"You could try."

"Try?" Manning's head looked about to explode. Sarah noticed that his shade of red had gone from rouge to maroon. She had to do something before this became a real situation.

"Director Manning, Xander, can I just remind you that we are on the same team?"

Xander scoffed while Manning turned his rage to her.

"Sarah Gilbright, nice of you to finally check in. Let me just remind *you* that your fate, just like Captain America here, also hangs in the balance of my good graces. And let me just tell both of you this"—he pointed between the two of them—"It ain't lookin' good for either one of ya."

Xander heard the accent of Manning's last sentence turn to hillbilly, and he knew he was making fun of Xander being from Kentucky.

Xander overexaggerated a country twang himself. "How original, Manning. That's right, I'm a hillbilly. I have a bourbon distillery and a farm, you know, where my seventeen-million-dollar *horsee* stays in a barn worth three times your house here in Virginia."

Kyle swore he could see steam piping out of Manning's ears.

Sam stood up; she'd had enough of the nonsense.

"Could we please step inside your office like adults and have an actual conversation? Regardless of the fact that our fates are in your hands, Mr. Manning, Sarah is right. We *are* trying to accomplish the same goals."

"Is that right, princess? And just what goal might that be? To avenge Xander's parents? I couldn't give a rabbit fuck less about them."

Xander stepped forward, but Sam caught him and stepped in front of him before he could rearrange the ugly on Manning's face.

"Well, that may be the case, Mr. Manning, but I do know that you care about having Xander working for you, and not against you. I think everyone, including *your* superiors, would agree with that."

Just then a man stepped out into the hallway from Manning's office. He looked like he was straight out of an old western. He held a tan suede cowboy hat down by his dark blue Levi's as he ran a hand through his medium-length silver hair. His matching silver mustache, red-and-black checkered flannel shirt, and battle-hardened, wrinkled face along with a good-looking pair of caramel, tan cowboy boots rounded out his Montana man persona. He stepped in front of Manning and reached his hand toward Xander. Xander accepted the handshake from the old, but still fit, cowboy.

"Jack Bronson." A real man's man voice.

Jack reminded Xander of a carbon copy of Sam Elliot. Voice and all. The man, like Xander, had a real presence.

"Xander King."

Xander reminded Jack of a hardened—whatever that pretty guy's name was in *The Hangover*, something Cooper. Real pretty, like him, but with a razor-sharp edge. An edge you can only obtain from war.

"Frogman?" Jack grunted, alluding to Xander's time as a SEAL. Something he and Xander shared.

"Oorah." Xander smiled.

"Oh, terrific, the two of you are fast friends." Sarcasm poured out of that comment as Manning rolled his eyes and motioned for them all to move inside his office. Had Manning made a massive error putting Jack on this?

Jack had managed to defuse the situation. Just before Sam and Kyle walked through the door, Manning held up his hand. "The help will have to wait in the lobby. Mary will be glad to get you a coffee and a copy of *The Washington Post*. I'm sure there is yet another story in there of how Captain Fuckup King here goes about his business."

And just like that, the tension shot back through the roof. Xander waved them in.

"Where I go, they go. You want to talk to me, you talk to them. We don't do a damn thing without them. Captain Fuckup, that's you, dick." Mr. Mature.

Manning puffed out his chest. "You don't make the rules here, King, and—"

"Boys," Jack spoke up. "If everything you two say turns into a pissing contest, that's all this whole meeting's gonna be. Tommy, it seems like what these two did over in Syria ought to be enough to get them into this meeting. They're the kind of people I want on my team anyway."

"I appreciate that, Mr. Bronson—"

"Call me Jack."

"I appreciate that, Jack, but *your team?*" Xander made a face.

Manning finally gave in and had everyone take a seat. After starting with his "this is how this is gonna go" speech, Manning proceeded to explain how their relationship was going to work. Xander's team, the CIA, and Jack Bronson would all work together. After some back and forth between Xander and

Manning not seeing eye to eye on things—well, on almost everything—they finally came to an agreement.

Jack Bronson would be the lead. Mostly, Manning explained, because he couldn't leave handling Xander to the— in his own words—"apparently inadequate Sarah Gilbright." But he at least let her be a part of this so-called team. Xander agreed to Jack being designated the lead because he knew he was going to do what he had to do, regardless. At least this way, Jack—who Xander liked immediately—would be the one to communicate with Manning. Something Xander would never do, and he was happy Sam wouldn't have to do it either. It was even easier to let Jack have this designation after he heard the similarities in their military experience. Both walked away from prestigious careers due to lack of trust in the US government. Manning at least had the foresight to see the need for bringing in someone Xander could relate to. However, Xander was no fool. He knew that no matter what, this was Manning's guy. All the important details would stay between Xander, Sam, and Kyle.

The jury was still out on Sarah Gilbright.

Sam's Cold Heart Might Just Have a Warm Spot After All

Xander, Sam, and Kyle gave Sarah time to pack a bag before they all boarded the jet bound for Lexington. Jack Bronson agreed to hold council at Xander's home there, but he wanted to drive himself down. Sam got to work immediately on preparing the next steps, but when she approached Xander, he made it very clear that he needed a break. Twenty-four hours. That's all he asked. He knew how quickly they needed to regroup, because at the very moment they were speaking about it, Nicoli Pavlovich and Vitalii Dragov would be trying to figure out a way to kill him. He just had to have one day to recover. She declined his offer of taking a break with them, but she understood.

Sam knew that Xander's hidden reason, the *real* reason, why he wanted to take a break. He wanted to get to know Sarah

Gilbright and where her allegiance truly lay. Sam was okay with this, because she knew Xander had a special way with women. She knew beyond a shadow of a doubt that by the time they all sat down together tomorrow morning to get serious, Xander would know exactly just how *in* Sarah Gilbright was. She also saw the way Sarah looked at Xander, and knew there would undoubtedly be some "complications" that came along with this so-called night off. Sarah was much too beautiful for Xander to keep his hands off of her. Especially with Natalie Rockwell off in Paris, trying to live without him. Sam knew that wouldn't last long either. She had never seen Xander look at a woman the way he looked at Natalie. He was in love, and when Xander loved something, it stayed around forever. The only thing that really made her nervous for Xander was that Sarah embodied a lot of the same qualities that she knew he liked about Natalie. Sam didn't do love anymore for this very reason. That, and she had been burnt by a love triangle once herself. She knew there was nothing she could do because Xander led with his heart. And while that is an amazing quality in a person, it can often lead to more heartache than anything else.

Sam let all of these thoughts wash over her as she looked out the window to see Kyle, Kate, Sarah, and Xander playing in the pool. Kyle had invited Kate—his "Lexington girlfriend"— over to relax with Xander and Sarah. She looked out beyond them toward the rolling hills of freshly cut green grass. Sam had never been much of a fan of anything but the city. That was because she had never known anything else. She had to admit to herself, as the afternoon sun shined down over the majesty of Kentucky, that she couldn't imagine going back after now being exposed to both ways of life. She, of course, could never tell

Xander this, but Lexington and the Internet had all the things in the world a girl could ever need, without all the shit the miserable people living around buildings all day try to sell you is good about where they live. Bullocks, every single bit of it. Big city living is for people who haven't figured out what to do with their lives. Sam realized that was why they loved all those distractions, to keep from having to actually work at figuring it out. Sam knew she didn't have it all figured out, but she was at least doing some real good with her life. A fact that, before she met Xander, she never thought would be possible. You just never know in life. She had that thought as she was looking down at Kyle and couldn't understand why it bothered her when she saw Kate touching him. For as long as she'd known Kyle, she'd thought him an immature wildcard, incapable of real love. But something was different about him since coming back from Syria. Or maybe something was different about the way she saw him. Whatever it was, the thought returned like a bullet through flesh.

You never know.

"Xander, thanks for being okay with me coming along. I'm not sure Manning would have let me keep my job if you hadn't insisted that I be part of the team."

"Sarah, if I haven't said it, thank you for everything you have done for me. You have gone way beyond to help me and to make sure that my friends and I were safe. I am forever in your debt for keeping that crazy son of a bitch alive." Xander smiled and pointed to Kyle who was leaning against the side of the pool talking to Kate. Xander was on his back on a float in the pool, being careful not to get the stitches in his stomach wet.

Sarah had pulled a sun chair over to the side of the pool, and was lying on her stomach looking down at him. She found him absolutely fetching in his swimming trunks. The sun glistening off of his lightly sweat-beaded body.

Before she could respond, Kyle and Kate waded over, and Kyle splashed playfully at them both.

"Would you all stop being so damm serious all the time? Sarah, I need you to be a positive influence if you are gonna be around. I have a hard enough time getting Xander to relax, I don't need your help making it worse." Kyle splashed again. "Now get your ass in the pool, girl!"

"Hey now, come on. Watch it. Don't get Xander's stitches wet!" Sarah laughed as she got up. She took a seat on the concrete, letting her legs dangle in the pool. The three of them stared back at Sarah like she was on fire. And, as far as Xander was concerned, she was hot enough to be. Her blonde hair looked lighter than usual against the darkening tan of her body. The only bathing suit she could find in her apartment in Virginia on such short notice was a pale blue bikini—Brazilian-cut bottoms with little tiny straps on the top. Far too skimpy to be wearing around people she hardly knew.

Kate said what everyone was thinking.

"Girl, you are sexy!"

"Well, thanks," Sarah blushed. "This bikini is a little much, but I hadn't been planning on a pool day. Can't remember the last time I had one, actually."

"Can I ask a personal question?" said Kate.

"Sure."

"Are those real?"

"You don't have to answer that, Sarah," Xander interjected.

"Oh, it's fine. I get that question a lot. They are real. Mom's great gift or burden, depending on which way you look at it."

"Burden? I'd kill for a set of those."

"So would I!" Kyle joked. That warranted a punch in the shoulder from Kate.

Sarah just looked at Xander and smiled. He didn't say a word. She really wished he had.

The afternoon grew toward evening, and the cicadas began their southern serenade from the tops of the live oaks that surrounded the property. The warm air carried the scent of honeysuckle. Every once in a while a horse whinny could be heard, possibly from the great King's Ransom himself. The group made their way to separate quarters to get cleaned up for the evening. They had reservations at Bella Notte, Xander's favorite Italian restaurant in town. On his way to the shower, Xander noticed a light coming from the bottom of Sam's room. He knocked on the door.

"Hey Sam, can I come in?"

"Of course."

Xander walked in, and Sam was sitting up against the bed's purple quilted headboard, her computer in her lap and hair in a ponytail. Xander didn't often see her so dressed down. It looked good on her. She was wearing a white V-neck T-shirt and a pair of black yoga pants. The same pants that seemingly every other woman on earth had decided necessary to wear all the time, regardless of their plans to actually do yoga or not. Xander didn't mind. Even a mediocre body looked great in them. Not that Sam needed help in that department.

"What can I do for you, Xander?"

"Come to dinner with us."

The soft yellow light of the lamp gave Sam's otherwise pale skin a nice warm glow.

"Oh no, no, no. I know better than that. Dinner with you and Kyle means coming home at three in the morning, snockered, the entire next morning lost."

"Come on, Sam." Xander turned on his best smile. "We haven't just hung out in forever."

"You know that smile doesn't work on me, so you can just go ahead and wipe it right off. I'll just order some takeout or something. I am eyeball deep in preparing a plan for us, and it is really starting to come together."

"You know that I appreciate, so much, everything you do for me, right?"

"I know."

"But just tonight, knock it off? All you do is work. You make me look bad, and all I do is work." Xander turned on the puppy-dog eyes.

"There you go, letting Kyle plant seeds in your head again. If it were up to him, you'd never do another thing but indulge his childish whims."

"Kyle's not so bad, you know. He loves you too, Sam. And ever since you dropped down to your underwear on the plane a couple of weeks ago, he hasn't stopped talking about you either."

"I would eat that poor boy alive."

Xander had a feeling that was absolutely true. "I don't doubt that, Sammy. Now come on, for me. Come with us?"

"I don't do fifth wheel."

"You don't have to. Kate can't make it. Help me get to know Sarah better. I need you to get a feel for her anyway."

"Get a feel for her? That what you're trying to do, Romeo?"

Xander laughed. Julia Sanders—she helped around the house when Xander was in town—came in with an ice-cold gin and tonic perched on an old-fashioned, round, silver serving tray.

"You're behind. I had Julia here whip you up a G and T. What do you say?"

Sam sat there for a moment eyeballing Xander, then the drink, then back to Xander. Just then Kyle poked his head inside the bedroom.

"Where's my date?" His goofy smile turned something in Sam's hardened heart.

"Sam?" Xander smiled and held his arms out to his sides.

She paused a moment longer and then a smile finally made its way to the surface. "Oh, all right. But just dinner!" she said as she slammed her laptop shut.

"Yes!" Kyle and Xander rejoiced collectively.

"I'll just call Melanie and have her work on a few things while we *eat*."

"Whatever gets your ass down to the driveway in thirty is what I want you to do."

Sam hopped up, grabbed the gin and tonic, and walked toward the bathroom.

"All right, go on then." She waved behind her.

Kyle and Xander both couldn't help but notice how great Sam looked in those ever flattering black yoga pants. Again, not that she needed the help.

Dean Martin, Bottles of Wine, and Cold Showers

The buttery voice of Dean Martin melting over sweeping violins and the thrumming beat of a bellowing upright bass filtered through the speakers of Bella Notte Italian Trattoria. Happy chatter and the clink-clank of busy silverware were the music being made inside. It was rare to see unsmiling faces gathered around a gluttonous meal. The inside of the restaurant vaguely reminded Xander of his villa in Tuscany, a place he hadn't visited in far too long. The restaurant floor, an antiqued cobblestone, and the walls, made up of broken stucco, were illuminated by the soft yellow light emanating from the outstretched branches of an olive tree that took up real estate in the middle of the indoor courtyard.

It was difficult for Xander to pass up pizza whenever he saw it on a menu, but tonight he opted for the lasagna. There was just something about layer upon layer of meat sauce, cheese, and noodles that could transform any mood to a great one. The Chianti they passed around the table certainly didn't hurt, but tonight no one needed the boost in morale. All of them had silently decided to save the darkness of life for the dealings of tomorrow.

Sarah finished the last bite of her pasta—Penne Gorgonzola—with a satisfied sigh.

"So, Sam, how did you get involved with the military in London?"

Sam pushed her plate forward and took up her glass of wine, gave it a swirl, then a sip.

"Honestly, it's entirely cliché."

"You know, I haven't heard this either." Kyle sat back in his chair and admired the bulge the overload of meatballs had created in his stomach. "You know everything about me and Xander, but you never share anything about you."

"It's really not very captivating."

Xander wiped his mouth and gave Sam a wry smile.

"Bullshit. That's precisely what it is. Don't let her fool you."

Sam returned his smile in kind.

"So, what is the worst thing that has happened to you while you've been on a mission?" said Sarah.

A chill fell across the table and there was an undeniable shift in mood. The question made Kyle instantly uncomfortable as his memory blasted him back to the bottom of Khatib's compound where he was forced to relive the answer to the question. It was also the worst thing he had ever seen himself. It was something that he still thought about every day. Sarah sensed the awkward silence and made everyone feel better by retracting the question.

"Sorry, that was horrible dinner table manners," she said with a bit of a slur. "Must be the wine. I don't normally drink more than a glass. I think this might be my . . . third?"

"Well, this was delicious, but we have a big day tomorrow. Maybe we should get home?" Sam suggested.

"What?" Not surprisingly, Kyle was near outrage at the thought. "It's only ten!"

"I agree with Sam, we can open another bottle on the patio, it's a beautiful evening," said Xander.

"Not you too! Sarah?"

"I could do a little more wine. The patio sounds lovely."

"Jesus Christ. What are we, ninety?"

"No, Kyle, we are not ninety," Sam said. "But we aren't nineteen either. We aren't trying to *find* ourselves and the three of us don't need our egos stroked by a drunken slut to make us feel like we've achieved something."

"Speak for yourself." Xander laughed. Sarah giggled tipsily as she smiled at him.

"Well, Sam, maybe I wouldn't have to chase after drunken sluts if you'd give me the time of day."

"Well, Kyle, I don't recall you ever having the balls to approach a real woman like myself."

That shut him up. He took an unnaturally hard swallow at the thought. Was that an invitation? Surely not, Sam had only ever held Kyle in contempt. Sarah and Xander got a kick out of seeing Kyle's normally cocky exterior get a jolt from the almighty Samantha Harrison. Xander paid the bill, making the waitress's day with his usual 100 percent tip, and they made their way back to the house.

On the way, Xander texted Julia to prepare the patio with wine and dessert. As they walked outside through the tall glass French doors, they were met with a gorgeous spread. Two bottles of port—Xander's favorite—had been decanted and were situated on the table alongside two bouquets of white roses, a plate of assorted chocolates, and a chocolate soufflé with a side of vanilla ice cream. Strands of exposed yellow rope lights hung above them, and Sarah had to pinch herself to make sure she wasn't dreaming. Her only hope at that point was that Kyle and Sam would somehow decide to forego this dream and leave her and Xander to it.

That wasn't the case.

"My, this looks outstanding. Julia, is it?" Sarah asked the dark-haired, eager-to-please young lady who began pouring the port into each of the four snifters on the table.

"Yes, my name is Julia. I'm happy you like it, Ms. . . . ?"

"Sarah."

"Ms. Sarah. If you need anything else, please don't hesitate. I'll bring out a pitcher of ice water as well."

"Thank you so much," said Sarah. Julia gave her a nod and went back inside. "She's lovely, and she does a fantastic job. You're lucky to have such great people," she said to Xander.

Sam took a seat and smiled.

"I assure you, Sarah, it isn't luck. Xander overpays everyone tremendously."

"I'm sure he does. That's sweet." Sarah smiled at him.

"Sweet isn't the half of it. Did you see that Porsche in the driveway?" Sam asked Sarah.

"I did. Gorgeous car, yours?"

"Julia's."

74

"Wow, are you always so perfect?" Sarah sat down next to Xander and gave his hand a squeeze. Xander smiled. When Sarah noticed Sam noticing her hand on his, she pulled it away.

The four of them continued to laugh and indulge in the warm summer evening. The humidity wrapped around them like a damp blanket, and the crickets sang them their very best lullaby. Everyone was getting well acquainted with the new girl, and they couldn't for the life of them find one thing about Sarah that they didn't like. Not for lack of trying on Sam's part. As they finished the first bottle of port, Xander became more and more enamored by Sarah's smile, and of course the plunging neckline of her blouse. His mind kept jumping back a couple of hours to her sun-kissed body in that baby-blue bikini.

"Well, this has been a lovely evening, but I am going to head on up," Sam announced.

"Come on, Sam, have one more with me down by the pool?" Kyle practically begged.

Sam didn't answer. She just smiled, shook her head, and walked toward the house. "Goodnight everyone." Just before she disappeared, she looked back over her shoulder and gave Kyle a wonderful tease of a smile.

"Damn, she's sexy. Why am I just now realizing this?"

"Easy, cowboy. She would chew you up and spit you out." Xander smiled.

"Exactly." Kyle smiled back. He let out a huff of sexual frustration, pushed his seat toward the table, and wished Sarah and Xander a good night. Even if he wasn't going to get lucky, bro-code emphatically states that you don't get in the way of your friend's chances. And everyone had seen at one point or another the way Sarah got a twinkle in her eye anytime Xander King came around. It was so bright that it was distracting, maybe distracting everyone from noticing Xander shining a little twinkle of his own.

"Thank you for a wonderful evening, Xander." Sarah turned toward him, all the sincerity in the world in her eyes. "It's been a while since I've had an evening of laughs."

"Well, you're very welcome. Does that mean you are calling it an evening?"

"I really better. Otherwise, I'm going to say something embarrassing that *sober me* will regret in the morning."

Xander wanted to invite her to his room. He really did. However, all he could hear was Sam's voice in his head, nagging him to death about making things more complicated. Women.

"I understand."

The two of them stood, and Xander leaned in and kissed her on the cheek. She smelled wonderful. Like vanilla and flowers, chocolate and wine. For a moment they stood face to face. Her hand on his arm, her eyes lost in his. Their hot breath, sweet with wine, rapid between them as their hearts found a quickened pace. Sarah nervously dropped his stare with a giggle and grabbed her clutch from the table as she took a step back. The temperature seemed ten degrees cooler just outside of his aura. They both could feel the heat.

"All right then." Xander broke the silence as he gathered the port and the stack of plates. "Sleep well, I'll see you bright and early. Thank you again for being here."

"There is nowhere else I'd rather be," she said. She took two slow steps backward, then turned to go inside. She hoped he hadn't noticed the way she was biting her lip. Or maybe she hoped he had.

Xander had noticed. He noticed everything. It's what made him such a fantastic lover. It was the way she bit her lip that left him hollow. It reminded him of Natalie. He walked inside, into the kitchen, and set the decanted port wine down on the counter. Julia turned from the sink and gave him a smile.

"Are you finished for the night, Xander?" Xander always insisted that everyone working for him called him by his first name. His pause before answering caused her smile to grow. "She's a lovely woman."

Xander knew what Julia's smile meant, and he couldn't help but laugh. "Can you get me two more clean glasses?"

Sam had just finished washing her face when she heard a knock at her door. She knew it was Kyle, come to attempt one last tipsy advance. She couldn't help but smile. He was going to absolutely love her negligee. She always wore some type of lingerie to bed. It made her feel sexy. She had never been happier about this little habit of hers than she was in that moment. She took a sexy stance, hand on her hip as she stood by the bed, ten feet from the door. Only the soft yellow light from a lamp in the corner helping her glow.

"Who is it?" She smiled.

"It's Kyle. Can I come in?"

"Of course."

Kyle slowly opened the door, and the look on his face made Sam warm in places that hadn't been touched by anyone but her in quite some time. Kyle couldn't have wiped the astonished look on his face off if he wanted to. Not even with bleach. There in front of him stood Sam in something Kyle had only dreamed of seeing. The tall, long-legged Brit had on a sheer black baby-doll negligee. The black bra was vaguely see-through and attached to the bottom was a sheer black veil hung down to the tops of her thighs. Behind that sheer he could see a flat stomach that met with perfect hips, covered only by a black thong. He could almost see her tenderness, if it wasn't for that extra sheer veil clouding the way. He couldn't help but swallow uncomfortably as a warmth of his own gathered below.

"You like what you see?"

Kyle stepped all the way inside the room. He couldn't speak. He just gave a nod.

"What? Have you nothing to say? The ladies' man himself is speechless? I don't know what to say myself."

"Y-you look amazing, Sam."

"You're sweet when you're vulnerable." She walked toward him, and she could see his body tense in nervousness. She was aware of the power she had over him. And she reveled in it. The closer she came to him the more he could see the outline of her nipples through the sheer bra.

So sexy.

Now she was standing right in front of him. "Whatever am I going to do with you?"

Kyle answered without hesitation. "Whatever the hell you want."

To his surprise she took him in her hand, feeling that he had become aroused. She absolutely loved the deep breath he couldn't help but take in his surprise. She moved closer, gently moving her hand back and forth.

"You like the way I look, Kyle?"

"I-I do."

He was a blubbering idiot. Putty in her hands. She leaned her head toward his, her luscious lips inching ever so close to his. She brushed up against them as she spoke. "Then I'm glad you got an eyeful, you pervert." She gave his body a shove out the door and gave him a wink just before she shut it.

Kyle bent over and put his hands on his knees. His breath was hurried and his manhood throbbing. "Fuck," he said to the walls in a huff.

"Everything okay there, buddy?"

Kyle jumped, not expecting Xander to be there. He covered the bulge in his black cotton pajama pants and looked up at Xander. The smile on Xander's face was priceless, and embarrassing.

"Sam put the ole tease on you, huh?"

"I think I'm in love."

The two of them shared a laugh, and Kyle gave Xander a wink as he looked at the wine and two glasses in his hands. "Looks like I'm not the only one? I'm assuming that's not for me."

"Easy."

Kyle threw up his hands. "I'm on your team, buddy." And he walked away with a laugh. "I need a cold shower."

Xander smiled to himself as he was left alone in the upstairs hallway. He'd accidentally seen Sam's regular sleep attire once. He could only imagine the look on Kyle's face when he saw it. With a shake of his head, he got back to tending his own business and walked toward the opposite end of the hall. The same hall that just a couple of weeks ago he had shot and killed nine men that had intruded on his home. He tried not to think of it, but every time he walked past the stairs, he couldn't help but recall seeing Natalie there, fear fixed on her face, tears running down her cheeks while she was held at gunpoint. The two of them never stood a chance of working out.

He shook it off and transferred the decanter to his right hand, balancing it and the wine glasses as he gave a quiet knock on Sarah's door. He waited a moment, put his ear to the door, but heard nothing. He gave one more quiet knock and turned the doorknob as he gave a slow push.

"Sarah?" He whispered, then immediately stopped movement as the bedside lamp showed him her quiet, eyes-closed face. She had already fallen asleep. He stood in the doorway for a moment. Captivated. He couldn't take his eyes off of her. She was gorgeous. The covers were pulled up tight around her chin, so he didn't feel like a pervert as he looked at her. He wanted nothing more than to wake her, but he just couldn't. She was so peaceful. As much as every ounce of Xander hated that the CIA was now a part of his life, he couldn't help but know that she was on his side. And, most importantly, if it came down to it, he knew he could trust her.

He stepped quietly across the carpet to her bedside and did his very best to shut off the lamp without waking her. He then poured a small amount of wine into a glass and left it on the nightstand. He wanted her to know he was thinking of her before he went to bed, silly as that may be. A strand of moonlight worked its way through a small break in the curtains and fell gently across Sarah's face. His mind flashed to seeing Kelly in bed on the yacht in a similar fashion.

Damn he loved women. He didn't have many vices, but a beautiful woman just might be the death of him. He softly brushed a lock of hair from her cheek, bent down, and gave her a kiss on the forehead. She rustled slightly, then fell back into oblivion.

Sleeping Beauty, he thought. Then he retreated to his bedroom at the other end of the house.

Kyle wasn't the only one that needed a cold shower on this night.

A Friend of the Family

The sun came up over Lexington, Kentucky, displaying the beautiful land in all its gold-tinted splendor. Downtown, the bankers, lawyers, and businessmen made their way into their concrete-and-glass boxes. Hardly a mile from there to the southeast, students, mostly hungover but a few of them lively and eager to learn, were making their way into classrooms at the University of Kentucky, bluebirds perched in the live oaks serenading their walk. On the edge of town, on some of the wealthiest land in all the world, trainers had their stopwatches in hand as their million-dollar horses thundered around the tracks for the amusement of their billionaire owners. King's Ransom, the reigning Kentucky Derby champion, was busy eating his breakfast as his billionaire proud poppa, Xander King, greeted Jack Bronson at the front door with a firm handshake and led him into his office.

"Beautiful land you got here, Xander."

"Thanks, Jack. How was the drive?"

"Quiet, just like I like it. That stud of yours stay here between races?"

"Sure does, he's in the stables out back. You like horses?"

"Love 'em. Grew up on a big farm in Montana. Used to break the wild ones for my daddy."

Montana man, Xander knew it.

"Whew, tough work. You're a better man than me."

"No question." Jack smiled, his little yellow Chiclet teeth giving a wave as he did.

Xander returned the smile. Jack's way reminded him of his father. Xander re-introduced Jack to Sam, Kyle, and Sarah, and they each pulled up a chair ready to listen to what Sam had to say. Everyone got the awkward from last night out at breakfast where they all laughed, and like Jamie Foxx, they blamed it on the alcohol. Sarah asked about the wine on her nightstand, and Xander played it off that he must have accidentally left it when he shut off her lamp for her. Sarah knew better and kicked herself for having the ability to fall asleep so easily.

Sam took her natural position at the head of the room, just in front of Xander's desk. "Good to see you again, Mr. Bronson. I know you are the lead, as designated by Manning, but I hope you don't mind if I begin, as I have already gathered several key points of intel."

Jack stood up and adjusted his jeans at the oversized and overwhelmingly hideous gold belt buckle. "Just so we're clear. Manning did appoint me *the lead*," he made air quotes with his fingers, "but, frankly, I am very aware that you are way ahead of me with what is going on. Now, I know my fair share about Dragov and his operation, but I am surprised that I was put on this team. I'm assuming Manning doesn't trust any of you, so he called in an old navy comrade out of retirement to be his eyes. That about how y'all see it?"

Xander couldn't help but be relieved that this wouldn't be a battle the entire way. "I think you hit the nail on the head, Jack."

"Okay, well good. But that don't mean I can't be of service to ya. I still have skills, and though my hair may be gray, I assure you, those skills haven't wavered."

Sam nodded and thanked him. "I am very aware of your skills, Mr. Bronson. And they will fit perfectly with what we need."

Xander wasn't surprised at all that Sam had done her homework on the new guy. She probably already knew how he took his coffee and how long it took for him to take a piss. "If you don't mind, what is your specialty?"

Sam answered for Jack. "He's probably one of the five most well-regarded snipers in your military's history."

Xander looked at him, impressed. Jack nodded to Sam.

"I'd say that about sums it up. I make a mean flapjack and can start a fire from sticks too, if the need should ever arise."

They all laughed. Xander liked Jack, but he was still put here by Manning. And he did not like Manning. There was something slimy about that son of a bitch, so it would take Xander just a little more time with Jack to give him the full green light.

Jack took his seat, and Sam went into full detail on everything she had learned about Vitalii Dragov, Nicoli Pavlovich, and the scumbags they associated with. She told them all about Dragov's multibillion-dollar crime ring. Some of her contacts were able to shed some light on the ghost that Nicoli had become, and she did everything she could to help them understand that other than Xander himself, there might not be a more proficient killer on the planet.

"The way it went down at the hospital was an anomaly, I assure you. Nicoli Pavlovich doesn't miss, and he won't miss again if he gets another chance."

"Okay, so why Xander's parents?" Kyle asked. He turned to Xander. "I don't get it, I knew your dad, he was like a second father to me. Sure, he was gone a lot, but he would *never* have been involved with a guy like Dragov. No way."

"If I may?" Sam jumped in. Xander nodded. He already knew what she was about to say. It was going to hurt to hear it out loud, but he was glad Sam had given him the info to read prior to the meeting. It would help the sting.

"According to a file that Manning sent over yesterday, unfortunately, Kyle, you are mistaken." Kyle just shook his head in disbelief. He wasn't going to buy a word that came out of Sam's mouth. "Martin King was an oil man—that, the entire world knows. He took what his father started and made it even bigger. He apparently did such a great job that it caught the interest of the world's largest crime boss, Vitalii Dragov. Now, Kyle, part of what you said I believe is true. Xander's father would not have been involved, I believe, if Dragov hadn't forced him. That being said, in a file I was able to *not so legally* get my hands on, he stayed on and together the two of them made a lot of money."

That sentence, though Xander didn't believe it, really hurt.

"It was when Dragov got wind that Mr. King was going to turn on him that he made the decision to get rid of him. Unfortunately, Xander's mother was caught in the crossfire. I'm sorry, Xander. I know this is tough to hear."

Xander stood and walked to the front of his desk. The sadness hung heavy in his eyes. Sarah and Kyle both looked on with empathy.

"Unfortunately, what we did in Syria a couple of weeks ago resulted in the loss of a dear friend. But I know Sean would be proud of all of us. He's somewhere in the great beyond cheering us on right now. You all know what it will mean to me to look into the eyes of the man responsible for the death of my parents, right before I take his life. But you need to know that this is my fight. Not yours."

"Let me just stop you right there, son." Jack stood up. "I know I don't know you very well, but I know by your track record that you're a righteous man. And I don't know any of the rest of you here, but I believe I know why you're here. 'Cause you would lay your life on the line for Xander, mostly 'cause you know he'd do the same for you. And though our reasons might be different, Xander, ain't a goddammed one of us letting you do this on your own. And we know full well what's at stake."

Xander let that set in. He appreciated what Jack was saying. He could see in his friends' eyes that they all agreed. The bridge he couldn't form was over the gap in what Jack's reasons were exactly.

"I appreciate that, Jack, but why exactly do you give so much of a damn? You have to see it from my eyes, we don't even know each other."

"I can't say exactly, but let me just tell you that Manning, though he wasn't aware of it, was influenced in his decision to bring me on board."

"Okay, but that isn't enough. You know why we are all here. If we are going to war together, it's only fair that we have that same level of familiarity with you."

"I can't."

"Then you can go, Jack. And tell Manning to go fuck himself while you're at it." The sincerity in Xander's statement could be read loud and clear in his eyes. Jack thought it over for a moment, then readjusted his belt.

"If I tell you why, you have to promise there won't be another question. Not one."

"I don't make promises I can't keep, Jack. Tell me why you're here so we can get down to business."

Jacked paused, considering.

"Jack, it was nice to meet you. You can see your way out—"

"Your daddy was a friend of mine."

A chill wrapped around the bottom of Xander's spine and slithered like a snake all the way up his back. And that was without knowing the full implications of Jack's statement.

He would know, soon.

Director Manning Has a Secret

Back in Langley, Virginia—just above CIA headquarters—a dark-gray rain cloud hovered ominously overhead. It was a metaphor for the darkness that hovered over Director Manning. He sat alone in his office nervously working his leg up and down, waiting for the untraceable old Motorola StarTAC cell phone to ring. The call was supposed to come in at nine in the morning. It was now past nine-thirty, and with each passing second Manning's mind raced. He couldn't understand how in the hell he had put himself in this situation. The Director of the CIA was afraid. How on earth is that even possible? How many bad decisions had to be made to get him to this point? His shaking leg only picked up speed along with the continuous rise of his blood pressure.

All of this was Xander's fault.

If he'd just kept on with his vigilante justice and not been so hell-bent on revenge. If Manning hadn't put a woman in charge of watching Xander, a woman who of course fell for the pretty son of a bitch, he wouldn't be in this spot either. All he wanted to do was make sure that Xander stayed in his lane. Stayed away from the big-boy business.

Away from Manning's secret.

The secret that now involved an inevitable clash of the titans—Xander King against Vitalii Dragov—and he had a sickening feeling that in the middle of all of it, the blame would in some way get shifted to him. He knew Sarah was compromised, so he just let her go deeper in with Xander. At least then he knew what she was up to. Jack would report anything to the contrary back to him. He still wasn't exactly sure why he put Jack on it. The suggestion came to him in the form of a report that showed the retired Special Agent Jack Bronson's dislike of pretty boys. He'd pretty much dedicated his life to hating them. He was a rugged good ol' boy, loyal to the core. Some of the men who had worked alongside him had reported back. That was the reason he chose him: someone who had been off the grid, didn't like pretty boys, and would be loyal to his boss to the end. He didn't like the way the meeting between Jack and Xander had gone, however. He hadn't counted on the fact that Xander was just a good ol' boy at heart himself. This factor could be a fatal mistake in this high stakes game of life and death. What's done is done. Manning would just have to count on that loyalty that everyone he spoke with said made Jack the man he is. Loyalty. He just hoped the pendulum of Jack's loyalty continued to swing his way.

Manning almost jumped out of his chair when the loud trill of the Motorola finally rang. He banged his shaking leg on the desk, and pain rifled up his body like a chased cat up a tree. By ring number three he had managed a couple of deep breaths so he could answer the call normally.

"You're late." Okay, not normally.

"And you are incompetent."

The guttural grunt of the voice coupled with the Russian accent made Manning's entire stubby body shudder.

"I have it under control."

"This is what you said just before your men ended up dead on yacht in the Virgin Islands. I don't think you have anything under this control."

"Oh, and I suppose you are one to talk. You killed eleven people at that hospital and not one of them was the target, all while blowing the cover of your number-one asset."

"Nicoli? Don't worry about Nicoli, he will get job done. Unlike you."

Manning couldn't sit still. He jumped up from his chair and began to pace the room. A waterfall of sweat cascaded down his lower back.

"Listen, Dragov—"

"No. It is your turn to listen."

Manning's legs stopped pacing, but his heart didn't. It thudded against his chest so hard it caused a shortness of breath.

"You have man now, in Xander King's camp, correct?"

"Yes."

"Can you trust this man?"

"His loyalty is his calling card."

"Calling card? What this means?"

"Yes, I trust him." Manning got to the point.

"Good. Nicoli is ready to move. As soon as your man reports to you, you tell me where Xander will be and Nicoli will kill him."

"One man won't be nearly enough."

"You let me worry about this."

"Just make sure you understand, one man won't be enough. And, there is no need to wait. I got a call from my guy a half hour ago. Xander held a meeting this morning; they are leaving for London tomorrow where they will be meeting with British intelligence that claims to know your every move. Jack tells me that Xander's closest confidant, Sam—ex-MI6—knows of a mole inside your organization. They are going to form their plan of attack after those meetings, then come directly for you."

"This horseshit. I have no mole."

"Apparently you need to tighten it up."

"Me? Dragov tighten it up? Fuck you, American pissant. The fact that I am in situation to begin with is your fault. Don't think I have forgotten this."

Manning's stomach dropped. For a moment, he had forgotten that fact and let his big mouth poke the proverbial bear.

"I-I haven't forgotten."

"So, your man inside this Xander's camp, he does not know our little secret, correct?"

"No one knows our secret, Dragov. No one."

"Makes no difference to me really, but for you, big difference. You better hope Nicoli Pavlovich get to Xander before secret somehow get to him first."

"Are you threatening me, Dragov?"

"Threat? No, no, no, no threat. Warning. If this Xander is legend that you say he is—which of course I doubt—then you better keep me in the loop on exactly where he is at every moment. Otherwise, maybe my enemy becomes your enemy. Вы понимаете меня?"

"Yes, Dragov. I understand. Just make sure this secret stays between us. You wouldn't want the CIA or the FBI taking any more interest than they already do in your business, would you?"

"Then we have understanding. But don't worry my friend, *our* problem ends in London. Nicoli will make sure of that."

It's a Long Story

Xander pulled up the shade of the jet's window, took a swig of his Red Bull, and let the warm sun wash over his face. Sam, Sarah, Kyle, and Jack were just rousing themselves from a night of sleep. They had decided to leave at night instead of in the morning like Jack had originally told Director Manning. Jack and Xander had just begun discussing the fact that Jack told Manning they were going to London, when in fact they were headed for Xander's villa in Tuscany. Xander liked the location of the villa: remote enough to have it all to themselves, but only about a three-hour flight to Moscow, about seven hours closer than leaving from Lexington, once they were ready to make the move to end this thing with Dragov once and for all.

Xander turned his attention from the sun floating over the Atlantic Ocean back to Jack. "And you're sure he bought it?"

"I'm sure," Jack answered.

"Why are you doing this, Jack? Why should we trust you?"

Jack tilted his cowboy hat back, revealing more of his hardened face. His bushy eyebrows matched the silver of his hair, and his deep brown eyes looked to Xander like the dark insides of one of those big liberty floor safes, stuffed full of secrets.

"Well, so far, I guess I've given you no reason either way. All I can tell you is that I have been investigating what happened to your father for even longer than you have. The way it all went down has always smelled fishy to me."

"The two of you were that close?"

"We go a long way back. He was a hell of a SEAL. Not like you, but still, hell of a good man too. We even worked a few cases together."

Xander's face drained of its color. A look of pure confusion formed on his face. Sam leaned forward from her seat in front of them. The silence between them was filled only by the hum of the jet's engines. All of a sudden, Jack's face looked just as confused.

"Wait, you mean you didn't know? Jesus. Manning never said a word about it being kept under wraps. There were at least five others from the CIA at your father's funeral."

"You were at my parents' funeral?" Xander's mind was reeling.

"I sure was. I remember seeing you and your sister there. Awful thing. I'm sorry, Xander, I just assumed you knew."

Sam, apparently slow on the uptake, tried to catch up. "I'm sorry, did I miss something? Assumed he knew what?"

"Dad was in the CIA," Xander said, not to anyone in particular. More just letting it settle in for himself.

"That can't be. You or I would have come across this information."

94

Jack cleared his throat. "Well, that's part of what I meant by smelling fishy. After the funeral, they never really even attempted to answer the question about who was responsible. Which I guess isn't all that strange. You know, it's a thankless job. When you are an undercover agent, and you die, they often think it better just to act like you never was."

"This makes so much sense." Xander looked over at Kyle who was also wearing a shocked expression. "Kyle, what you said was true. My dad would never have been involved with someone like Dragov. Not unless he was trying to take him down."

"And that's exactly what he was real close to doing too," Jack explained. "Last time I spoke with him, he didn't give me details, but he was in Russia, and he seemed excited. I can't believe you didn't know. I mean, I know yesterday you were speculating on whether or not your dad would have dealings with him, I just assumed you meant outside of working the case. I'm so sorry, son."

Xander cleared his head. He actually felt a weight lifted. "So, you said fishy. You had to have meant something else."

"It's a long story." Jack shifted in his seat. He wasn't sure he should share the information on the tip of his tongue. However, the very reason he had himself put on this assignment with Xander was because of this information. And, as loyal as he was, it was at this very moment where he had to decide who his loyalty was with. He searched the faces of the people surrounding him on Xander's plane, then back to Xander. Not only had he heard all of the stories of Xander's time in the military, but he had also followed it himself with a keen eye. That would probably be enough to swing his loyalty Xander's way. It is the information about Director Manning he happened across in Russia last year that made the decision easy.

Xander could see Jack arguing with himself. "I have a feeling it isn't that long of a story. Besides, we're still an hour outside of Florence. Take your time."

Jack shifted in his seat, took a sip of his coffee, and thought for a moment about his classified mission in Russia. And then he thought about who he called just before he boarded Xander's jet a few hours ago.

"Well?" Xander interrupted Jack's train of thought.

"That's a deep subject." Jack stalled.

"Really?" Xander began to grow impatient. Usually he could appreciate stupid jokes, but now he wasn't in the mood.

"I'd rather you hear it from the horse's mouth."

"I don't get it. Another bad joke?" Sam asked.

Jack leaned forward, elbows on his knees. He had already chosen Xander's side. "I've got someone meeting us at the airport in Florence. I'll let her tell you and you can make up your own mind."

"Her?" said Xander.

Jack clasped his hands together and nodded his head.

"Vitalii Dragov's daughter."

Did I See a Wood Fired Pizza Oven by the Pool?

The gorgeous and sleek Gulfstream G650 landed in Florence, Italy, about an hour later. In that hour, Xander had time to throw exactly two conniption fits, one of which ended with Sam untangling the collar of Jack's ugly plaid shirt from Xander's iron grip. As they came down the steps of the jet, Xander stopped his stride toward the helicopter and turned back to Jack one last time.

"Explain to me again why I am going through with this?" Then he looked at Sam. "And you, you're okay with this? With Vitalii Dragov's *estranged* daughter coming with us to my home in Tuscany? Literally letting the wolves into the pasture?"

"I made some calls before we landed, Xander. You heard me make them." Sam spoke over the winding down of the jet engines. "My source in Moscow confirms everything that Jack is saying about her. She not only has no contact with Dragov, but she testified against him in court. She is as much an enemy to him as you are."

"Is this source as reliable as your source was in Syria?"

The look of shame on Sam's face was enough to let Xander know that he had gone below the belt. Sam had apologized over and over again about James. She was deeply hurt when he turned out to be a traitor, and Xander knew it.

"I'm sorry, Sam."

"No, you're right."

"I'm not. I trust you, and your judgment. You know that."

Sam nodded, still stinging from the comment.

"It's just that this seems crazy to me. Am I wrong?"

"You're not wrong, Xander. It does seem crazy." Sarah interjected.

"Thank you. Kyle?"

"I don't know man, is she hot?"

Xander was too upset to give that an answer. "I'm serious, Jack. If she's so estranged, then how does she have any information whatsoever about Dragov that could help us?"

"Because her best friend is Nicoli Pavlovich's niece. The two of them grew up together. I swear to ya, Xander, she can help. Just let her explain."

Every ounce of Xander's intuition screamed at him to not let this happen. He very rarely didn't listen to it. The tension between the four of them was thicker than a pine knot. Sam felt obliged to relieve it.

"To answer your question, Kyle, I sure as hell hope she isn't hot. The last thing we need is another distraction for the two of you."

"Dibs." Kyle smiled at Xander. It took a moment, but Kyle had the magic touch.

"Fine. But it must be said, this just doesn't feel right to me. And, Kyle, she is all yours."

Xander turned toward the helicopter. It was bad enough that she would be inside his home; there was no way in hell he was going to let Dragov's offspring in his bed too. He enjoyed living far too much to take that risk. Kyle was a little more careless in that regard.

As the five of them approached the helicopter, a tall, fiery-red-haired, long-legged, hourglass-shaped woman stepped out of its cabin. She wasn't hot, she was a total knockout. If Xander didn't hate her father so much, he would have immediately turned to Kyle and made him take his dibs back. Her white blouse flapped open from the stirred wind the rotors above had created, enough so to reveal a milky-white skin that was rounded into two amazingly curved mounds. Her tight black pencil skirt revealed that her curves didn't stop at her torso. She was truly a sight. As Xander approached, he looked deep into her cat-shaped bright-green eyes, the skin around them almost translucent, and then couldn't help but move his glance to her naturally pink, pouty lips that would have made Angelina Jolie jealous. Then he walked right past her outstretched hand and pulled himself up into the helicopter. For once, he let his big head make a decision. Kyle quickly took that empty hand and introduced himself, apologizing for Xander's behavior. Sam shook her hand and pulled herself inside, taking the seat next to Xander.

"So much for no more distractions," she shouted over the sound of the helicopter. Xander just turned and focused his attention out the window.

Twenty minutes and one hell of an awkward helicopter ride later, they were hovering over a sprawling estate in the vine-filled hills of Tuscany. Xander paid twenty million euros for it early last year and had only visited once in the meantime. He looked out his window, and all of Tuscany stretched out in front of him. The first thing that came to mind was Lexington. The terrain was stunningly similar. Beautiful rolling hills, acre after acre dedicated to farmland, alcohol production, and at the end of it all, a city that held almost an identically sized population. Obviously, the history was much longer here, but the people in Kentucky had a similar pride for their home as the Florentines. His home was directly below them now. It stood atop a hill in the town of Greve in the Chianti region, a town in the province of Florence. The manor house, constructed in the sixteenth century, had multi-shade red clay tiles for a roof and matching sand-colored stone with red accents as its walls. The pool area extended out the back and had breathtaking views of the vineyard below it, and beyond. The grapes in the vineyard should be in the fruit set phase, and would just be showing the signs of the fertilized flowers developing a seed. This would be Xander's first year of growing here. He had Cabernet, Canaiolo, and Sangiovese grapes currently on the vine. He couldn't wait to combine them to make his own Chianti. King's Ransom Chianti, no less. If it ain't broke, don't fix it.

The helicopter made its way down to the open grass field at the front of the manor. The manor had plenty of room for everyone to have their own space. Ten bedrooms. And even if it were without the extra bedrooms, any one of the seven farmhouses on the property would have sufficed.

"Are you kidding me?" Kyle shouted as he put his arm around Xander, who was smiling. He had forgotten that this

VANQUISH

was Kyle's first time at the villa. "Did I see a wood-fired pizza oven out by the pool?"

Xander smiled again. "I'm making pizzas tonight."

"Of course you are. A little vino too?"

"Indeed."

The chopper let everyone out, then immediately lifted off and headed back toward the airport. Just like that, the silence of the countryside surrounded them.

"Man, I love that sound," said Jack.

"There is no sound." Sarah laughed.

"Exactly."

Xander couldn't agree more. The older he became, the more he enjoyed being out of the fray. And this place was officially out of the fray.

"Xander!" Melanie shouted from the front door. Her infectious smile nearly knocked the black-framed glasses from her face. Xander always loved her quirky style. Her short black hair bobbed up and down as she ran to him.

"Melanie?" said Kyle. "I didn't know you were going to be here!" Kyle stepped in front of Xander and took her in his arms. Kyle and Melanie had been a flirt-a-minute ever since Xander had brought her on board to assist with all of his toys and business affairs.

"Oh yeah, I've been here a week and never want to leave!"

"Hey Melanie, how are you?" Xander gave her a hug.

"Never been better. And so happy you all are here!" She smacked Kyle on the ass. "I've got us all set up for this evening. Everyone's room is ready, and the chef will be here at five to start working on the pizza!"

101

Xander loved her infectious personality. He literally had never seen her in a bad mood. He assumed, if she ever got bad news, it probably bounced right off the gleam of her smile.

"Great, thanks, Mel."

The day turned to evening and Melanie made sure that everyone was settled in. Xander managed to avoid Dragov's daughter entirely. So much so that he didn't even know her name when she approached him as he sat in a lounge chair by the pool, staring off at the countryside.

It startled him when she stepped in front of the sun. Her long legs made their way into a pink sundress, and her red hair blew in the warm breeze.

"I am sorry that my presence here is disturbing to you, but I thank you for having me at your beautiful home." Her Russian accent was thick, and even though the dress didn't seem to be her style, she wore the hell out of it.

"One of Melanie's?" He nodded toward the dress.

"Oh yes. There is something off about her if you ask me, but she is very much a sweetheart."

"That she is. Why are you here?" Xander cut to the chase as he stood up from the chair. The soft grass billowed between his toes, and he was forced to look away from her mesmerizing eyes. They reminded him of Vegas Kelly's emerald pair.

She held out her hand. "Xander, I am Zhanna Dragov."

Xander glanced down at her hand, and then back to her eyes. He made no move to take her hand. "Why. Are. You. Here?"

She took back her hand and then ran it through her hair. Xander could tell by the way she moved that she was used to getting men to do whatever the hell she wanted. The wind rustled through the surrounding olive trees, and down the long private drive he could see it blowing through the quintessentially Tuscan pencil pines.

"I am here to help you," she answered.

"Bullshit."

"It's true. And I am here for myself as well. My father is monster."

"That's right, he is. He killed my parents. Give me one reason I should believe you are here for any other reason than to lead Dragov's dog—Nicoli Pavlovich—right to my doorstep."

"Because you and I have common goal."

"You and I have *nothing* in common."

"Xander—"

"Enough!" The volume of Xander's shout caused her to jump. "Sam took your cell phone, correct?"

"Y-yes."

"Good. And you have no other electronic devices with you?"

"No, why—"

"Then just sit by the pool, look pretty, and enjoy my hospitality. I don't want to hear another word. I am going to kill your father with my bare hands. I'm going to watch the life drain right out of him for what he did to my family. If you're lucky, I'll spare you their fate."

"But I need to tell you—"

"Xander!" Melanie called from the house, interrupting Zhanna. "The pizza is ready! I've got us all set up by the pool. I even hung those pretty string patio lights you like!"

Xander waved to her and then turned back to Zhanna. "Save it for someone who gives a fuck, okay?" Then he walked away.

Zhanna was left alone, frustrated. Valuable information hung on the edge of her lips.

Expect the Unexpected

Just as Xander was all but telling Zhanna Dragov to go to hell, Nicoli Pavlovich and eight of his finest men stood on the tarmac at the London Heathrow airport, growing very tired of waiting for Xander's G6 to arrive. Nicoli had been there for hours; he wanted to make sure Xander didn't arrive early. But now he was beginning to think they had received the wrong information. Then his cell phone rang.

"I gave you the wrong information."

"Wrong information? Xander is not coming?"

"Not to London. I'm sorry, I couldn't risk calling you until now."

"Where is he?" Nicoli's voice sounded as if it was losing patience.

"Tuscany."

"Are you certain?"

"Of course I'm certain, I'm here with him now. I'll text you the address. When will you come?"

"I'll be there by morning."

"Are you sure you want to try to take him alive? He isn't like the low-life thugs you are used to dealing with. He—"

"He must be taken alive. You will be there to help, no?"

"Of course. But—"

"Then we will take him alive. There is no other way."

"I'll be ready."

Xander took a seat at the long, reclaimed wood table beside the outdoor bar area at the edge of the lagoon-shaped pool. The smell of burning applewood and the baking pizza crust filled the air around them. The chef was hard at work shuffling the pizzas around in the oven while Sam and Kyle were catching up with Melanie. She had done a fantastic job with everything. The soft yellow patio lights were strung above their heads like she'd promised, and somewhere in the distance, the sun was dipping its toes into the Ligurian Sea. That thought helped settle Xander's nerves. He would do his best to forget Zhanna even existed. He couldn't help noticing, however, just how gorgeous she was as she walked around the corner of the manor, the orange sky and rolling green hills as her backdrop. Sam was right: she was, if nothing else, distracting. Sarah and Jack walked out of the manor at the same time, and before Xander knew it, he was sharing a meal with his mortal enemy's daughter.

Ain't life grand.

Other than a few contentious staring contests, Xander made it through the meal. And a glorious meal it was. The chef

106

started them with caprese salads—fresh sliced tomatoes and creamy burrata cheese topped with basil-infused olive oil.

Delicious.

They paired the salads with a 2010 Castello di Ama, Chianti Classico Gran Selezione.

Delizioso.

Then came the pizzas. Perfectly smoked thin crust, a sweet and flavor-filled tomato sauce, and fresh burrata cheese topped off with more of the basil olive oil.

Magnificamente perfetto!

Everyone agreed, dinner was perfect. It was full dark outside now. Xander couldn't help but notice that everyone around the table was beautiful. Except for Jack, of course, but the rest of them, beautiful. It didn't hurt that they had just finished the fourth bottle of Chianti.

After Kyle finished flirting with Zhanna, Melanie, *and* Sam, he walked around the table with a chilled bottle of Pallini Limoncello in his left hand and two snifters in his right. "How 'bout dessert, me and you?"

Xander answered in the voice of a southern belle, "I do declare, *Mista* Hamilton, you know how to make a girl swoon . . . I'll grab some cigars."

"I love it when you talk dirty to me. I'll be in the lounge chair." Kyle motioned toward the other end of the pool toward a lounge chair that sat in front of a wood-burning fire pit, and walked on by. Xander went to stand up when Sarah grabbed his arm. Xander was halfway up but sat back down to hear what she had to say. He leaned in as she began to whisper in his ear. He didn't catch what she said the first time because her short, yellow cotton dress had ridden up her long tanned legs, and he could just make out the white panties that hid underneath. He felt a warmth move through his lower midsection.

"What was that?" he whispered in her ear. She smelled amazing. Like lavender and honey.

Sarah giggled and leaned back in, whispering, "I said, when you are finished with dessert, maybe we can have some of our own?"

Xander smiled. "Why, Ms. Gilbright, are you coming on to me?"

A devilish look flashed through her eyes. "I want to do more than that."

Xander was a little taken aback. He wasn't expecting her to come on so strong, but a lightning bolt of want struck through to his core, the sparks from which tingled all the way to his fingertips. He was going to have to hurry through his cigar. And that wouldn't be easy, because Davidoff Oro Blanco cigars should never be rushed. He had a feeling it would be worth it.

"I don't think that will be a problem."

Just as he spoke, he noticed Zhanna staring at him from the end of the table. A sincere look flashed across her face. Could he be wrong about her?

"No, I don't expect it will be a problem. I know I've had a little too much to drink, but I'm ready for what you were going to give me in Lexington." She separated her legs and took Xander's hand. She turned slightly to shield this from the others, and slowly she moved his hand onto her silky smooth leg. He gave her soft skin a subtle brush of his hand as she nuzzled his neck. Xander took his hand away and let out a deep breath. Sarah did the same. "I'll be in my room. Don't be long."

"Don't worry, I won't be," Xander assured her. Just then he noticed Zhanna noticing the moment. She didn't shy from him catching her staring. In fact, she raised an eyebrow and took another sip of wine. Xander held her stare with a coldness that could have extinguished the fire in the pizza oven.

He kissed Sarah on the cheek, stood from the table, doing his best to hide his arousal, and grabbed the cigars from a humidor that sat atop the stone outdoor bar. He took a moment to watch Sarah saunter into the house, and he took a deep breath as he grabbed his lighter. When he turned back around, Zhanna was standing right in front of him. He really needed to stop hanging out with such gorgeous women. He had a feeling one of them would be the death of him. No coincidence that thought hit him as he stared into the eyes of a Dragov.

"Xander, can I please have moment with you now?"

"Not now, I'm busy."

"Xander, I talked to Sam a moment ago, but now I must speak with you about this. It is important."

"Then I'll let Sam fill me in."

"But—"

"Listen, goddammit." Xander's tone was sharp. Everyone at the table turned toward him. Even Kyle turned from the far side of the pool to see what was going on. Xander lowered his voice a few decibels. "Listen to me. I don't give a shit what you have to say. The only reason you are here is because Jack vouched for you, and Sam confirmed it was safe. But I don't buy it. So, steer clear of me, and we'll get along just fine."

"Just let me say one thing, then I'll let Sam fill you in."

"Fine." The annoyance in Xander's tone was unmistakable. She was walking a thin line.

"Thank you."

"Thank you? I didn't do anything."

"By letting me come here, you saved my life. So, thank you."

"Whatever."

Xander walked right past her toward Kyle. Though he completely blew off the thank-you, Xander was a pretty good read of people. Women in particular. His read at that moment was that she meant what she said. He was going to have to find out what was going on from Sam. Sarah might be waiting a while.

Xander walked around and sat down beside Kyle. He sank into the rust-colored cushion that covered the brown wicker lounge chair.

"There he is." Kyle handed Xander a glass of limoncello. "Everything okay over there?"

"It's fine." Xander cut the tip of a cigar and handed it to Kyle. Kyle put it in his mouth and Xander lit it for him.

Through the side of his mouth as he got the cigar going, he joked with Xander. "You realize that talking to her like that only enhances my chances of getting her in bed before you do."

"She's all yours."

"Seriously? I mean, I know you've looked into those eyes."

Xander thought it over as he lit his cigar. They were amazing eyes. Windows to the soul, and what he saw in there was deep. He decided to change the subject. "Sarah just made a pass at me."

"What? Just now? I hate you. She is so beautiful."

"So beautiful," Xander agreed.

"Where is she now?"

"Waiting for me in bed." He grinned.

"Jesus, X, get your ass up there. She's top shelf."

"It can wait. I'm right where I want to be." Xander clanged his glass against Kyle's.

"This place is unbelievable. You gonna make some wine this year?"

"Oh yeah, grapes should be starting to grow as we speak."

"Awesome. So, joking aside, what do you think of Zhanna being here? Pretty f'd up, right?"

"Right."

"I tried to play it off, but I know it must bother you. I mean, her dad . . ." Kyle decided not to ruin a good moment, and left it at that.

"Something about her eyes, though," Xander said as if he were in another world.

"Right? I told you."

"No, I mean, something sincere. I don't know. Maybe she's just gorgeous."

"Well, she's definitely that . . . shit, she's hotter than a whore's ass on nickel night."

"I hate to break up this little bachelor party, but we need to talk," Sam said as she came around the lounge chair, Jack following close behind. Xander normally would fight it, but after Zhanna said she spilled it to Sam already, he was too curious to deny her. Instead, he scooted over, handed Jack a cigar, and let Sam have the floor.

A half an hour went by in a time that felt more like five minutes. Xander's world had shifted on its axis. Was he losing his touch? Was Sam losing hers? For no reason whatsoever, the slogan to the reality TV show *Big Brother* flashed in his mind.

"Expect the unexpected."

111

"What's that?" Sam asked.

Xander took a final draw from his cigar and placed it on the ashtray. His chiseled jaw protruded as his mind sifted through the overwhelming information.

"Nothing. I'm just trying to get my head around all of this."

"It's a lot, I know."

Xander leaned forward in his chair and took a hard look into Sam's and Jack's eyes. "So . . . you think it could be Sarah?"

"We can't be sure," Sam replied, her eyes full of anguish.

Zhanna had it on good authority that there was a mole in Xander's camp. Someone was feeding information to Pavlovich. Xander didn't want to believe it was Sarah, but he knew it wasn't Sam or Kyle, so who else could it be? Xander stood from his chair and stared out into the darkness. "I just can't believe it." He started to walk back toward the mansion.

"Where are you going?" Sam stopped him.

"To find out for sure. I can't stand this shit not knowing who to trust. That's why it has always just been me and you, Sam. And Kyle, of course. Jack, I'm sorry, my man, but I don't even know you."

"So what do you propose we do?" Jack asked him as he settled into the chair and crossed his leg, cowboy boot lying across his knee.

"Trial by fire."

"What are you suggesting, Xander?" Sam asked.

"Jack, you said Zhanna was KGB, right?"

"Yep. The two of you have a lot in common. She joined up to take down her father, you joined the military for the same reason. You just didn't know that you both had a common enemy in Dragov."

"And tell me again, why is she so set on taking down her father?"

"Same as you. She watched him kill her mother. She's been stewing on it ever since. It wasn't until she heard about what happened to you that she thought she could actually make it happen . . . take him down, I mean."

"And she heard about me through who again?"

"Her friend. Nicoli Pavlovich's niece overheard Pavlovich making a deal to send the Middle Eastern militia to kill you at your home in Lexington a couple weeks back. It stood out to her because she had never heard of Kentucky. When Zhanna heard you killed them all, she reached out to me. She thought maybe the two of you, working together, could take Dragov down."

"And Director Manning?"

"I'd had my suspicions for a while now, but when Zhanna told me about the secret bank account he has in the Caymans and the two-million-dollar deposit he'd made to it last month, I knew he was working with Dragov."

"Mother fucker!" Xander shouted. His voice echoed through the hills. A cool breeze blew through the pencil pines and rows of grape vines, a welcome sensation for Xander because at that moment his blood was at a full-on boil.

"Xander, I am sure that Dragov is the man who had your parents killed, but I am just as sure that Manning is the man who set your daddy up," Jack explained as he stood from his chair and joined Sam. "There is no way of knowin' how far back Dragov got to Manning. And as for your question about Sarah, she has only been involved with tailing you for the last six months, when Manning put her in charge of monitoring you. It's obvious now why he wanted you watched. He didn't give a good goddam about you taking out criminals in your spare time. All he cared about was making sure you didn't find out about Dragov without him knowing, so he could give Dragov the heads-up. When Manning thought you found out who killed your parents, that's why he had Sarah's team go to Moscow instead of Syria. He didn't know you were on the wrong scent by going after Khatib."

"This is fucked up," Kyle said as he sidled up beside Sam and Jack.

Xander didn't know what to say. His head was spinning. "Why the hell would Sarah go through all the trouble of saving my ass if she is in on it with Manning? Why wouldn't she have just let them kill me on the yacht in the Virgin Islands?"

Sam stepped forward. "Maybe to make sure you wouldn't come after her if the truth ever came out?"

"But she killed Dragov's own men when the two of you saved our ass on that boat."

"Wouldn't that give her plausible deniability?"

"Jesus, Sam. Is all of this really that messed up? The head of the CIA worked with a mob boss to kill my father, and now because I put a wrinkle in the plans to keep it covered up, he's helping Dragov take me out too? How much money does it cost to pay off the CIA these days?"

"Xander, you know as well as I do that double agents happen all the time," Sam said.

Xander pondered that for a moment, then turned his eyes to Jack. "You're right, Sam. Double agents do happen all the time."

"Now, Xander—"

Before Jack could finish, Xander had closed the ten-foot distance between them and had Jack by the shirt collar for the second time that day. Fury rumbled in Xander's eyes. "Give me one reason not to end your life right here, Jack. One reason!"

Kyle stepped forward but stopped himself when Xander shot him a clear "stay out of it" look.

"Your father was a friend, Xander."

"Manning put you on this detail, Jack. If Manning is in on it, then you are too! Why else would he put you on my case if he thought for a second you might help me?" Xander threw Jack onto his back and pulled a pistol from the back of his belt. Jack held out his hands and just before Sam could form a protest, Zhanna stepped out of the darkness and into the lights that were still glowing above the pool.

"Because I made sure Manning put him on it."

Xander swung the gun in Zhanna's direction and held it there. "Bullshit! There's no way you could make that happen. I'm going to bury you right beside Jack and let you both fertilize the grapes that will make my Chianti!"

Xander was losing control. The one thing he couldn't stand was a liar, and the thought of being surrounded by liars was driving him mad.

"It's not bullshit, Xander."

Xander pulled the slide on his Glock 19. Zhanna didn't flinch.

"We are not so different, you and I."

"You'd better do better than that. Jack already tried that one."

Zhanna walked from the poured concrete around the pool into the grass, putting only inches between her and Xander's gun. "Fine. The KGB has a mole inside my father's inner circle. I needed Jack to be in yours. All I had to do was make sure that my father got wind of this retired cowboy agent that had a falling out with Martin King, and just like that, my father made certain that Manning put Jack on the team."

Xander swung the gun back to the now standing Jack. "Well, Zhanna, you are a little late with that make-believe story, 'cause Jack already told us he was friends with my dad. Jack, you have three seconds to tell me the truth, or I'll just shoot you both."

"We were friends, Xander."

Xander put the gun back on Zhanna. The moonlight swam in her eyes, eyes that held no fear of Xander's gun. "So you're the liar then, Zhanna."

"Xander, we aren't lying. What Jack doesn't want to tell you is that after he slept with your mother, your father and Jack's friendship ended rather abruptly."

Xander lowered the gun as rage coursed through his veins. "My mother . . . would *never* do that to my dad. Never!"

"It's true, Xander. I made a horrible mistake. Your mother and I both did."

"Shut your mouth, Jack!" Xander turned toward him, his chest heaving, and his heart pounding.

"I tried to make it up to your father, but that is when the two of them were killed. That's why this thing has haunted me for so many years. I figured the least I could do for your father was find out who killed him and make it right. When Zhanna reached out to me with the plan, I immediately reached out to Manning."

"Then why didn't you reach out to me to tell me all of this before we met with Manning?"

"Because I needed Manning to know for sure that we didn't know each other. I couldn't risk anything else."

116

Xander's head was doing cartwheels. How could all of this have been going on and he and Sam didn't know about it? He hated to admit it, because it was admitting a mark against his own mother, but it did make sense to him. His mom and dad hadn't been the same that last year. That was why Xander was so surprised when his dad was coming along to the amusement park on the morning they both were killed. They hadn't been spending time together at all before then. They had been so distant.

"I'm sorry you had to find out this way, Xander." Zhanna tried to console him.

Xander just looked at her, a blank expression on his face. Kyle stepped forward, took Xander's gun, and looked between Jack and Zhanna. "Can the two of you just leave us the hell alone right now?"

"That's a good idea," Sam agreed. Without another word spoken, Zhanna and Jack went inside.

Kyle put his arm around Xander's shoulder, but Xander quickly shrugged it off. Kyle didn't know what to say, neither did Sam. Xander turned his back to the two of them and looked up into the star-dotted blackness above him. From behind, Kyle and Sam could see Xander's chest heaving more and more as he stood staring at the sky.

"Xander," Sam whispered. "Can I get you some water?"

Xander turned toward her. His look frightened her. She'd seen him angry, but the cool, calm, and collected Xander had never given off madness. He took in a deep breath and held her stare.

"Sam, no matter what you hear, promise me you won't interrupt me."

"Xander? Calm down. What do you mean, Xander?"

"Promise me."

"I promise, Xander, but please, don't do anything rash."

"Yeah, man, let's just sit out here and have another cigar," Kyle urged. Xander had gone to a place he'd never seen. It truly scared him.

"I will not sleep in this house with a traitor. I must know, right now, if Sarah is with us, or with *them*."

"Xander, I promise you I will find out by tomorrow morning. I promise."

"No, you promised you wouldn't interrupt." Xander started to walk away. "That's the promise you'd better keep."

"X! Don't! Just stay out here and chill with me!" Kyle shouted to him.

It fell on deaf ears.

The Calm Before the Storm

Xander rolled his neck in a circular motion and took a deep breath to calm himself as he gave a light wrap against Sarah's closed door with his knuckle. He didn't know if he could go through with this. His head was swimming from the conversation with Jack and Sam. He didn't know if he would be able to put all of that out of his head long enough to be with her or not. He slowly pushed open the door, and lying on her back on top of the comforter was Sarah, wearing only a light-pink lace bra and matching panties.

He *could* do this.

He stepped inside the bedroom, walked past the bed, and over to the window. The restored cobblestone was cool beneath his feet, and the only light in the room came from the crack in the bathroom door. He shut the door and pulled back the thick burgundy curtain. The stars were magnificent in the country, and they were really showing off tonight. The moon laid into view the rolling hills that stretched far beyond the second story window where he stood. His life was like a symphony. Sometimes it could be the sweetest of melodies; at other times, it was the theme from *Jaws*. Right now it was as if both tunes were playing in some tumultuous harmony. On one side, the sweet melody—this beautiful place, all the people he loved around him, and in a moment the warmth of a gorgeous woman—then, the *Jaws* side of his life—his parents' murderer, Dragov, living through another night, his rabid dog, Nicoli, coming to kill Xander, Natalie in Paris, and of course all the unknowns that surrounded Sarah. A woman he had really grown to like. A woman who, as he looked back at her lying atop the comforter, might as well be the sexiest thing he'd ever seen. What a swirl of emotions. He looked back out the window and up at the wondrous night. He wondered if it were possible that Natalie could be thinking of him at that very moment. It was then—as a star shot across the sky—that he realized: every other woman he ever came across would leave him wanting her. He shouldn't be in the room with Sarah right now. Without knowing if he could trust her, without knowing if he could control himself at the thought of betrayal.

"Xander?"

Sarah had awoken and propped herself on her elbow. Her curves were intoxicating. It angered him that he wouldn't be able to stop himself. He should have stayed outside with Kyle.

"I didn't think you were going to make it. I'm sorry I was so forward earlier. I really should never have more than two glasses of wine. I was out of my head."

Xander didn't say a word. He turned from the window, removed his shirt, then his pants and crawled into the bed on top of her. Sarah went to speak but Xander covered her mouth with his hand before she could get anything out. There was wildness in his eyes. He could tell by the way she looked back at him. She didn't fight him. She let his hands have free rein over her luscious curves and soft skin. Without hesitation she grabbed him and began to stroke him. He ripped her bra off of her chest without undoing the clasp. Sarah let out a moan of excitement and tried to pull him into her, but as soon as she reached for him he caught her arms and pinned them back behind her head at the wrists with his left hand. He tasted her soft skin that had already grown salty with her sweat. The scent of lavender and honey returned to him and his desire for her was strong enough to blind him. She let out another moan, this one more in pleasure. Xander dropped his grip from her arms and pulled himself on top of her. He couldn't wait any longer, he wanted—needed—to be inside of her. He grabbed her by the hips and rolled her over. She moved to her knees, grabbed the headboard with both arms and Xander moved in behind her. As bad as he wanted it—wanted her—the thoughts of her lying to him, betraying his trust, were too much for him to overcome. Just before he slid her panties down her legs, he backed away from her, got up from the bed, picked up his T-shirt, and threw it to her.

"Xander? What's wrong?"

"You tell me."

Sarah pulled his shirt over her breasts, and one last zing of desire almost made Xander reconsider. But he couldn't.

"I don't understand. We don't have to do this if you don't want to. Was it something I did?"

Sarah's expression changed when she saw in Xander's eyes the madness that Sam had noticed earlier.

"No more games. How long have you been working for Dragov?" Xander growled.

"Dragov? Xander, what the hell are you talking about?" Sarah's face turned quickly from concern to anger. "After I've risked my life for you, you're going to ask me this?"

Sarah was too spun up to stay seated. She got up to her feet, deep breaths coming fast, her hands on her hips.

"No more bullshit, Sarah. Tell me the truth!" The muscles in his neck tightened, looking like cords. Sarah could see he was truly angry.

"Xander, what are you talking about? I'm CIA, you know this. I would never work with someone like Dragov!"

Xander rounded the bed and pinned her against the wall. "Okay, then you are working with that motherfucker Manning to take me down!"

"What? Why would Manning . . . Xander, I saved your life on that boat! What the hell is wrong with you? What was that about on the bed? Why would you almost make love to me if you doubted me?"

Xander could see the hurt in her eyes. What the hell was he doing?

The bedroom door busted open and Zhanna rushed through the door. Without hesitation she stepped in between them and shoved Xander onto the bed.

"What the hell are you doing, Xander? Who do you think you are?" Then to Sarah. "Are you all right?"

Sadness washed over Sarah's face. Xander knew at that moment that he had made a terrible mistake. "No, I'm not all right!" Sarah moved away from Zhanna and stormed off into the bathroom. Xander had no words. He covered himself with his pants and left the room immediately. Zhanna's intense judgment followed him out of the room.

Once inside his room, Xander headed directly for the shower and stepped inside. As the warm water washed over his body, for the first time that he could remember, he was disgusted with himself. He let his past affect his present, and worse, he had let it affect Sarah. She didn't deserve to be accused like that. She had more than earned the right at a chance to explain herself. He knew he had just completely humiliated her, and hurt someone who had done nothing but care for him. And he cared about her. What had he done? The water continued to massage his back, and as he tilted his head into the shower, letting it fall upon his face, Natalie flooded back to his mind. She would be so disappointed in him. For so many reasons. Why was he doing this? The selfishness of revenge? Or was he thrusting himself further inside this madness, subconsciously doing things to push Natalie away, to keep her safe? Or was he denying himself Natalie to keep from losing someone else he loved?

Xander had never been good at introspection. Not on the level that he would ponder an uncomfortable thought. That's what the whiskey and women had been for. That's part of the reason he had let Kyle in, because he knew his friend could distract him from truly feeling something. But regardless of his lousy introspective skills, Natalie had awakened something in him. Something that wanted more. More than revenge. However, he knew he couldn't stop now. He finally knew for certain who killed his parents. He finally could put an end to all of this bullshit and heal. No matter what, he had to finish it. For his sake, for Sam and Kyle's sake, and for Natalie's sake. She may not know it yet, but Xander had plans for her. For them. He would do everything in his power to make her the happiest woman in the world.

If she would have him.

Xander shut off the water, toweled dry, and collapsed onto the bed. He realized as he stared up at the old reclaimed wood beams in the ceiling that it could be a while before he could make all of that happen. He just had to make sure he wouldn't be hurting anyone, like Sarah, in the meantime. He knew he had to be patient. He couldn't bring Natalie into this underworld. Not again. Not until he had cleared the evil from his life and they could truly be together without worry of another incident like the one at his home in Lexington. He had been lucky that she hadn't been hurt, or worse. If it wasn't for that text, they both would be dead. It was the first time in a while that he had thought about that anonymous text. He let it bother him for a moment, but he was tired, and his body finally gave out on him.

Special Delivery

The smell of bacon and a relentless beam of sunlight finally tore Xander from a deep but tormented sleep. It didn't take him more than a second to feel sick about what he had done to Sarah. He had never been in such a prolonged state of rage. He knew that Sarah wanted him, but not like that. Not with that rage inside him. No matter what he did, she would never forgive him for that. He'd become a real charmer with the ladies. He was starving, but the thought of facing Sarah at breakfast made him want to bury his head under the covers.

A knock at the door.

"Xander?" Kyle called to him through the door.

"Come in."

Kyle pushed the door open, and Xander sat up when he saw the look on his friend's face.

"What happened?"

"You tell me."

"I don't understand."

"What happened with you and Sarah last night?"

"Oh, you heard." Xander felt that rush of disappointment in himself. Not to mention how embarrassed Sarah must have been seeing everyone this morning.

"I haven't heard a thing, that's why I came up. Zhanna said something happened between you and Sarah last night, but she said it was up to you to tell us." Kyle never lost his look of concern.

"So, Sarah didn't tell you?"

"Xander, Sarah's gone."

Xander jumped out of bed and put on a shirt. "Gone?"

"Gone. We've looked everywhere. Thought she may have just gone for a walk, but none of her stuff is here."

"Damn it. I fucked up, Kyle."

"It's okay, just tell me what happened."

"I was such an asshole."

"It can't be that bad."

"I stopped just short of making love to her, then demanded that she tell me how long she'd been working for Dragov."

"Oh . . . yeah, that's kinda messed up."

Xander didn't know what to say.

"So, how'd you two leave things?"

"We didn't. Zhanna came in and kept us from tearing each other's eyes out. I left and took a shower, then fell asleep."

"And now Sarah is gone."

"And now Sarah is gone." Xander repeated, trying to work through it.

"Shit." Kyle took a seat on the bed. "Now what? I thought you two were really getting along."

"We were, she's fantastic . . . I just . . . I lost it last night. I don't know who I can trust and it made me crazy. I took it out on Sarah, and she was the last person that deserved it. I should have directed my anger toward the obvious, Vitalii Dragov's daughter."

"Xander," Sam shouted from somewhere in the house. "There's a delivery truck coming up the drive, should we be concerned?"

Xander looked at Kyle. "You're sure Sarah actually left? I feel awful."

"We looked everywhere, man. And like I said, her stuff is gone."

"Xander?" Sam walked into the bedroom. "Did you hear me? There's a delivery truck—"

"Probably just something for the winemaker. I know he's working on the fermentation tank this week."

Sam made a face, then went over to the window and pulled back the curtain. A white BRT parcel service truck came to a stop at the front of the circular driveway. A man in a BRT uniform stepped out of the truck with a large package in his hands. They were hiring some really muscle-bound drivers these days. Sam also noticed a large tattoo running down his left arm. Alarm bells went off in her head.

"Jack!" she shouted down the hallway.

"What is it, Sam?" Xander asked.

"Jack!" No answer.

Sam walked back over to the window, and just as she heard Jack call back to her and noticed the truck begin to back away from the villa, a massive boom reverberated through the house and pieces of the front wall blew out toward the truck. The shock of an explosion brought the three of them to their knees,

127

shoulders hunched in a protective reaction. From the other side of the villa they heard a woman scream, and Sam got back to her feet just in time to see armed men in full tactical gear jumping out of the back of the delivery truck. Her alarm bells had been correct.

They were under attack.

"Xander, Nicoli Pavlovich and his men are here," Sam relayed.

"Is everyone all right?" Jack asked as he walked into the room, his .357 Magnum Colt Python held down by his side. "We got company."

"Sam, find Melanie and make sure she's safe," Xander said as he ran out the bedroom door and down the upstairs hallway to Zhanna's room. Smoke filled the main level, and debris from the blast covered the great room that led out to the back pool area.

"Zhanna!" Xander shouted as he approached the door to her room. He could hear instructions being barked in Russian by someone just outside. He opened the door to her room, and the only thing he saw was a black boot leaving through the open window. "Zhanna!" he shouted again, running over to the window. When he looked out, he saw a man pointing a gun at him and a bullet ricocheting off the stone right above his head. He would have to deal with Zhanna later.

BOOM!

Another explosion rattled the villa, this time from the backside. The blast refocused Xander, and he turned back toward the room and over to the closet. Inside the walk-in closet, on the left, there was a full-length mirror attached to the wall. Xander bumped his fist against the right side of it, and it popped open like a medicine cabinet. However, its contents in no way resembled medicine. Xander reached in and pulled two Glock 19 pistols off their hooks, one Glock nine, and ammunition and quickly strapped a replica of his favorite tactical knife, Rambo, to his leg. He could now hear the shuffling of feet echoing up the stairs from the foyer. Time was up. He turned back toward the hallway as he tucked the extra magazines and a gun down into the shallow pockets of his white linen lounge pants and broke into a dead sprint. As he entered the hallway, two men were coming up the stairs. He didn't have time to cock the pistol and fire, so he ducked to the height of the rail and sprinted past them. Shots—most likely from two Uzis—sprayed all around him, but he managed to keep from getting hit. He saw Kyle exiting the master bedroom window in front of him, a window that led to the roof of the connected pool house.

As the gunmen rounded the stairway into the hall behind him, Xander racked the slide on the second pistol and yelled for Kyle, "Catch me!"

Unsure if Kyle heard him, he was going to have to chance it. He knew more gunmen would be right behind the two who now had an open shot at his back, and his pistols were no match for their fully automatic weapons. Simply turning toward them and firing would most likely cost him his life. So he did what any badass motherfucker would do: he ran straight for the window, jumped, rotated toward the two gunmen in midair, and, just as his ass was clearing the bottom of the window seal, he put two bullets in each of them while falling in full backward extension through the window and into the waiting arms of his best friend on the roof.

Kyle had heard him.

Xander wished he'd been wearing a GoPro camera.

Jack missed the action due to the fact that he was loading his gun.

Sam just reached out her hand for the extra pistol, as if all he'd done was pour her a drink.

Tough crowd.

Xander passed her the gun and extra magazine with a disheartened look and then did the same for Kyle. Shouts in Russian filtered out the bedroom window to them. Xander pointed in the direction of the rows of grape vines across the pool area that led to the south. "Sam, you and Kyle make your way south and as soon as you are out of view, turn to the west and make your way to La Castellana. Ask for Antonia. She'll tell you where to go from there, Jack and I will meet you there.

"Just come with us now, Xander." Sam hurried.

"Did you find Melanie?"

"No time."

"Well, I have to."

"Xander, it's too late."

He ignored her. "And I have to find Zhanna."

"Why, Xander?"

"To kill the bitch."

Blurred Lines

By the time Sam and Kyle made it across the pool area and out to the vines, Xander had shot two more gun-toting thugs through the still open master bedroom window. Sometimes, at the most inopportune times, weird thoughts popped into his head. Like just how unbelievably odd it was that his life had brought him here to Tuscany, standing on a roof, shooting moronic, under-trained thugs through his bedroom window. Truth is stranger than fiction.

Xander turned back toward Jack. When he did, he had another thought. All of that other stuff about shooting people through his bedroom window in Tuscany was weird, until you turned around and saw a real-life, honest to god American cowboy standing there with you.

"Jack, I'm going to go around front and come in behind them. I have to find Melanie. Stay here and smoke anyone that comes through this window. Just make sure no one comes up behind me."

"Roger that."

Jack tipped his hat and pulled the hammer back on his shiny cowboy pistol. Xander backed up, dropped off the roof until he caught the edge in his hands, then dropped the last ten feet to the grass below. The smell of smoke and explosives was heavy in the air; the front of his beautiful Tuscan home was completely blown to shit. He stepped over the broken stones that used to be his front wall, pistol in hand, crouch-walking around to the front. Behind him he heard Jack's Colt Python doing its job. Three shots fired so far. Xander sidled up to the only standing pencil pine, peered around it, but didn't see any movement. Then there was Melanie. Just as Xander made a motion to move, she put her hands over her head. He couldn't see her face, but he could only imagine the horror it displayed. She was backing up toward the delivery truck, and then Nicoli Pavlovich came into view, a gun extended in front of him, directly in Melanie's face. Five men followed directly behind him, their guns positioned upon her as well. Rage flamed through Xander like a backdraft blowing through an opened door in a house fire. He went to move again, then noticed a glint of light in a tree just over Melanie's head in the distance.

A sniper.

Xander propelled himself onto his back, and just as he did he heard a crack in the distance, followed by the whiz of a bullet, rifling through the branches of the tree he'd just been crouched behind. Then another gunshot in the distance, this one from the east. Almost simultaneously a bullet collided with the stone of the wall just above his head. Pieces of it showered down around Xander.

They were surrounded.

This was orchestrated.

Zhanna.

Xander knew if he tried to play hero and save Melanie in that moment, he would only get them both killed. He would have to hope they would make the mistake of using her as bait. He heard the horde of gunmen shuffle as Pavlovich ordered them after him. Xander pulled his knees to his chest and did a kick-up to his feet. Two more cracks from sniper rifle blasts rang out in the distance, but somehow they missed.

"Time to go, Jack! Follow the path Sam took, I'll catch up!" Xander yelled as he ran around the side of the house.

"Roger!" Jack yelled back. "They's five more of 'em come around the back, Xander, I'll try to get a couple of 'em on my way out!"

Xander didn't respond; he was busy running a zigzag pattern, trying to maintain a moving target for the snipers. The god-awful snipers. He heard a couple of blasts from the unmistakable boom of Jack's Python and made it around the corner of the pool house. He paused for a glance around the corner, and he saw Jack disappear between the vines, two men nipping at his heels about fifty feet back. Before sprinting after them, Xander walked around the corner toward the pool, glanced back up at his bedroom window, and saw the front end of a rifle pointed in Jack's direction. With the accuracy—or lack thereof—that these snipers had so far displayed, Xander almost ignored him and took off after Jack. But even a blind squirrel finds a nut from time to time, so he leveled his pistol on the middle of the window and squeezed the trigger. The rifle fell forward out of the window, out onto the roof.

"Good thing they don't have me shooting at me," he said aloud to himself as he broke into a full sprint toward the grapevines. Jack's Python only held six rounds, and Xander was pretty sure he'd already spent those. He'd better hurry before the gunmen caught up to him. Older men were still good for a lot of things, but running away wasn't one of them. Xander didn't know how great he'd be at running either. The gunshot wound in his stomach was sore, and the wound in his calf was sending pain through every inch of his nervous system.

Xander hit the dry soil stretch between two rows of Sangiovese grape vines at a full sprint. Faintly, he heard the delivery truck start up behind him. They were taking Melanie with them. No need to come after him when they had Melanie. Xander was aware that they knew his weakness for his loved ones. They knew Xander would come to them, and as Xander turned to the west in between the vines, the image of Pavlovich's eyes bulging out of their sockets from the pressure Xander's hands were putting on his neck flashed gloriously through his mind. The next thing Xander knew he tripped over something heavy at his feet and did a nose dive forward onto his stomach, sliding head first, arms stretched out in front of him.

Pete Rose would have been proud.

Xander was not. He shot up to his feet and pointed his gun at the body lying in the dirt path. Just to the right of that body lay another two men in full tactical gear. A cowboy hat emerged from the vines where they lay.

"Didn't expect that, did you, young buck? You ain't the only one with a few tricks up his sleeve."

Jack. A wide, proud smile on his face. He chuckled at the somewhat bewildered look on Xander's face. "What, you didn't expect me to just outrun 'em, did ya?"

"No." Xander lowered his gun and raised a smile. "No, I most certainly did not, old man."

"Now let's go save that pretty woman and your girl-crazy friend."

"Yes . . . let's."

Xander and Jack did their best to look normal as they crossed over Via del Castello Street, walking toward Xander's favorite little restaurant in the area, La Castellana. The exterior was mixed brick and stone, and the back patio gave patrons a view of the rolling hills of Chianti. The Pappardelle Bolognese was off the charts there. One of his all-time favorite meals. As a few locals walked by, their eyes fixed upon the two of them as they approached the restaurant. Xander realized how ridiculous he and Jack must have looked. Xander in his white V-neck T-shirt and white linen pajama pants, barefoot, and then Jack, well, looking like Jack. They must have looked like they were on their way to some warped Las Vegas-themed Halloween party. *The only person this would look halfway normal to would be Antonia,* Xander thought. She'd seen Xander in his pajamas before. Just then a beautiful dark-haired, olive-skinned stunner walked out of the side entrance of the restaurant.

Speak of the devil.

The look on her face was not what Xander wanted to see. Something was wrong.

"Xander!" She ran up to him. "I tried to help them, but there wasn't time!"

"Slow down, Antonia, time for what?"

Just as the question left his lips, out of the corner of his eye he saw a BRT delivery truck. His stomach dropped when he saw Sam getting thrown into the back of it. It dropped again when he saw Kyle at the wrong end of a machine gun. A flash of Sean getting his head blown off that night in Syria flashed in front of his eyes. On reflex, Xander whipped his pistol forward, and without the need to take aim he shot the man pinning Kyle with his gun in the throat. Kyle dove to the right, and the BRT truck lurched forward. Sam's eyes met Xander's just before the back doors were slammed shut.

Xander turned toward Antonia, and she tossed him a set of keys. Xander had prepared for this day. Antonia knew this was the moment he would use it.

"Jack, make sure Kyle is all right. If I don't come back, I think we all know where I'll be."

"Dead?" Jack had never been known to mince words. There was no time for that old-dog-new-tricks thing. The BRT truck full of gunmen and two of Xander's favorite women sped off in the opposite direction.

Xander glanced over at Jack. "No matter what, you find Sam and Melanie. I suspect they'll be in Moscow before the night is over. Bob will be ready for you at the airport. He won't trust you, but he'll listen to Kyle. Promise me you'll find them."

"Son, they're getting away."

A gleam came to Xander's eye. "Don't you worry about that, Jack."

"Okay then, I promise."

Xander bolted for a carport behind Antonia's restaurant and made a beeline for a covered vehicle. The gleam in Xander's eye came from knowing why the BRT truck would never get away. He tugged at the front of the cover, and in one motion a jet-black Lamborghini Aventador was free of its restraints. Xander jumped into the cockpit and fired up the engine. Seven-hundred-and-fifty horsepower roared to life when Xander popped the clutch, then slammed the gas and squalled out of the parking lot, sideways, smoke from the tires filling the air and the smell of burnt rubber teasing his nose. Like a jet pilot headed down a runway, Xander corrected the supercar and just like that, the fastest Lamborghini ever made launched forward down the road toward the enemy.

Five short miles later, Xander could see the back of the BRT truck in the distance. At 190 miles an hour, it didn't take long. The rolling hills covered in delicious grape vines were going by in a blur that could only be described as suicidal. They looked more like random streaks of light, like those pretentious pictures photographers take of blurred streetlights. Their version of showing the city's emotion, or some dumb shit like that. Rather apropos, the satellite radio played "Blurred Lines" by Robin Thicke. It would have made for a fantastic moment except for the fact that Xander absolutely hated that song and the guys who were found guilty of stealing the music to create it.

Before Xander could react—because at 210 miles per hour it would be absolutely impossible to react—something large and black clipped the back end of his Lamborghini. After an outstandingly violent yet glorious and seemingly never-ending, world-class crash full of twisted metal and broken glass, everything went dark.

Keep Your Enemies Close

After over an hour of pacing around the restaurant, it occurred to Kyle that Xander wasn't coming back. He didn't know what that meant exactly, but something didn't feel right. Jack had told him what Xander had said to do, but it didn't mean he had to like it. The thought of not going after his friend made him nauseous. The three espressos Antonia had given him weren't doing anything to help the cause.

"Son," Jack started from his seat under the hanging garlic, "we gotta go."

Kyle didn't respond. He knew Jack was right. And he knew Xander said what he said for a reason, but he had never been in this position before. No Xander and no Sam. He walked out of the restaurant and onto the back patio. The quintessential white-and-red checkered tablecloths on the tables and the lattice along the walls covered in daisies didn't even register to him. Neither did the bright green grass covering the hills sprawled out in front of him. He took his cell phone from his pocket and scrolled down to Sarah Gilbright in his contact list. He had her number still saved from the night of the King's Ransom bourbon launch party on the rooftop in San Diego. Though it had only been a couple of weeks ago, it seemed like light years. He pressed dial and her phone rang, unanswered, until her voice mail picked up.

"Sarah, this is Kyle Hamilton. Xander and Sam have been taken. I really don't know what to do. Jack is here, but I don't know him well enough to trust him. I know Xander had his suspicions. I know you think Xander has suspicions about you too, but I assure you that he doesn't. Not anymore. He feels horrible about . . . Listen, I need your help. It looks like Zhanna has set us all up, and now I don't even know where to go. Jack says he does, but can I trust him? Please call me back, Sarah. Please?"

Kyle ended the call, his shoulders slumped, his mind lost. The door rattled behind him and Jack walked out onto the patio.

"Kyle, I know you don't trust me yet, and I understand that, but you're gonna have to. If Xander and Sam are alive, I know where they are gonna be. But son, they ain't gonna be there for long. Not alive anyway."

"With Dragov?" Kyle said to the hills.

"That's right. Dragov's. Now, I know where that sum bitch lives in Moscow, but I can't call this in. Director Manning is compromised. I can tell by the messages he's left on my phone. We call him, and not only would we have to deal with the Russians, but we'd also have to contend with the CIA. I can guaran-damn-tee ya that Manning is spinning up some story of betrayal about us right now. We can worry about that later. Right now, look at me." Kyle turned toward him. "It looks like

139

it's just me and you. I reckon I was wrong about Zhanna. I can't believe it, but I don't know what happened to her. And Sarah, I guess Xander ran her off. So as I was sayin'—"

"Just you and me," Kyle interrupted.

"That's right. I heard how well you did in Syria. We'll need that and then some if we're gonna have a shot at savin' your friends."

"Why are you doing this, Jack?"

"Like I told y'all last night, Xander's daddy. I did him wrong, and though I know I'll never make up for it, I can sure as hell die trying. Especially if I can save his boy."

"You think Xander is okay?"

"Don't know, but we gotta act as if he ain't. That means get our ass to the airport and get our ass to Moscow. I know you don't know me, but this ain't my first rodeo, son. I've got friends in all the right places and I'll have us as good a plan as we can get before we land. But . . ." Jack grabbed Kyle's eyes with a look that gave Kyle a chill. "You gotta understand something . . . We do this, we are pretty much signing up for a one-way ticket to the great beyond. You get me?"

"I do."

"You ready for that?"

"I would do anything for my brother."

"Well, you just might have to."

Kyle called and got things squared away with Bob. He said he would have the jet ready to go. Bob couldn't believe that something had happened to Xander, but he seemed ready to stay in it for the long haul in order to see Xander safe again. One common theme amongst anyone who was ever around

Xander very long was the loyalty that the people in his life had toward him. Kyle knew why: it was because Xander would die for them, and everyone who ever got close to Xander knew it too.

Antonia had let Kyle borrow her catering van, and now he and Jack were pulling up to the private aircraft division at the Florence airport. When they walked through the glass doors and into the holding area, a flash of fiery-red caught Kyle's eye in the corner of the room. As soon as he realized it was Zhanna, something lit a fuse in his adrenaline box. His fists clenched and everything around him blurred as he stomped toward her and violently pinned her up against the wall by her shoulders.

"Didn't quite make it out of here in time, huh, bitch?" Kyle's face was as red as Zhanna's hair.

Zhanna's demeanor did not change.

"I'll let that slide because I realize how me not being able to help you at Xander's villa must have looked."

"Must have looked?" Kyle was going nuclear. "Bitch, you set us up!" He pulled her off the wall and then immediately slammed her back up against it.

Kyle was so inside his own rage that he wasn't prepared for it when Zhanna snaked her left leg around Kyle's right leg and pushed abruptly with her upper body, sweeping him off his feet, landing him on his back and her on top of him. Instinct and Xander's hours of jujitsu lessons kicked in. He immediately bucked his hips and rolled over on top of her. She wrapped her legs around him, in full guard, and held him in place.

"Listen to me! Stop! I did not set you up," she screamed.

Kyle broke her arm grip and postured up. He wanted to hit her, but at that moment he saw the same thing in her eyes that Xander said he had seen. Genuine concern. He stopped his fist mid-downswing, and the two of them glared at each other, their bodies heaving for air.

"Then, where the hell were you?"

"Get off me and I'll explain."

Jack came over to Kyle and coaxed him off of her.

"Zhanna, what the hell happened back there?"

"Jack, you know I would never abandon fight."

"Well, I didn't think so, but Xander said he saw you escape out the window. I said that wasn't like you, but it sure wasn't a solid argument."

"Xander must not have seen me fall."

"You fell?" Kyle asked. "From the window?"

"Sort of. I was attempting to get around behind Pavlovich's men, but I didn't see the man watching the window."

Zhanna looked down at her leg. It was wrapped in a blood-soaked bandage at the calf.

"The bullet knocked me off balance and I fell into bushes below window. I hit my head, and when I woke, everyone was gone. They must have thought I was dead. I did not know where else to go, but I knew if Xander survived, he would eventually have to come here for plane. Is he on his way? Is he all right?"

Worry washed over Kyle's face. "We aren't sure. He and Sam were taken by Pavlovich."

"Shit. I am sorry, Kyle. This is no good. But if we hurry, we might have chance. My father will want proof of Xander's death. That way he will not have to ever be paranoid about him again. Pavlovich will do everything he can to make sure Xander stays alive. It will be only way he get paid."

"I'm sorry I pushed you up against the wall."

"I am not sorry I put you on your ass." She gave a sideways smile.

Jack interrupted the apologies. "Well, now that the two of you are on the same page, we have work to do."

Zhanna said, "It is roughly five-hour flight to Moscow. If we both reach out to our contacts, we can have good plan in place at landing. We will land at secluded airfield to stay under radar. Father will have eyes on airports."

Kyle's stomach took a nasty twist. Talks of foreign countries and secluded airfields hit too close to home. He still wasn't anywhere near over what happened in Syria. And if Zhanna said something about a trusted ally coming along with them, he was going to have to object. The memory of pushing James's dead body over the side of the boat into the Mediterranean after James had turned on him was enough never to trust another *ally* again.

"Wheels up in five," Bob announced from the doors that led out to the tarmac.

Kyle nodded.

Zhanna looked . . . disappointed?

"Something wrong," Kyle asked.

"Not to hurt your feelings, but I expected more from your precious Xander."

Kyle's face knotted up.

"This coming from the supposed amazing KGB agent that took herself out of the gunfight in the first five minutes by falling out of a window?"

"You have no idea what I am capable of, Kyle."

"And you could multiply whatever you are capable of by a hundred and still not catch up to Xander."

She could tell she had hit a nerve. "It's just . . . I expected to be taking out Vitalii Dragov with Xander, not saving Xander from my father."

143

"Don't worry about X, Zhanna. Whatever situation he is in, no matter how dire, he'll turn it around. You'll be lucky to witness your father's death at all, 'cause Xander may have already finished the son of a bitch by the time we get there."

Tom Petty Would Be Proud

Just about the same time that Kyle, Jack, and Zhanna lifted off the runway in Florence, heading straight for their suicide mission in Moscow aboard Xander's G6, Xander could swear he heard a jet engine of his own. Yep, that definitely sounded like an airplane. The problem he was having is that even though he knew his eyes were open, he couldn't see a damn thing. He sure as hell could feel, though. Every single muscle and bone in his highly tuned body gave off the feeling of being run through a meat grinder. Flipping and rolling car accidents at 200 miles an hour tend to have that effect on the soft tissue of a human. The floor under his ass where he sat, hunched forward, legs out in front of him, was hard like metal. Whatever aircraft he was in, it wasn't a G6. Some sort of cargo plane, by the sound of the engine. His arms were behind his back, and when he moved them, he heard and felt chains weighing him down. That black blur, the last thing he saw before his Lamborghini was airborne, must have been Pavlovich. They had set Xander up. They knew about La Castellana. They knew Xander would flee there if pushed. The image of Zhanna's boot sneaking out the window flashed in his mind. He knew he had been right not to trust her. She must have been gathering intel on him for months, and sure enough they walked right into all of this. Xander wondered what that meant for Jack. He's the one who brought her in. Xander's gut told him that Jack had been fooled too, blinded by the need to make things right for his betrayal of Xander's father. Now, here Xander was, chained to a plane, a bag over his head, on his way to be Vitalii Dragov's latest victim. In the meantime, Xander knew he had unfortunately sealed the fate of poor Melanie and Sam.

"Xander?" He heard a whisper come from his right.

"S-Sam?"

"Xander, are you all right? I saw the crash from the back of the delivery truck. I was certain you were dead."

"What, and miss out on all this fun?"

"Lean your head to the right."

Xander did as Sam asked. He felt a tug at the top of his head and the next thing he saw was Sam with a mouthful of the bag that covered his face.

"Jesus, did you have to pull out my hair too?" Xander smiled. Damn, it was good to see Sam's face. Alive. "How much trouble are we in?"

"The worst kind. We are fifteen thousand feet in the air and there are fifteen of them." She moved her head in the direction of the men behind her.

Xander was right: they were in a small cargo plane. Most likely one of BRT's fleet, the same company as the delivery

146

truck that started this mess. It was almost entirely empty except for the men seated in rows along both sides of the outer walls. There were a few weapons packed against the walls and a couple of parachutes, but other than that, it was just the two of them and a bunch of Russian thugs.

"Fifteen? That's all? Cake walk."

"I'm afraid not this time, Xander."

"How long have we been in the air?"

"Two hours, we have around three to go."

"Two hours? So, you have already figured a way out of here then." Xander looked at his partner with unwavering confidence.

"I have. But it's risky."

"My favorite." He smiled.

"We both won't be able to make it, but as long as one of us does, there is hope."

"I'll follow your lead."

A shout came from one of the men. "Shut the fuck up back there!"

Sam shifted around to face him.

"I have to use the ladies' room."

"There is no ladies' room. Go in panties."

"Come on, where is there for me to go? We are stuck in a plane, for god's sake."

One of Pavlovich's cronies stood up from his seat and began to walk toward them. The sun cast rays through the windows and showed a smug, thick-necked, and ass-ugly Russian man walking their way. He had a parachute strapped to his back, and as Xander looked beyond him, he could see that all of the men did. They were prepared for anything, it seemed.

"You think I am going to fall for oldest trick in book, unchain you, so you can have chance at getting free? You think I am that stupid?"

"No comment." Xander spoke up.

"Ah, I see superman is finally awake."

"It's X-Man to you, needle dick."

Needle dick? What is this, middle school? The look on Sam's face confirmed that apparently it was.

"Big talk coming from little bitch who was so easy to catch."

"What, that whole car crash thing back there? All part of my plan."

"What is plan now, big talker?"

"I was thinking about ordering a pizza, does Domino's air deliver yet?"

"So, death of you and pretty lady here is joke to you?"

"Not as much of a joke as that stupid mustache you got there, Magnum, P.I."

Sam knew Xander was baiting the man. And though Xander didn't know it, Sam had counted on this. The Russian stiffened and looked as if he was going to lunge at Xander, but he stopped short, coming right into Sam's range. Sam snap-kicked the muscle-head in the groin, and he doubled over. She followed that with a snap-kick to the forehead, and he fell forward, flat on his face. Sam's chains extended just enough to allow a powerful axe-kick levied directly down on the back of his head which knocked him out cold. Fortunately, the plane had hit some turbulence at the same moment, so it didn't draw the attention of the others. Sam immediately pulled him toward her with her legs, turned around, and fished a set of keys out of the man's pocket. Xander quickly turned his back to her, and they lined up their hands.

"See, piece of cake," Xander added as she undid his shackles. "Now what?" He took the keys from her.

"This was as far as I got."

Just as Xander was moving to undo her chains, they both heard a shout from the front of the plane as one of the men stood and pulled a gun.

"Shit," Sam grunted.

He squeezed off a round, and it ricocheted off the metal floor and managed to bore a hole in the back of the plane.

Xander dropped the keys and moved the body of the unconscious Russian in front of him and Sam as a shield.

"STOP!" a man yelled from the front of the plane. "We are in plane. You can't shoot gun, you imbecile!"

It was Pavlovich. When he noticed Xander was free of his chains, he instinctively pulled his gun. Xander and Sam were in a real pinch. Sam was still chained. Xander had no weapon, and no protection. The only thing he had going for him was the fact that Dragov clearly wanted him alive, or he would already be dead.

Big mistake.

Maybe.

That fact, coupled with how seriously dumb it would be to fire a gun in this plane, gave Xander a chance. But what the hell could he do?

The unconscious Russian's gun. Of course!

As the men all stood and started to make their way to Xander, he reached for the Russian's belt and pulled out a pistol and pointed it in their direction. They may be afraid to shoot in there, but Xander was not.

"Hold it right there, boys."

Pavlovich looked to his left and to his right. "What, you going to kill all of us?"

He had a point. His gun only had a twelve-round magazine, and besides, once he started shooting, he had nothing to hide behind in there; he would be a sitting duck, and so would Sam. All fourteen of the rest of the men were standing now, their guns trained on Xander. The sound of their weapons clicked and clacked as they collectively locked and loaded.

"Don't be stupid, Xander." It was a Russian woman's voice, but he couldn't see her. He could hardly hear her over the roar of the plane's engine, but there was really only one person it could be.

Zhanna.

Xander almost fell over in shock when he saw Melanie come out from behind the wall of gunmen.

"Melanie?" Xander managed.

"Melania," she corrected him. Her demeanor was no longer the nerdy girl with the black-framed glasses. Her ever-present smile was still there, but now it looked far more sinister than sunshine.

Xander looked at Sam. "You're so fired."

"Get him restrained," Melanie—Melania—ordered.

"Kyle is going to be so disappointed in you," Xander told her as he quickly searched the plane for a way out. Four of the men moved toward him. Time was running out. This was the only chance he was going to have to save himself and Sam. If they got him chained once again, the two of them were dead. Barring a miracle Hail Mary from Jack and Kyle, of course. Xander's noticing last night of a genuine quality in Zhanna may still have merit after all. More likely, however, she's on this plane too, or somewhere in place just in case Dragov needs a plan B.

Dragov is going to need a plan B.

Just then, the cargo latch release button at the back and far side of the plane caught Xander's eye.

"Xander, don't do anything stupid," Sam pleaded when she followed his eyes to the release button.

"Who, me?" Xander shrugged.

Xander shot the unlucky grunt, directly in the forehead, who was in the front of the pack of four goons headed his way, then immediately turned and shot the release button on the cargo hatch. The pressure in the cabin changed almost instantly. They were just above the safety zone for jumping, but Xander didn't have a choice. The gunmen coming toward Xander dove to the floor for cover in anticipation of another shot. Instead, Xander grabbed the unconscious Russian and began to drag him backward toward the slowly opening hatch. The plane filled with gusts of cold air, and as Xander brought the Russian up as a shield, the group of gunmen began to fire at him. Between the sound of the howling wind and the blasts of guns, Xander could only hope that Sam could hear him when he promised he would be back for her. He figured she probably could since he heard Melanie—or Melania—or whatever the hell her name really was—shout to take Xander alive. However, it was clear when Pavlovich stepped forward that he had made a decision otherwise. There was no time to undo the parachute from the Russian meat shield that Xander was carrying in front of himself. So, as bullets whizzed around him, he backed his way right off the platform, and the back of the plane quickly grew farther and farther away as he began free-falling into the deep blue sky. Probably not what Tom Petty had in mind when he wrote the song. Xander had managed to wrap his arms and legs around the unconscious man and was holding on to him like a cat falling down the trunk of a tree. It wasn't a second later that he saw Pavlovich and four other men dive out of the back of the cargo plane after him.

A Thin Line Between Love and Hate

"What the hell do you mean you just left?"

Sarah was sure this time, she actually saw smoke coming out of Director Manning's ears.

"What the hell is going on over there, Sarah? You were supposed to be in London, then I find out—no thanks to Jack, 'cause he all of a sudden isn't communicating—that you all were in Tuscany the entire time? Now you're here? Needless to say you are gone if you don't have an absolutely perfect explanation!"

For the first time since her encounter with Xander in the bedroom of his Tuscan wonderland, she understood why he had been so paranoid of her. Just moments ago, on the way to Manning's office in Langley, Virginia, she was stopped by a sort of nerdy looking man just outside CIA headquarters. He identified himself as Marvin "you can call me Marv" Cameron. Which meant nothing to Sarah. Then he said he was friends with the late Sean Thompson, which vaguely rang a bell, and finally he explained that he had been helping Xander King and Sam Harrison for a few years now. Though she still didn't know the name, she was able to make the connection. Marv went on to explain to her that Xander was in some real trouble, but he couldn't get a hold of him. Sarah didn't let on how much she knew, but when Marv said he tracked her down because he was given a request to check into a few things by a man named Jack Bronson, who was currently with Xander, Sarah took a moment to catch her breath and let Marv have his say.

"Why aren't you with Xander in Tuscany?" Marv asked her.

Sarah was a little weary, but she took the time to explain that Xander had the impression that she was compromised. That is when Marv explained the conversation that he had with Jack, and that is when her world shifted on its axis. She hadn't listened to the voice mail that Kyle left a couple of hours earlier. So she didn't know that Xander and Sam had been taken. She was immediately infuriated with herself for leaving when Xander needed her most. She was even more distraught when Marv explained to her that he found out that Melanie, Xander's trusted assistant, was actually a mole for Dragov, and the one who told Pavlovich where they were in Tuscany. Sarah felt horrible. Xander had reacted poorly, granted, but there really was a mole. He just got caught up and took it out on the wrong person.

"I have to relay all of this to Manning, right now! Come with me!" she told Marvin. That was right before he blew her mind again, forcing the world to re-shift its axis entirely.

"Sarah." Marv glared into Sarah's eyes. "That is the last thing you're going to want to do. Manning is working for Dragov."

"No way."

"He knew all about Melanie."

"No way."

"And he knew all about the attacks that you helped save Xander from in the Virgin Islands and at the hospital in San Diego."

"That—that's just not possible. Manning is the one that put me in charge of watching Xander in the first place."

"Exactly. So you would be able to keep him informed on exactly what Xander was up to, and who he was targeting."

"So that Manning could then relay it to Dragov," Sarah said to no one.

"That's right, Sarah. And when word got back that Xander had found his parents' killer, that's when Dragov began to take action. Dragov was lucky that my intel wasn't good."

"Your intel?" Sarah looked baffled.

"Yes, I'm the one that told Sean that I thought Sanharib Khatib could be the guy. I told Sean to not let Xander know until we were sure, but Xander can be very persuasive. And now, because Director Manning kept the info from Xander that Dragov was actually the murderer, Sean is dead."

Sarah didn't know what to do with all of that information. The only thing she wanted to do was get back on a plane and get to Moscow so she could try to help Xander. Now, here she was, taking a tongue-lashing from this turncoat, wrinkly-ass, fat shit Manning because Marv told her it would be best to act like they knew nothing. Marv said Manning would ask questions, probe her, to see if Sarah was on to him.

155

Sure enough . . .

Manning grew tired of waiting for Sarah to pull out of her silent stupor. "You'd better tell me that Xander tried to turn you against me, but then you decided to do the right thing and come back here instead of listening to him!"

And there it was. Marv was right. The only thing Manning cared about in that moment was if he was burnt. He would want to know if she'd contacted anyone. But she hadn't. She would let Xander take care of Manning. Right now she just needed to get out of there so she could meet her new friend Marv at the airport so they could get their asses to Moscow!

"That's exactly what happened, Director Manning." Sarah managed her most impressive pouty face. "Xander took advantage of me. The only reason he wanted so badly for me to be around was to find out what you were up to. I told him to go fuck himself when he said you were compromised." Sarah was impressed at the way her own voice sounded. Convincing.

Director Manning's entire demeanor changed. As if the storm clouds of concern in his mind had lifted. "Good. Compromised," he huffed, liking the sound of that.

Sarah's skin was crawling. She wanted to shoot that old fucker right in his blood-red wrinkly forehead. Time to make for certain once and for all whether Manning is truly working against Xander, and possibly for Dragov.

Sarah probed, "I'll grab a team and go take him down. He won't see us coming at his villa in Tuscany."

Here it was. If Director Manning was on the up-and-up, he of course would want to put an end to Xander's free rein. However, if he wanted otherwise, that meant he knew that Xander had already been captured. Sarah waited. The air in the room seemed thick enough to see.

156

"You know what, Sarah? Fuck Xander King. Let him try to go in there and take out Dragov. No matter what happens, we win."

And there it was. Sarah was disgusted. She couldn't believe the uphill climb that Xander had unknowingly been up against. Sarah stood and told Manning that she would await further instruction. Manning told her to be ready in case he called.

She sure as hell would be.

An hour later, Sarah was sitting aboard a Gulfstream jet beside Marv and across from the CIA's director of espionage, Mary Hartsfield. It seemed that Jack Bronson and Mary Hartsfield "go way back" and Jack had made a phone call to her from Xander's G6 as it was making its way to Moscow, letting her know that Xander and Sam were taken.

Sarah was devastated. Once she caught her breath, she was shocked when Mary wasn't all that surprised to hear about Director Manning's corruption. The fact that it came from Jack probably helped; Mary's eyes twinkled when she mentioned his name. They clearly had a romantic history. It also probably didn't hurt that Mary would be at the top of the list to replace Manning as the head of the CIA. She had to be sick and tired of his shit by now.

All she could do now was hope that Xander, though clearly in trouble, was at least not in any immediate danger.

Pistols and Parachutes
(not a good mix)

The power of the wind against Xander's back as he plummeted toward the earth below was strong enough to pin him against the Russian—aka his parachute. Before he could deploy the parachute, he would have to turn the man around so that they were face to face. Using his jujitsu grip, he slowly turned the man toward him. As he did so, Pavlovich and his four merry men arranged their bodies into aerodynamic dive positions, arms at hips, legs together straight out behind them. They were currently rocketing toward him. Gaining fast. Xander, because he had to hold this rhino of a man in order to use him as a parachute, didn't have the luxury of a dive position.

Xander finally managed to get the man turned around, and as the first of the Rocket Men approached, he managed to acquire a firm grip on the pistol. He had seven shots and *maybe* five thousand feet to get himself out of this mess before he had to open the chute.

"Help!" Xander shouted as the first Rocket Man fanned out his arms and matched the free-fall pace of Xander and the bullnecked Russian parachute, now clearly dead. "Help!" he screamed again, trying to feign being out of control. And what were these guys, expert parachuting Russian mafia thugs?

The first Rocket Man moved closer through the air and made an attempt to latch on. Xander smiled, put the gun to the man's head, and pulled the trigger. Blood and brains splattered upward in spectacular fashion, all over the face of Rocket Man Number Two who had moved in right behind Rocket Man Number One. As the wind whipped around him at a deafening pace, Xander struggled against its upward push, managed to squeeze the trigger, and subsequently managed to make Rocket Man Number Two's head explode in a similar fashion. Rocket Man Two never even saw the gun, or the bullet coming, because the goggles over his eyes were still covered by Rocket Man Number One's guts.

"Did you see that!" Xander grabbed the head of his dead-man-parachute and gave it a shake. "Seriously man, you are missing out!"

Xander couldn't wait to tell Kyle about this. At least *he* would appreciate it.

It was then that a look back over his shoulder at the unrelenting rise of the ground below brought him back to reality. Xander reestablished his grip on the dead-man-parachute, squeezed his legs around him with all his might, and pulled the rip cord. Pavlovich and Rocket Man Three and Four went flying past him. Rocket Man Three and Four pulled their chutes but Pavlovich continued to dive toward the ground. The yank of the parachute deploying was almost enough to shake Xander loose, but his training paid off. The burn in his legs was fierce, but he held on. Rocket Man Three and Four began to pull on their lines, and it slowed them enough to where they began to rise up to Xander's level. Below them, Xander could see that Pavlovich had finally pulled his chute. He was smart. He knew his best chance at killing Xander would be to be there waiting for him on the ground. After he got rid of the oncoming Rocket Men, Xander would have to try to steer away, at least to give him a chance to land before Pavlovich came after him. The ground below Pavlovich was a plush green open valley that ran into what looked like a small forest, which just so happened to be nestled right up to a vast mountain range. Xander figured it was most likely the Carpathian Mountains. Great, even if he did survive this battle, he was going to be stranded in the middle of a massive mountain range, in the middle of Ukraine.

Sigh.

Rocket Man Three floated slowly up to Xander. He let go of his lines and now had both hands on his semiautomatic weapon. Xander did his best to sink his limbs in behind the big Russian in order to shield himself from the spray of bullets. He heard a succession of crackles and heard bullets smack into the back of his dead-man-parachute. Xander reached over the shoulder of his human shield, and just as he was about to pull the trigger on a clear shot, he heard a succession of crackles behind and a little below him. Rocket Man Four, in an attempt to cover his comrade, sprayed a line of bullets up toward Xander. Xander still managed to squeeze off a shot, but it was sent flying off course because one of the stray bullets from behind him ripped clean through the right line on his parachute. The parachute began to fold in on itself, and Xander had a decision to make. He was in the middle of the sky, holding on to a sinking ship, two men shooting at his front and back.

No time to consider the consequences.

Shots rang out behind him through the deep blue sky, and Rocket Man Three was now right in front with his gun trained on Xander, barking something in Russian. Xander squeezed with his legs, unclipped the parachute strap from the dead man's right leg, then his left leg, and just as his hand hit where the clip snapped around his waist, Xander felt a bullet hit just above his leg, causing the automatic reaction of flailing, making him lose the grip that his legs held around the dead man. All of a sudden he was hanging by his fingertips from the clip of a parachute, the iron grip of his hand being the only reason he wasn't dropping his way toward death. He clung to the clasp like a vice, his hand burning with ache. Rocket Man Four was now at Xander's level, and once again he was forced to act. He pulled himself up with one arm as he tucked the gun into his waistline. His half-parachute had begun to cause him to circle, and the earth, blue sky mixed with clouds, swirled around him. Rocket Man Three had floated too far away by then, but Four sprayed bullets that zipped all around Xander and smacked into his human Russian shield several times. There was no time to think. Xander gripped the left shoulder strap of the parachute at the same time he unbuckled the last clip. The parachute shifted, pulling the dead man's arm out of socket, but it stuck just long enough for him to get a grip on the second strap. The chute above him continued to swirl in the wind and this time folded onto itself, and Xander dropped quickly away from Rocket Man Four, plummeting to the ground that was maybe a thousand feet below him now. With both hands death-gripping each strap, Xander spread them out away from each other as far as he could. With the wind whipping around him, his lungs on fire from the struggle, his arms and hands failing him from muscle fatigue, he summoned just enough strength to bring his legs up and kick the dead Russian straight back. Finally, the parachute was free.

It's amazing what you can do when death is relentlessly rising toward you at near warp speed.

Xander quickly pulled himself into the parachute, pulled the gun from his waist, used two of his last three bullets to cut free of the line that held the original parachute and yanked the chord on the reserve chute. It jerked him upward again as it plumed out into the deep blue above him like a cloud of yellow smoke, and finally the ground below began to come at him more slowly once again. The problem was, he hadn't had time to steer in all of the madness, and now he was dropping straight for an armed and deadly Nicoli Pavlovich.

Shit.

As his adrenaline finally took a moment off, it allowed the pain from a bullet in his leg to come screaming to the surface. It was a familiar pain, in a familiar place. It couldn't have been too far from the bullet he had taken in the calf muscle out on the yacht in the Virgin Islands just a few days ago. This was getting ridiculous. He'd had more holes put in him in the last two weeks than a goth chick on a piercing binge. And his stomach was still sore from its own recent healing.

Putting the pain aside, he yanked down on the right line and began to turn to his right. Below him, he could see Pavlovich running after him. He would be in shooting range in a matter of seconds. He yanked hard on both lines, trying to float along as much as he could. Pavlovich was running through the middle of an open meadow, through a carpet of purple saffron flowers.

The serene landscape that surrounded him was in stark contrast to Pavlovich's sinister intentions. There was a canopy of pines at the foot of a mountain just in front of Xander. If he could float that far, that was his best chance. The air was much warmer than it had been fifteen thousand feet ago, much more abundant as well. Xander closed his eyes and took in a couple of in-through-the-nose, out-through-the-mouth breaths and steadied his heart rate. He was about three hundred yards from the trees and about fifty from the ground. A rabid and relentless machine of a man was sprinting about a hundred yards behind him. With only one bullet left, and a leaking hole in his leg, it dawned on him that given all that he'd heard about the skills of Nicoli Pavlovich, even though Xander had been through many unbelievable battles over the years, he was about to be in for the fight of his life.

Here Comes the Cavalry

Outside the window of the Gulfstream, a never-ending light blue sky cradled the golden glow of the afternoon sun. Below, another never-ending, though darker blue ocean rolled out into the same great beyond like an infinite floor of carpet. The warmth coming through those windows served as what felt like a tranquilizer, melting Sarah into her seat. However, no matter how drowsy, she couldn't relax enough to fall asleep. Not with the thought of Xander being *taken*, and not with the thought of her boss being a turncoat, Benedict Arnold, super-sized, lying-ass-traitor son of a bitch.

"You all right, Sarah?"

Sarah actually jumped when she heard Marv's voice. Marv could tell by the look on her face that she absolutely was not all right, and he felt obligated to lend her an ear after all she'd been through. Sarah gave a fake smile and nodded her head.

"I'm okay. It just seems like we've been on this plane forever, and it's only been like three hours."

"I know. There is no reality worse than the unknown."

"So true. I mean, I know Xander is the very best at what he does, Marv, but if he's been taken . . ." Sarah took a deep breath. Marv gave her hand an "it's gonna be okay" pat. "I mean, you've known him longer than I have, do you think he's okay?"

"Well, to be honest, it doesn't sound good. Though I've never known Xander to let emotions dictate his decisions, it seems lately that is exactly what he's doing. And with Manning turning on him and having two of the meanest men on the planet after him, it really doesn't look good."

"So much for encouraging words." Sarah slumped in her seat.

"But . . ."

Sarah perked back up immediately. Marv could see that Sarah didn't really want the honest truth, just a pep talk. Marv was so terrible at this sort of thing. He didn't get the "how to comfort women" gene. He didn't even get the "how to talk to women" gene. Xander was always the one who handled this stuff when they were working together. Marv gave it the old college try anyway.

"But if there is anyone on this planet that can get himself out of the most impossible situations, it's Xander King. Or X-Man, as Sean used to call him. We all thought he was some sort of superhero."

"So, maybe he's all right then?"

Just tell her what she wants to hear, Marv. Damn it. For once in your life don't screw it up with a gorgeous woman!

"I think maybe he is."

Sarah leaned over and wrapped her arms around him. *It worked!* At first, Marv was like a deer in headlights; it took him a moment to hug her back. She smelled so good. Lavender and honey.

"Thanks, Marv. I needed—"

Sarah's phone chirped. A new e-mail. Mary roused from a deep sleep in the chair across from Sarah and immediately tuned in to the commotion. Sarah's heart jumped into her throat when she saw it was a message from Xander. She clicked on the e-mail notification, her eyes serious, ready to take it all in. It didn't take long.

"I'm sorry I doubted you. Melanie is a traitor. Sam is prisoner on way to Moscow. Don't trust Manning. Call Marvin Cameron. I need a chopper ASAP."

After that last sentence, she saw where Xander had dropped a pin to divulge his location. Sarah's heart was still racing as she clicked on the pin, and her phone loaded Xander's exact location.

I'm sorry I doubted you.

She and Xander were okay.

"You okay?"

Sarah jumped out of her zone when Marvin spoke. "Oh god, I'm sorry, Marv, it's Xander. He's okay!"

"He messaged you? That son of a bitch made it."

"I know, right? He dropped a pin and said he needs a helicopter. But, he's in . . . hang on, it's loading . . . Ukraine? How the hell can we get him a chopper in the Ukraine? I don't know anyone there."

"Shit. I don't either." Marv rubbed his chin and pushed his black-framed glasses back up his nose. "But I spoke with Jack while you were in with Manning and he said they are with Zhanna. She's ex-KGB. She might have a contact."

Mary leaned forward. "I spent some time in Ukraine years ago. I have a contact there. His nephew used to fly for their military . . ."

"But?" Sarah asked. She could see hesitation in Mary's eyes.

"But he got kicked out. Now he just lives off of his father's money. I only met him once, he's like a ten-year-old. He's out of his mind, always getting into trouble doing stupid stuff that almost always gets him killed. One of those adrenaline junkies. He's a total wildcard, but his daddy does have a helicopter."

Marv's chin almost dropped to the floor. "You're serious? Xander just so happens to somehow escape in Ukraine, needing a chopper, and you actually know someone there that has one? You can't make this stuff up."

"Can you make a call?" Sarah asked, her doe eyes doing their very best pleading.

"I'm telling you, he might end up getting Xander killed. He's bat shit crazy."

"Sounds to me like they're kindred spirits. Both of them having a death wish and all," Marv mused.

"What should I tell Xander?" Sarah asked.

Mary let out a sigh. "I guess this is the best we've got. I'll make a call."

Sarah jumped out of her seat, but her seat belt was still latched and it yanked her back like a yo-yo. It barely even slowed her down, though; she unlatched the belt and ran over, throwing her arms around Mary. Mary gave Sarah a pat on the back and over her shoulder gave Marv a double-eyebrow-raised "wow" face. Marv just smiled and winked.

"Oh my god!" Sarah said in realization as she pulled away from Mary. "I never called Kyle back. He must think I have abandoned them completely!"

The satellite phone in Xander's airplane rang, pulling Kyle, Jack, and Zhanna from their plotting positions on the couch. Kyle shrugged his shoulders at Jack and Zhanna and then walked over to the opposite side of the jet, sat down, and answered the phone.

"Hello?"

"Kyle! It's Sarah."

"Sarah? Are you okay? We looked everywhere for you but—"

"I know, I'm sorry. I panicked when Xander . . . listen, I know about Xander and Sam."

"You do? How?"

"Marv."

Kyle had only met Marv once, but he remembered Jack mentioning that he had him looking into things. He also remembered that Xander called him the smartest guy he'd ever met.

"Yeah, okay, I know of him. We are on our way to Moscow now to get Xander back."

"So are we. Listen, Kyle, I just got an email from Xander—"

"What?" Kyle stood up, his heart leapt into his throat.

"I know! He got away!"

"He got away?" Kyle repeated her words but mostly to let Jack and Zhanna in on the news. Both of them jumped to their feet.

"Yeah! Ha-ha! Can you believe it?" she screamed.

"How did—"

"I don't know how, but I know where. The Ukraine. We have someone on their way now to try to find him."

Kyle could hardly process her words. His nerve endings had fried hours ago when he knew his friend was in trouble. But he got away. Of course he did.

"What about Sam?"

"All he said was that she was still a prisoner, and still on her way to Moscow."

"Shit! I'm gonna kill that motherfucker Pavlovich as soon as I see him." Kyle pounded the back of a chair with his fist.

"I've got to go, Kyle. How far out are you?"

"Only about an hour now."

"You?"

"Ugh, still about five or so."

"Wow, where are you coming from?"

"I know, I'm sorry. Virginia. Hey, Marv wants to talk with Jack and Zhanna to help coordinate. He says if Zhanna can tell him where Dragov will be, he can get online and work up a blueprint."

"Of course, let me put you on speaker."

The six of them came together like they had been working with each other for years. Kyle didn't understand a lot of the lingo, but he'd been around Xander and Sam long enough to get the gist of it. It didn't take long for an extraction plan to come together. The last piece, of course, was Xander and whether or not he would be involved. They would have to make their plans without him. That thought brought Kyle a sense of emptiness like he had never felt before. No Sam and no Xander. They had to have Xander. But if they didn't, Kyle was ready to do whatever it took to get Sam out safely. That was his only goal. Get Sam out safely. When Xander made it to Moscow, and Xander *will* make it to Moscow, he would let him deal with Dragov and Pavlovich.

For now, this was a rescue mission.

Belly of the Beast

Vitalii Dragov slammed his fist against his oversized, cherry wood desk. The globe with the golden accents that sat on its corner toppled and crashed against the floor, and Dragov followed that up with a violent sweep of his arm, raking all of the papers off the desk, and they fluttered violently through the air. His face was red, his mouth slobbering, like a pit bull going for the neck. He stood from his chair and waddled over to the window. Then he turned back to Melania.

"What the fuck you mean he just jumped? How was he ever unshackled? How you manage to fuck this up?"

"Nicoli jumped after him, sir. I am sure by now Xander is dead." Melania's voice held zero confidence, and Dragov could sense it.

"Oh, you're sure, are you? Just like Nicoli got him last time?"

One of the three men standing behind Melania stepped forward. He was still dressed in his all-black tactical gear from the plane ride from Tuscany. "Boss, it's not Melania's fault. Xander tricked Boris."

Dragov shifted his eyes to this man. A man he did not know. Without a word he picked up a letter opener, took two steps forward, and jammed the blade into the side of the man's neck. Hot blood shot out onto Melania's face, and the soldier went down writhing to the floor. No one moved. Dragov pulled out a handkerchief and wiped the spatters of blood from his face and hands. His eyes were black as coals. An evil aura surrounded him. A chill ran down Melania's back.

"I want to see her," Dragov finally said.

"She is in basement cell. May I speak?"

"Speak," he growled.

"Sam is one of Xander's closest friends, more like sister. He will do anything to save her. If Xander does make it back here, which I assure you he will not, but if he does, we can use her as bait."

"Bring her to me."

A few moments later, after a couple of cigarettes and a few fingers of ultrarare, forty-year-old Balvenie scotch, Dragov's fire had reduced to a simmer. As he waited for Melania to bring Sam in for a chat, he stared out the window of his fortified mansion at the south end of the richest subdivision in all of Russia. He bought the surrounding lots, giving him many acres all to himself and his business. He took another sip of scotch and lit another cigarette as he contemplated the empire he had grown. The media calls it the largest organized crime ring in the world. Dragov chuckled to himself. They didn't know the half of it. His empire, built on the blood of lesser men, was double the size of the six billion dollars they all said it was worth. He took a long drag of his cigarette, arched his back, and puffed smoke into the air, the way a man does when he is on top of the world. All of a sudden he became very relaxed. Why was he worrying about this pissant, Xander King? Of all the men Dragov had dealt with in his life, of all the kingpins and drug lords, he couldn't figure for the life of him why he had let this one American ruffle his feathers.

"Dragov is real king. Not this Xander King," he said to the walls of his office.

He was impressed with what Xander had done in Syria. He was impressed with the way he dispatched the men he'd sent to his home in Lexington, and he was impressed with the way his *team*, headed by this *Sam*, had been able to bail Xander out not once, but twice this week. But Dragov had defeated entire gangs. Rival organizations that had hundreds of associates, not just one man and his measly two or three. Dragov knew he had fought wars, and he decided right then not to waste another second worrying about this Xander. If Pavlovich hadn't already disposed of him, his men would easily do so when he showed up here to save his precious Sam.

"Mr. Dragov, we have Sam in the hallway. Shall we bring her in?" Melania, from the doorway behind him, interrupted Dragov's train of thought,

"Dah." Dragov nodded, ashed his cigarette, took his scotch over behind his desk, and remained standing as he lit a cigar this time. Chimneys had nothing on Dragov.

Melania stepped back out into the hallway.

"Sam, I suggest you keep mouth shut unless Dragov expects answer. Then give answer and nothing more."

Sam was still a bit taken aback by Melania's Russian accent; she had disguised it well while inside her company.

"Melanie"—Sam was sure not to use Melania's real name—"I suggest you pull a one-eighty and join the correct side. Before it's too late."

Melania gave a short but mocking laugh. "I suppose you would rather I be the nerdy and submissive woman, you like me better in this role, yes? Before it's too late." She made air quotes. "Ha! You are delusional. Too late for what, Sam?" Melania held an arrogant smile. The smile someone wears when they believe themselves untouchable.

Sam looked dead into Melania's eyes, unwavering, cold as ice. "Before I squeeze your neck so hard you won't even have the chance to beg for your life."

Melania punched Sam in the face. Then spit at her. Just the reaction Sam was hoping for. Stupid bitch hit just like a toddler. The three men who had shuffled her up four floors nudged her not so gently into the room where a huge fat ass stood behind an oversized desk. Sam observed the walls that were covered in books—books she knew were all for show, she'd be surprised if this blob could even read—and took in the stench of the smoke-smothered space. The men continued to nudge her up to the desk where Dragov stood, smugly continuing to fill the room with cancer clouds. Sam was the stark opposite of Dragov. To him, she reminded him of Kate Beckinsale in one of his favorite movies, *Underworld*. To her, Dragov reminded her of the dad in one of her least favorite movies, *Shallow Hal.* Pockmarked

174

face, three chins, and a waistline the size of the Equator: disgusting.

Dragov spoke first.

"So . . . this is famous Sam? You don't look so special to Vitalii Dragov. Though you are more beautiful than I imagined." His lazy Russian accent almost hypnotized Sam to sleep. Dragov ashed his cigarette, tabled his scotch, and slithered around the corner of his desk with the grace of an anaconda that just swallowed a human. Two men held Sam in place as Dragov walked right up to her. His mouth smelled of whisky and smoke, his face uglier the closer he came, and his eyes, dark and gray. Lifeless. Sam held those eyes, unafraid, as he ran his fat-fingered hand down the soft skin of her left cheek. Though revolted by his touch, she didn't dare flinch.

"Yes, very beautiful." He continued to slide his hand down her neck, then down around her black leather-covered breast, and he finished by cupping it over her crotch. Again, Sam didn't flinch. However, her mind did flash back to the basement of Sanharib Khatib's compound, his urine running down her naked back as one of his men raped her from behind. Still, Sam didn't so much as shudder. "This"—Dragov pushed up with his hand—"this is all you are good for now. Your precious Xander cannot save you here. You will be mine, over and over again until I tire of you. Which I am sure will not take long."

It took everything in Sam's will to keep from snap-kicking that pudgy mound of sleaze in his tiny little balls. It also took everything she had to keep from vomiting. The thought of that fat shit, naked and sweating on top of her, almost triggered a gag reflex she didn't even know she had. He removed his hand from her crotch and forcefully wrapped it around her neck. His face scrunched in anger as he continued to clamp tighter around her throat.

"Listen to me, bitch. As soon as Pavlovich returns with Xander, I am going to gut him right in front of you." Dragov spat as he released his grip.

Sam cleared her throat and spoke evenly through the pain. "You are? Or do you mean you will have someone do your dirty work for you?"

"I will personally end him. Just for you. Would you like that?"

"What I would like is for you to consider popping a mint. I recommend Altoids, curiously strong little buggers."

Dragov backhanded Sam in the face, almost twisting her head in the opposite direction. She snapped her head back, taking his eyes, slowly letting a smile grow across her face. Blood trickled from her bottom lip. Dragov nodded to the two men holding her, and they kicked the back of her legs, forcing her down to her knees. He stepped forward, his crotch now directly in front of her face.

"You have very smart mouth. Let Dragov see if that mouth is good for anything else." Dragov reached for his zipper and pulled it all the way down. Just as he reached in his pants, Melania's phone chirped.

"It is text from Pavlovich." She unlocked her phone. Dragov's attention moved to Melania, and he zipped his pants. "He says he has Xander cornered. He has already called for helicopter to escort them back after his capture. He says three hours maximum."

Before Dragov could react to Melania's words, Sam responded, "That is the last time you will ever hear from Nicoli Pavlovich."

Dragov let a slow and guttural laugh roll from his big round belly. He shook his finger at Sam in a tsk-tsk fashion. "You must not know about skill of Nicoli Pavlovich."

"Don't need to, I know about skill of Xander King."

Welcome to the Jungle

"I must admit, Xander, I am impressed." Pavlovich shouted through the rows of pine trees. "You've got balls. You're stupid, but you've got balls," He motioned to his men on the left and right of him to fan out and flank around. He had a good view of Xander floating from his parachute into the tree line, and there was still plenty of sunlight to see into the shadows to determine which direction he ran. "Unfortunately for you, I am going to cut those balls off. You didn't actually think you could get away from me, did you? I am not like other men you have faced in past. I am greatest assassin in the world." Nicoli's voice echoed through the trees and up the mountain that lay just beyond them. His men had fully loaded AK-47s, and Nicoli himself had two nine-millimeter pistols and a backup magazine.

Xander was outnumbered three to one. His enemies had ninety-six bullets, he had only one. Ninety-six to two if you counted his trusty knife, Rambo, which he always kept tucked against his right calf muscle. These weren't the worst odds he had faced, not by a long shot. As he leaned his back against the sturdy pine and listened to Pavlovich stroke his own ego, a flashback to Syria ran through his mind when he killed eight men with a smoke bomb and a knife. However, according to Sam, Pavlovich is definitely a far more competent killer than all of those men would have been, combined.

Overhead he heard the scream of a hawk, and now on his left and right he could hear the crunching of twigs and pine cones. They were surrounding him. With one bullet and a knife, Xander's options were limited. Ahead of him, he could just barely make out the edge of the trees where it met the mountain range. It would do him no good to run there, he would be even more exposed than he was at the moment. Plus, the hole in his leg was really starting to ache.

"Come out, come out wherever you are," Pavlovich shouted.

Real original.

Pavlovich must have learned his trash talk from old JeanClaude Van Damme movies. Wait, maybe that was Steven Seagal. Either way, this guy was a total cliché. Even though it seemed so dismal, Xander couldn't help but smile. It was in these moments that he felt most alive. It must be the reason he always seemed to end up in them. He could feel his adrenaline leaking into his veins, and at that moment he just couldn't imagine a life without this. How boring? Most people get off on other things, normal things, like business. And while horse racing definitely got Xander going, it wasn't the same. Most people would feel at the pinnacle of their lives when they are told that their bourbon brand just got picked up in ten more states. That made Xander happy, proud even, but *this*—being out there in the middle of nowhere, outnumbered, outgunned, nowhere to hide, and death knocking at the door—*this* was living.

Like a lion outnumbered by elephants, Xander had to thin the herd. It was the only way he was going to get out of there alive, and get back to Sam. There was a branch above him, so he pulled himself up into the tree. A couple of branches farther up and he was semi-hidden, and had a decent view of what was around him. The footfalls of his enemies grew closer. He strained his eyes to his left, and through the branches he finally saw movement coming his way. He crouched on the branch, freeing his hands. He took his gun in his right and reached across with his left and slowly slid Rambo from its sheath. The man to his left was heading directly under his position. As he prepared for the drop, he saw movement to his right. The second gunman had turned toward them, walking directly for his comrade. The man coming from the left was only steps from being under him now.

"Come on, Xander, give it up. I could beat you alone, but it's even worse for you, it is three against one."

Xander dropped from the branch, and as he landed, with his left hand he drove the razor-sharp blade of Rambo into the gunman's neck, and with his right hand he shot the other gunman walking toward him in the forehead, before he could fire off a single round.

"I demand a recount," Xander announced, before the echo of his gunshot had even made it out of the trees.

The herd had been thinned.

180

"Admit it," Xander said loud enough for Pavlovich to hear as he pulled his knife from the man's neck and wiped the blade clean of blood on his white linen pants. "Your butthole puckered a little bit just now."

From only a few yards behind him, Pavlovich answered, "What this mean, butthole pucker? You think Nicoli Pavlovich is scared?"

"Enough with the third person, who do you think you are, Elmo?"

"Elmo?"

"Yeah, you know, *Sesame Street*. Elmo want to play. Come on man, don't you have a TV in douche-bag-ville? My niece loves Elmo."

"You talk, Xander King, because you are nervous."

Xander re-sheathed Rambo and traded his empty nine-millimeter for the dead man's AK-47. A pool of the dead man's blood gathered around Xander's feet as he threw the gun's strap over his head and shucked the lock on the machine gun, making a loud click-clack.

"You hear that, Pavlov? Does that sound like I'm nervous?"

"Name is Pavlovich, and any coward can shoot gun. Real man fight with hands."

Xander took a quick glance around the trunk of the tree and saw Pavlovich standing behind a tree of his own, a pistol in each of his outstretched hands. "Then why don't you drop those pistols and fight like a *real* man?"

With the quickness of a deadly cat, Pavlovich dove out from behind the tree and sent bullets whizzing past Xander's head. He was barely able to get back behind his own tree. Bullet-stung bark scattered around his head. Pavlovich was quicker than Xander expected. It was time to stop underestimating him. Xander was ready to retaliate when he heard a familiar thump coming out of the sky from off in the distance.

"You hear that, King? That is your ride back to Dragov. Question is, will you be dead or alive on way back? Makes no difference to me. You are a dead man in the end, either way."

Xander hadn't had a chance to see if Sarah e-mailed him back. He had no way of knowing if the e-mail he sent her even went through, or for that matter, if she even wanted to help. It was far more likely that Pavlovich got through to have a chopper sent here, so it seemed that things had just gone from bad to worse. He had no idea if there would be more armed men waiting for him in the helicopter, so he had to act now.

Xander had seen instances on a number of occasions while in Iraq where a man had dropped his AK-47 onto the ground and, because the trigger was so loose, bullets scattered into the air. It certainly would make a good distraction now. With the thumping of helicopter rotors getting closer by the second, it was time for action, not reaction. Xander tossed his AK-47 as far as he could to the right of where Pavlovich was hiding. As the machine gun floated through the air, Xander sprinted around the left side of Pavlovich. Halfway there, the AK-47 landed in a thud on the ground, and sure enough, bullets sprayed up into the air like fire off a freshly lit sparkler. Pavlovich's reflex was the one Xander was counting on. He turned immediately and began firing at the unmanned AK-47. Now, only about twenty-five yards in front of him, Pavlovich's back was turned, his attention on the distraction. In just a few powerful strides, Xander was at full speed and only a few feet from Pavlovich, when Pavlovich pivoted around and extended two pistols out in front of him, there was a mixture of surprise and anger cloaking his normally hardened face. Xander planted his left foot and launched himself forward in a dive that ended in a collision with the much smaller Pavlovich, just before he was able to squeeze either of the triggers on his guns. They landed in a crash to the ground, and Pavlovich managed to roll backward, freeing himself from Xander, though losing hold of his weapons in the process as they went flying several feet from him. Xander rolled to his feet, Pavlovich rose to his. It was a sight of sharp contrast. Pavlovich stood with more the frame of Pierce Brosnan's James Bond. Xander stood more like Captain America. After the injection. Pavlovich was known all over the world for his skills as an assassin, but only because of his cunning and his skill with weapons. He was not known as a master assassin because of his hand-to-hand combat abilities. This wasn't going to end well for him, and he knew it as he stared into Xander's adrenaline-sparked eyes. His only chance was to get a weapon in his hands. For a moment, they stood, locked in a battle stance, their chests heaving as they both steadied their heart rates.

The helicopter was now hovering at the tree line's edge. Waiting.

"There is no way you can win." Pavlovich sneered.

"Did you kill my parents?" Xander asked, his voice cold and flat.

Pavlovich's eyes darted, only for a split second, from Xander's to one of his guns.

No more questions.

Simultaneously, they both launched themselves in the direction of the gun. However, Xander wasn't going for the gun; he launched himself where Pavlovich was going to be, and it paid off. Just as Pavlovich got his hands on the gun, Xander had his hands on him. Xander straddled him and clasped his hands around Pavlovich's grip on the gun and forced the bullets off course just as he squeezed the trigger. The bang of the gun clamored in Xander's ears, and a high-pitched whistle stayed behind, stinging through his eardrums. Before Pavlovich could once again squeeze the trigger, Xander forced his arms over his head and banged them against the ground. On the third slam, Pavlovich released the gun but was able to roll Xander over because of his lack of balance. He was now straddling Xander in an immensely dominant position. The worst position you could be in if you are fighting a man. Flat on your back, pinned underneath him, with only your arms to protect yourself.

A look of satisfaction grew over Pavlovich's face, but it quickly turned to surprise. Not surprise because Xander had managed to grab the gun, and he wasn't surprised because Xander had managed any other weapon either. He was surprised because when he looked down from his dominant position, ready to end this deadly encounter, he was shocked to find the look on Xander's face. Not only did he see no fear, but Xander was smiling.

"You smile?" Pavlovich grunted as rage washed over his face. He pulled his fist back and launched it at Xander's face. Xander slapped it away like he would a child's hand reaching for a hot pan. Pavlovich immediately drew back his other fist, launched it, and had it easily slapped away again.

Xander was toying with him.

"Nicoli Pavlovich, a world-renowned assassin, hits like a little fucking girl." Xander maintained his smile.

Pavlovich reached back once more, but Xander didn't give him the chance to try again. Xander took Pavlovich's dangling arm, pulled it down as he pushed up with his hips, then swept

184

him from his dominant position, turning the tables, and now Xander was on top. Xander quickly passed Pavlovich's guard and straddled his rib cage.

"Let me show you how this is done." Xander's smile was now nowhere to be found.

But his elbows were.

Those elbows rained down upon Pavlovich's face like a superstorm of ominous clouds opening up and pouring down cinderblocks on his head. With each annihilating blow, hot purple-red blood spattered Xander and the ground around him. Pavlovich's skin split like a block of firewood under a razor-sharp axe. Each merciless thud resulted in a pain-filled whimper. Just before Xander thought he might kill him, he sat up on top of him, took Pavlovich's face in his hands, forcing eye contact, and asked him one last time.

"Did you kill my parents?" His voice was cold enough to freeze boiling water.

Pavlovich's jaw was slack, clearly broken, yet he still managed to slur his final words. "Fuck your parents, and fuck you."

Xander let go of his face.

Xander rose to his feet.

Xander crushed what was left of Pavlovich's skull with the bottom of his heel.

It took a moment for Xander's wits to return. His heart raced and his entire body heaved with rage. He stalked back and forth beside Pavlovich's dead body like an animal boasting over its kill. It wasn't anything Xander thought or saw that broke his murderous trance; it was what he could no longer hear.

The helicopter's rotors had stopped.

Kyle Hamilton Has Trust Issues

Kyle, Jack, and Zhanna landed at a remote private airfield, not far, but far enough from where Zhanna knew her father would be. Sarah, Marv, and Mary were still a couple of hours out, and Kyle had no idea where Xander was. As Bob taxied the plane toward the hangar, Kyle was having a hard time fighting the panic rising from within. These were the moments he could look to his stoic friend, Xander, and his calm would become Kyle's calm. He looked around the cabin of the airplane. While he was sure the beautiful Zhanna, ex-KGB, and the vastly experienced Jack Bronson were formidable allies, to Kyle they were still strangers. And though they seemed as eager as he was to see this thing through, their motives were their own. Zhanna didn't really care about Xander. She just wanted to avenge her mother's death and kill her father. Jack barely even knew Xander, so Xander really wasn't his concern either. The only thing Jack cared about was clearing his conscience of putting Xander's mom in the pretzel behind his friend—Xander's dad's—back. Kyle heard the phrase on many occasions, the enemy of an enemy is a friend, and while Kyle didn't see these strangers as enemies, they were friends because they shared Dragov as a common enemy. But was that enough to band them together? Would they lay down their lives for Xander? For Sam? For Kyle himself? Would Kyle lay down his life for them?

The questions and anxiety surrounding the horrible situation they were all in swirled around his consciousness.

Bob chimed in over the intercom, "Kyle, can you come up here for a minute?"

Kyle jumped when the pilot bonged in. It hit him then that Bob was more of an ally than the two seasoned veterans in front of him. Bob had held off the enemy and saved their asses back in Syria. He could have just left them in Syria and worried solely about himself, but he didn't. It was proven that he was willing to risk his life for Xander. For all of them. A dash of hope sparked somewhere inside of Kyle.

As Kyle got up, Jack asked, "What's this about? Any idea?"

"Not sure. Be back in a sec."

Kyle walked to the cockpit. In the few short seconds it took to get there, the plane had stopped and Bob was turned around in his chair waiting for Kyle.

"I don't like this, Kyle."

"What's wrong?" The look on Bob's face killed what little spark of hope flashed in Kyle just a moment ago.

"Something's off. I've been doing this a long time, and something is not right here."

"You mean at this airport?"

"Yeah, it's too damn quiet."

"Didn't we choose this place specifically for that reason?"

"We did, but we weren't going to an abandoned airfield, just a remote one. No working airport is *this* remote. And I've communicated with thousands of air traffic controllers in my day, and I'm telling you, the guy that saw me in . . . I—he wasn't an air traffic controller." Bob's eyes conveyed nothing but sureness.

Kyle had to ask anyway, even though he could see the answer in Bob's eyes. "You're sure? He couldn't just be new?"

Bob just lowered his head and gave it a shake. "No. I'm positive we've flown into an ambush. That's why I stopped at the end of the runway instead of taxiing in."

Just then the radio on the plane chirped. "N800XK, you are cleared to taxi in. Please proceed to hangar three. N800XK, I repeat, please proceed to hangar three."

Bob said, "What do you want me to do?"

"What do you think? I'm out of my league here."

"Should we ask one of them?" Bob nodded his head toward the cabin. Zhanna and Jack looked on with focused curiosity.

"Shit. I was just having this argument with myself before you called me up here. I think we can trust them, but I hardly know them."

"Do you trust me?"

Kyle looked dead into Bob's eyes. "I remember Syria. I trust you with my life."

"Then sit down and buckle up. We're getting the hell out of here."

Blood, Sweat, and Urine

Xander's ears were pricked, waiting to hear something—anything—from the direction of the helicopter. He waited to hear the voices of soldiers, the rustling of weapons, footfalls crashing on the ground toward him; still there was nothing. The air around him had begun to cool. The sun's golden light turned to the orange beginning of its descent. The air smelled of blood and fuel. Before he moved forward toward the helicopter at the edge of the trees, he picked up the late Nicoli Pavlovich's famous ones and twos. Pistols that had seen the end of many an enemy. There were only a couple of bullets left in each magazine; he could tell that by the weight. He quickly ran up another ten yards and behind another tree, his leg throbbing the entire way, inching his way closer to the helicopter. The helicopter that showed absolutely zero signs of life. Almost as if a ghost had flown it in. One more ten-yard move forward and he would be able to get his eyes on it and assess the situation. An eagle screamed overhead, followed by another bird of prey. Soon, Nicoli Pavlovich's skin and muscle would be picked clean to the bone. A fitting end for a human vulture. Xander's end may be coming soon, but it was not going to happen out here. Not before he could get to his friends. Not before Dragov's cold, dead eyes stared back up at him as he joined Pavlovich in the afterlife.

Xander lunged forward and sidled up behind another tree. Through row after row of pine branches, he could see the tail rotor on the army green chopper. He couldn't see anyone standing around it. Something was off. There is no way Pavlovich would have called for a chopper with no one in it. Maybe this helicopter was meant for him—

Just as the thought crossed his mind, off in the distance that familiar thumping sound echoed across the sky and made its way through the trees to Xander. Another helicopter. So was the first one just a scout? Sent to find our location, then radio for the fully manned chopper? That didn't seem logical, but he was stuck at the foot of a mountain range in Ukraine.

Two weeks ago Xander would have laughed had you told him that would happen. He should be at home preparing his magnificent racehorse for one of the sport's greatest glories: the Triple Crown. Instead, more murder. More pain. More of his friends in danger. Xander figured he was becoming more like a cancer than a friend. Everything around him was shrouded in his personal quest for vengeance. Though he felt like sulking, he knew he really didn't have the time for that, or the time to further speculate on who this bird was meant for. It was either the good guys that flew in first or the bad guys. And only one way to find out.

Xander maneuvered his way through the last hundred yards of trees, zigzagging as gracefully as a man with a bullet in his calf muscle could possibly zig and zag. After just a few moments he came to the edge of the trees, the helicopter only twenty yards in front of him. The second helicopter closing quickly from the sky. Xander saw zero movement inside the cockpit. Quickly, he turned to his left, then his right, then behind him. Even though he did a scan on his way to the tree line and saw no one, it made him paranoid when the pilot was nowhere to be found. He, or they, could very easily have gone off and hidden while Xander was stuffing his heel through Pavlovich's forehead. But Xander had a certain feel for these things. At least he used to. His judgment in general lately, especially about people, had been at best a little suspect. He didn't like the feeling of questioning himself. He wasn't used to it, because it simply never happened.

Xander turned back toward the helicopter, determined. He couldn't wait any longer. If he was lucky enough to have an ally in this chopper, he knew he wouldn't be that lucky twice as the now visible second helicopter was closing fast. Xander sprinted for the front of the chopper, his arms extended in front of him, pistols in hand. He made it to the chopper and put his back up against the exterior, looking right, toward the open-air entrance on the side.

"You've got five seconds to exit the helicopter, hands on your head, before I come in and kill you. FIVE."

"FOUR!" He heard nothing.

"THREE!" Nothing but the closing thump of sure death that was the second chopper.

"TWO!" Still nothing, Xander readied himself for an entrance.

"ONE—"

"WAIT!" Xander heard as he turned the corner. His finger almost too heavy on the trigger to stop the shot. Inside the empty cabin of the unmarked military chopper, a scrawny, wild-haired young man lay on the floor, his hands above his head, and the fear of God on his face. As soon as he saw Xander, the fear on his face went from scared to piss-your-pants terrified. "Aaaahhhh!" A high-pitched, teenage-girl scream leapt from the lungs of the man.

Xander asked, "Who are you?"

A pause, then "Aaaaahhhh!" Another shrill scream as the eyes of the man went from Xander's eyes, roamed over Xander's body, and back up to his eyes.

Xander looked down; he was absolutely covered in blood. From head to toe. He wiped his face with the top side of his forearm, and even more blood must have been covering his face. Xander could only imagine the horror movie character he must have looked like.

"Please! Please don't kill Viktor! I should never have come here! I am good guy!"

"Viktor? Viktor, calm down, I'm Xander. Who sent you?"

Viktor's face changed in an instant. He went from fear to utter elation. "Xander? You are Xander! Ha-ha! Yes, man! Viktor knew that! I am just playing with you, man!"

Xander looked on, lowering his weapons, confusion on his face. He couldn't tell if this guy was playing with him or just trying to cover the fact that he was scared out of his mind.

Viktor got to his feet. He was maybe 140 pounds soaking wet, tall and wiry. He wore a white wifebeater, baggy khaki cargo pants, a scraggly beard, Albert Einstein-wild dirty-blond hair, and the goofiest expression on his face that Xander had ever seen.

"I had you, huh? You thought Viktor was really scared!"

The closing in of the helicopter shortened Xander's assessment of Viktor. "You gonna get me out of here or are you just going to stand there and try to convince me that the wet spot on your pants is from a drink you spilled earlier and not piss that leaked from you as you were screaming like a little girl?"

Viktor's head snapped down toward his crotch, then he looked back up with an embarrassed smile. "Oh, Xander King is funny man. I like funny man! Sure, let's get out of here." He motioned over his shoulder in the direction of the oncoming helicopter. "Viktor not so sure that next ride will have hero like Viktor waiting to save you."

Xander smiled internally as he pulled himself up into the helicopter. "Then we'd better get going." He walked past Viktor and straight to the passenger seat in the cockpit.

Viktor followed him to the front. "You did not really think Viktor was scared, did you? Come on! I know you would not think that."

Xander didn't say anything as he buckled up. Viktor took the seat beside him, a worried look on his face. "Seriously, I was not scared. I've killed hundreds of men. Nothing scares Viktor Panchak!"

Xander's eyes roamed over Viktor's physique. Clearly not a man who had ever served in any sort of actual combat. "Whatever you say, Viktor, just make sure you crack a window on the way up. I don't wanna smell urine the entire flight to Moscow."

For the first time Viktor's face sagged a bit. Then the smile popped right back on. "Oh, Viktor get it. You funny guy!"

Xander looked up at the incoming helicopter and let out a sigh. Viktor fired up the chopper. If they made it off the ground, it was going to be one hell of a long flight.

Upside Down and Inside Out

As the engines of the G6 screamed to life, Jack, Zhanna, and Kyle peered out the window and watched as jeeps, cars, motorcycles, and vans poured out of every orifice of the airport like an ant colony taking on water. There must have been over a dozen of them coming straight for the runway.

Kyle turned in his seat, one eye on the oncoming army, one toward the cockpit. "Bob! It's now or never!"

Just then the engines began to wind down, almost like they were letting out a sigh of relief.

"Bob! What the hell, man?"

Kyle heard a seatbelt click, and then Bob came walking down the aisle. "Bob, wh—"

"They have surface-to-air missiles," Bob said, dejected. "There's no way out. Believe me, if there was I would find it."

"We have to try. They take us and we're dead!"

Zhanna unbuckled her belt. "He is correct, my father would not hesitate to shoot us down. This way we at least have chance. Not good chance, but chance."

Kyle's face knotted up. He'd been captured before, and it was absolutely the worst memory of his life. "So, that's it? We just . . ."

Kyle's voice trailed off. He noticed Jack reaching for the phone. Outside, the horde of Dragov's bloodthirsty minions began to surround the plane.

"Mary, this is Jack . . . There's no time, just listen. We are in Moscow, and we are being taken. All of us. Domodedovo Airport is compromised. I would imagine any other airport near here will be as well. You, Marv, and Sarah have to find another way in." He paused. "No, no word from Xander. Mary, no, no Mary, they are approaching the plane now. We should have known better."

Viktor fired up the engine, and the rotors began to whirl to life. At the same moment, the second helicopter was descending toward them. Viktor pulled back on the yoke, and they began to lift off the ground.

Xander shouted, "How well can you fly this thing?"

Viktor looked over at Xander wide-eyed with a grin full of tobacco-stained teeth. "Viktor is best pilot in Ukraine!"

Xander couldn't tell just how off his rocker Viktor was, but he certainly had no confidence in his self-proclamation. As he pulled the bird into the air, the other chopper followed, its front end seemingly grimacing back at them. "I saw the missiles were stripped, this thing got any ammo in the chain gun?"

"They make Viktor get rid of ammunition."

Oh hell.

"But Viktor never really get rid of ammunition!"

Oh hell, yes.

"Viktor thought, just in case, when I left, and put ammo in chain gun! Ha-ha!"

Off his rocker or not, at that moment, Xander wanted to kiss that crazy bastard. "You ever been in a dog fight?"

"I play lots of *Call of Duty*, so don't worry!"

Oh hell.

Viktor turned the yoke to his left and then pushed it forward; their helicopter lurched forward and the Russians followed immediately behind him. Xander unbuckled his belt and made his way back to the opening in the side of the chopper. The wind whipped around the cabin as Xander grabbed the metal handle and looked back behind them. He really couldn't be in a worse spot. He felt helpless. Just then sparks flew from under the Russian chopper's fuselage. A split second later, bullets zipped under Xander's feet and then he heard a clank-clank-clank-clank as several of them bore into the side of their helicopter. Xander dove back inside the cabin and pulled his pistols.

"Viktor! We have to get behind them! It's our only shot!"

Before Viktor could respond, a buzz-buzz-buzz clamored from the cockpit.

Missile lock.

Viktor shouted after he jerked the yoke, "Hold on to pecker, Xander King!"

The helicopter jerked east and Xander slid toward the opening of the cabin. Just as his feet dangled out into the open air, Viktor jerked the yoke in the opposite direction, sending

Xander flipping toward the other side of the chopper. *BUZZ-BUZZ-BUZZ* continued to scream from being locked in the Russian's missile sites. Xander jumped to his feet, slid back across the chopper, and looked back out the opening just in time to see a missile dislodge from under the Russian bird.

"Countermeasure! Hit the antimissile flares!" Xander screamed, hoping against hope that they had never been removed. The missile was halfway to them now, and just as Xander was about to turn away in hopes of finding a parachute, sparks flew out from behind their chopper. Viktor had released the flares. Their helicopter launched upward, and Xander saw the missile explode midair.

"Ha-ha-ha!" Xander heard from the cockpit. "So that is what that button does!"

Xander's stomach rolled, and it wasn't because of the helicopter's steep ascent. It was because he was hanging on for dear life, which was currently in the hands of a madman. Xander fought against gravity and worked his way back up to the cockpit, just in time to hear the *BUZZ-BUZZ-BUZZ* alert of another oncoming missile.

"Any more flares?" Xander screamed, stabilizing himself by holding on to the backs of the cockpit seats.

"No more flares," Viktor said calmly. Then he yanked back on the yoke again.

"What are you doing? We'll stall!"

BUZZ-BUZZ-BUZZ!

Xander looked at the altimeter: only three thousand feet. If they stall here, there would be no time to recover.

"Viktor!"

BUZZ-BUZZ-BUZZ!

The nose of the helicopter was now completely vertical, pointed directly toward the heavens. The heavens that Xander figured he'd be seeing the inside of in a matter of seconds. He death-clutched the back of the cracked leather seats, and his feet dangled out behind him.

Viktor pulled the yoke back to his stomach and screamed, "Do not worry, Xander King! In simulator I have done this many times!"

"How often did it work?" Xander yelled back, hanging on with all he had. The helicopter began to pitch backward and the engine began to sputter.

BUZZ-BUZZ-BUZZ!

"Almost once!"

"*Almost?*" Xander shouted as the helicopter stalled and the nose dove downward, the ground coming into view through the front windows of the cockpit. The next thing Xander saw was a missile flash in front of them, just missing the helicopter. Viktor didn't even notice the dodging of the missile. He had already shut off the engine and was desperately attempting to get it roaring again. The crazy fucker *had* done this before. Apparently, however, this next part was as far as he got.

"Come on!" Viktor shouted at the helicopter's dash. "Don't do this to me, not now!"

As Viktor madly fiddled with the electronics, Xander held his ground against the seats in front of him. The ground grew larger and larger through the windows. It looked like a bad CGI job in a terrible crash scene of some underfunded B movie. Out of nowhere, Xander wondered what Natalie might say about this predicament. Amazing where the mind goes when it is panicked. He wished he could see or touch her one last time. He thought of Sam, alone, awaiting her execution. There would be no reason to keep her alive once Xander was dead. And Kyle, would he die trying to save Sam? Most assuredly so. He could tell his best friend was falling for her. It seemed to Xander that Sam's hardened heart was maybe growing a soft spot for him as well. But neither would ever get to explore that if Xander didn't make it out of this. Viktor continued to pluck at the controls. They were at the point of no return. The last face that popped into Xander's mind was Zhanna's. A bolt of hatred crashed through him. Everything in the cockpit turned red.

Bob lowered the door on the G6. A cool breeze filled the plane. Aggressive shouts from a baritone Russian man sounded off just outside the door. Bob put up his hands and started the long walk down the short set of stairs. Kyle's mind had gone completely blank. It was as if he were a part of a terrible dream. Jack passed by him and started to walk down the stairs. With his mind numb and senses overloaded, like a zombie, Kyle blankly followed behind him. When he reached the top of the stairs, cold wind hit his face, but it was the number of guns staring back at him that *slapped* him in the face. In front of him were Hummers, cars, and vans pulled in at different angles, all of them having in common men with guns surrounding each open door. They were officially screwed. Not screwed like Sam and Kyle had been in Syria; this was far worse, because most likely there was no X-Man on the way to save them. Kyle knew from what he'd heard over the last week that their deaths would not come fast, and they would not be painless. He reached the bottom of the stairs and looked up to find Bob and Jack staring back at him. One big Russian man pointed his gun in Kyle's face and was screaming at him. Kyle had no idea what he was saying, but he kept motioning over Kyle's shoulder. Kyle assumed he was talking to Zhanna. But when Kyle looked back over his shoulder, she was nowhere to be found.

The Russian bull smashed Kyle in the forehead with the butt of his gun, and purple sparks exploded in front of his eyes. Instead of the sounds of vehicle engines, all he could hear was a buzzing sound in his ears as pain rattled around in his brain. Two other men rushed past Kyle and up inside the jet. Kyle gave his head a shake, trying desperately to regain his wits. From his knees he looked back up at the entrance to the jet. A man reappeared in the doorway, looking down at the man that struck Kyle. As he shook his head from side to side, he said something in Russian that made the man pick Kyle up from his knees.

The man, his face twisted in anger, looked into Kyle's eyes and in a thick Russian accent addressed him. "Where is girl?"

Kyle looked back to the jet, then back at the man. "I-I don't know."

The man punched him in the stomach. Shock waves of pain spread through Kyle's midsection, and he desperately sucked in air.

"Where is Zhanna?" the man shouted.

Kyle had no idea; she was just there behind him when he exited the plane. At least he thought she was. Where could she have gone? Kyle just shrugged his shoulders and took another punch in the gut. As he dropped to his knees, he couldn't believe he let her come along. Zhanna must have radioed ahead and told them they were landing there. She had set them up. This must have been her plan the entire time, to spy on them in the plane and then disappear. But why run now if this was her plan? The pain in Kyle's body was jumbling his brain. Nothing was making sense to him. He could barely even think. All he could hear now was Xander's voice in his head about Zhanna being no good. All he could do now is hope that for once, his friend was wrong.

The image of Zhanna and thoughts of her being a traitor blew away from Xander's mind's eye the moment he heard the engine come to life and the rotors fire up overhead. The ground was closing fast in front of them, but maybe there was still a chance. As Viktor put two feet on the control panel in front of him and put all of his might into pulling back the yoke, Xander jumped into the copilot seat and pulled with everything he had as well. As what used to be dots slowly became trees in front of them, the nose of the helicopter began to rise. The two of them maintained their strain, almost yanking the yoke right off its hinges, and gradually the ground shifted in front of them, and just as they were about to become eagle dinner, Xander saw a hint of evening sky.

"Pull, Viktor! Pull, you crazy son of a bitch!"

Viktor's voice strained as he used all of his might. "Viktor . . . is . . . pulling!"

As they continued to pull, the helicopter finally began to level out and the tops of the trees that had come inches from swallowing them finally crept farther away. Off in the distance, against a wall of the dying fiery light, there was a little black dot.

"Viktor did it! Xander King, Viktor pulled off loop! Ha-ha!"

A rush of relief flooded over Xander, but he wasn't quite ready to celebrate with Viktor. He knew if they didn't go right after the little black dot in front of them, and take them out, they would be right back where they were a moment ago.

"Viktor, have you ever shot down a chopper in that simulator?"

Viktor smiled big. "Are you kidding me? That is Viktor's specialty!"

This time Xander believed the psycho little man. Ten minutes later, after Viktor went back to the chain gun, the Russian helicopter was a ball of flames in the middle of the Carpathian Mountains. Xander and Viktor shared celebratory high fives and hugs as they floated along toward Moscow. The happiness inside that cockpit was a stark difference from the darkness that awaited them. Death had knocked on the door far too many times already that day. Unfortunately, the night was young.

A Roomful of Worry

Sam sat alone, her butt on the concrete floor with her back against a cold cinderblock wall. The holding cell they were keeping her in was more of a room. Four gray walls and a white door. The only connection to the world beyond the room was a small sliver of light that squeezed its way through the gap between the floor and the bottom of the door. She couldn't help but let her mind wander back to the concrete room she shared with Kyle and about ten terrorists just a couple of weeks ago. That didn't go so well, and she figured this wouldn't either. However, if she was lucky, it would end the same way.

Watching Xander fall backward out of that cargo plane gave her hope as silly as that may sound. Most of the time when a man falls out of a plane, no parachute on his back, bullets flying all around him, and four assassins jumping out after him, *hope* would be one of the last things someone would have. But, amazingly, she had seen Xander in worse predicaments, and heard tale of some from his Special Ops days that would make today in the plane seem like a day at the fair. It also gave her hope that Kyle hadn't been taken. Though he didn't have the experience, knowledge, or even the skill necessary to form a rescue mission, he had the thing that mattered most. The thing you couldn't teach, and the thing that Xander had in spades. He had heart. She knew that he would fight to the death, literally, until he saw her and Xander free.

Kyle.

When she first met him, not long after she and Xander decided to work together, she couldn't stand him. He was arrogant for no reason, a chauvinist, and it seemed that the only direction he had in life was determined by whom he could poke next with his pecker. Though she found him physically attractive from the beginning, it wasn't until she went into battle with him in Syria that she saw what Xander saw in him. Loyal, strong willed, and full of *heart*. She couldn't help but smile when she thought about him.

The door to her holding room pulled open, and immediately her smile was wiped away. It was replaced with as dejected a look as one could ever wear. The crazy thing was, the very person that made her smile a second ago was the reason she now wore a frown. Kyle, Jack, and Bob were pushed inside with her, and the door slammed behind them. Sam let out a long, disheartened breath as Kyle raced over, brought her to her feet, and wrapped his arms tightly around her. She had never been so sorrowful and happy to see someone in all of her life. She returned the hug in kind, squeezing him tightly, not a word spoken between them.

After a minute, Bob broke the silence. "Any word about Xander?"

Sam released Kyle's embrace as the three of them looked at her expectantly. "No. Last time I saw the crazy bastard, he backed out of a cargo plane at fifteen thousand feet, without a parachute, holding on to a man that did have one."

"What?" Jack was visibly shocked.

Kyle said, "Sounds like something Xander would do. At least he's okay. Well, was okay, a couple of hours ago."

Sam perked up. "You heard from him?"

"Oh shit, that's right, you wouldn't have known if he made it down safely or not. Sarah got an email from him. He dropped a pin showing his location somewhere in Ukraine."

"I knew he'd make it." Sam's eyes filled with hope. A catch in her voice.

"Last we heard they were trying to get him a helicopter. Don't know how that turned out. Sarah, Marv, and some woman from the CIA—"

"Mary Hartsfield," Jack informed.

"Yeah, Mary, they were on the way here from Virginia, only a couple of hours out when we were taken."

"What happened?" Sam asked.

"Zhanna must have set us up, they were ready and waiting for us as soon as we landed."

Jack interrupted. "I know you are having a hard time believing me, Kyle, but I'm tellin' ya, Zhanna did what she did to give us a chance."

Kyle looked annoyed. "Jack, she left us high and dry. She just disappeared."

"I know that, and I'm tellin' ya it was the best thing she coulda done. Now we have somebody workin' for us on the outside. Someone that knows this place inside and out. I know her, Kyle. She ain't workin' for her daddy."

"What do you think, Sam?" Kyle asked.

"Doesn't matter. I don't know her. All we can do is hope that either Zhanna, Sarah and crew, or Xander gets here fast. Dragov has no need for more than one hostage."

With those dark words, they all let a morbid silence fall over the room. Kyle took Sam's hand and gave her a hopeful gaze. He didn't need words. They both knew that as long as Xander was out there, he wouldn't rest until he saw them all safe. The only unspoken question, which both of them knew hung in the balance, was how many of them would be alive when he finally made it.

A Moment of Clarity

Darkness successfully swallowed the last of the dying light of day. A damn long day. From the cockpit of the helicopter that was approaching Moscow, Xander and Viktor noticed the dots of light on the ground below had begun to outgrow the specks of fire scattered like broken glass in the sky. The air around them had finally begun to cool, but the smell of urine still lingered. Xander could hardly harp on it; Viktor *had* saved his life, for God's sake. After a while the sense of smell has a way of deadening such strong scents, good or bad. Much the way life has a way with a man's feelings. No matter how much of a high you are on in life, or how low your depths, just hang on, because something will change, and it can always go either way. Xander's life was no picnic before Sean spilled the beans—or thought he had spilled the beans—about Khatib a couple of weeks ago, but ever since that day it has been a gradual descent from controlled chaos to bouncing around on a razor-blade trampoline.

One minute he's getting revenge, the next it's gone. One minute he's celebrating the launch of his bourbon company, the next his good friend is executed in front of him in Syria. His newfound love is lost—his partner in crime, Sam, is raped and degraded—he celebrates victory with his best friend and then gets raided by his real enemy—gets shot a couple more times— gets blown out of his hospital room—gets attacked at his hideaway home in Tuscany—falls out of an airplane without a parachute—avenges the capture of said partner in crime, Sam, by killing a known assassin in Pavlovich—and now, here he is, ticking his way back up the steep incline of the roller coaster.

God only knew what awaited him once he got to the top and looked down. Xander had no way of communicating with Kyle's group, Sarah's group, or Sam, and he had to watch his back not only against the world's most notorious gangster and his goons but also against his enemy's daughter—Zhanna— who may or may not be working with him. And—oh by the way—his father's life was a lie; he was actually a CIA operative.

Things were not good. Not good at all.

And though it seemed things could only get better from here, Xander knew it could still get so much worse. So far, as far as he knew, everyone was still alive. A fact he knew wouldn't last long.

"We've reached landing point that CIA lady, Mary, said would be good to attack from. You think they have sandwich?"

All was not lost, Xander *did* have good ol' Viktor.

"No, Viktor, I don't think the middle of the woods in the middle of nowhere will have sandwich. Sorry. Just drop me and get the hell out of here before you get shot down. We're only about a mile from Dragov's compound, he's probably already watching. And I doubt the window of clearance the *CIA lady* managed to get us to fly into Russian airspace has a very long shelf life."

"Shelf life? There is shelf? Then maybe there will be sandwich, no?"

Jesus.

Xander ignored the ridiculous question. "Sit this bird down as fast as you can, and as soon as I jump out, get the hell back to Ukraine, understand?"

"Viktor like Xander King. I no leave. I stay and fight, then maybe Xander let Viktor come work for him in USA? Viktor bored in Ukraine. Plus, Viktor love American women."

"Viktor, I appreciate that, but this is serious. If I make it out alive, it will be a miracle."

"Viktor knows of this Dragov. One man can't make it in compound. Xander need Viktor. Remember, Viktor is killer."

Viktor said this without a hint of sarcasm. Xander could see in his eyes that he had already made up his bat-shit-crazy mind. *Call of Duty* has made every gamer think they can survive and even thrive in real combat.

Ignorance is bliss.

"Whatever you say, Viktor. Just make sure you stay behind me. If you wanna be a soldier, you've got to be able to follow orders."

Viktor flashed a snaggletooth grin and did a little shimmy in his seat; he was clearly excited to be coming along. On the ride in, Xander found a pile of military clothes in the back of the chopper and finally was able to shed his blood-soaked pajamas. Now he at least felt like a soldier going into battle.

Familiar army-green cargo pants, black combat boots, and a matching black V-neck tee. It wouldn't much keep him warm, but he didn't plan on standing still very long on this mission.

As they approached their landing zone in the middle of the woods, only about a mile behind Dragov's compound, his fresh clothing sparked the memory of the first time he met Samantha—Sam—Harrison, and subsequently, the reason she was still his loyal partner in crime to this day:

Six years ago, Xander had just finished up a successful Black Op for the US government in Paris. It had almost been spoiled by an overzealous MI6 agent who had come over from London. Wires had been crossed and they were pursuing the same target, an extremely dangerous terrorist faction that had been wreaking havoc in Europe for more than a decade. Taking down the leader of this group would certainly carry along with it a large notch on the belt of whoever had managed the successful eradication. Sometimes the promise of such recognition can get in the way of better judgment for agents, and Sam had nearly gotten herself killed when Xander was finishing the job. The problem for her was that the second in command of this terrorist faction never saw Xander when he successfully performed the assassination, but he did see Sam. So he held Sam responsible for the death of his leader, and took her.

Xander had already vowed to himself that he would be, at the very least, having harsh words with whoever this "Samantha Harrison" was who almost cost him the mission. That's why he declined to help retrieve her when the call came in from his superiors in the US government. He remembered having no desire to put himself in harm's way because of her, again. But—and this is why only months later he left the military—

when *the man* gives you orders, you have no choice but to follow them.

So Xander did what he does best, and with the help of US intelligence, he found where they were holding Sam in London, infiltrated with ease, and it was what he found there, in that dark abandoned room, that forever changed his mind and heart about Samantha Harrison. He had just taken out the two armed guards at the door and opened it when he saw, chained to the wall in front of him, a mostly naked woman, wearing only a pair of white, blood-covered panties, which matched the rest of her blood-covered body. Xander's throat tightened and his heart sank. She was hanging by her arms that were chained above her head, both shoulders torn out of their sockets. At first he thought her dead; her head hung limply, her chin against her chest. Then she introduced herself in only the way a tough-ass-bitch like Sam could. Without looking up, she spoke in her sharp British accent to who she clearly thought was her captor.

"I told you, until you find me someone with a bigger knob to shag me, I'll not say a word."

Xander instantly loved her. How someone who had clearly been so brutally tortured, raped, and God only knew what else, could have such wit and toughness. He knew that Sam was his kind of woman. He walked toward her, distraught to the core by what he saw, but managed to play back.

"Well, I definitely have the size you're looking for, but I have no plans on giving you the pleasure."

The look on Sam's face when she raised her head was one Xander would never forget. It brought tears to his eyes just remembering it. When she looked at him, the emotion in her eyes was so powerful that it nearly brought Xander to his knees. It was the look one would give when they awoke from a near-death experience to find the face of a loved one; this woman had seen hell and lived to tell about it. Sam didn't say another word that night. Xander, with the care of a mother for her child, removed Sam's chains and took her down from the wall. He took his black V-neck T-shirt off and put it on her, taking great care not to further damage the multitude of whip marks on her bloody back. He then took her over his shoulder, killed six more men on their way to safety, and together they have been a force of nature ever since.

"Xander King, I put chopper down right there." Viktor broke Xander's trance pointing to an opening in the trees. Xander jumped when he heard his voice and quickly wiped a tear that had streaked down his right cheek. He gave Viktor a nod and looked over the canopy of trees toward the lights of Dragov's mansion. The same mansion that held captive his precious Sam.

Xander had no idea how he would do it, but he *would* find a way to save her again. She was in there because of him. All of the people who were in danger on this night were there because of him, and he wasn't going to let them suffer for it any longer than they already had..

It was in that moment that everything changed for Xander. The switch had finally flipped; he had finally realized what was important in his life. No longer was his life going to be about the past. Xander had far too much to live for in the present. If he made it out of this night alive, all of his relationships intact, things from here on out were going to change.

Things would be different.

In the Pines

The helicopter's rotors finally came to a halt. A deafening silence filled in around them. The air was brisk, somewhere in the low forties. Xander knew without a doubt that their helicopter would draw the attention of Dragov and his men. Time was of the essence, so unfortunately there had been no other way in. Xander consolidated the two half-empty magazines in Pavlovich's pistols into one full magazine and traded the empty pistol for one Viktor had brought along with him. With Rambo tucked under his right pant leg, Xander felt good about his weapons. It was Viktor doing something stupid with his shotgun while trailing Xander that made for a much larger concern. Xander didn't like unknowns in combat, and a wildcard like Viktor scared the hell out of him.

"You sure you know how to use that?" Xander whispered to Viktor as they stood outside the helicopter.

Viktor smiled, "Viktor shoot plenty. Viktor also head of number-three clan in all of Ukraine in *Black Ops 3*."

Great, more *Call of Duty* arrogance.

"Please tell me you have done more than shoot in a video game."

Viktor shucked the slide, loading a shell into the twelve-gauge shotgun's chamber. "Let's go, cowboy."

Shit.

"All right, just stay behind me. There is no doubt a few men are already on their way out here to us after seeing us fly in. And Viktor?"

"Yes, boss?"

"Don't fucking shoot me."

"You worry too much, boss."

Xander shook his head and turned toward the trees in front of him. The grass below their feet was about ankle high, and as they entered, they were surrounded by endless rows of birch and aspen trees. There wasn't much of a wind; therefore, their footsteps sounded more like the symbol section of a marching band than a walk through the woods. It was much darker under the cover of the trees as well. The fingernail moon and scattered stars offered almost zero visibility. Xander's senses were on high alert. Viktor kept rhythm with his footsteps, which helped Xander maintain a focus on what might lie ahead. He tried to stay as far as he could from the tree trunks, hoping to avoid snapping fallen branches, but it was a useless endeavor. About halfway in, only around a half a mile to go, Xander held out his hand behind him to slow Viktor. He figured if men were coming to see who had flown in on the chopper, they would be getting close.

To his left he heard footsteps crashing toward him, and before he had time to react someone plowed into him, driving him into the ground. As soon as he hit the ground, he heard a smattering of gunfire from the trees out in front of him. At the same moment, the person who tackled him was already returning fire, apparently hitting their mark because grunts of pain came back to them from the darkness. Viktor let out a squeal and dove to the ground with them. Xander's instinct was to react, but he felt a light hand on his chest, and as he squinted up at the person leaning over him, he could see that he was wearing night vision goggles. He fired his weapon a couple more times, then turned toward Xander. If it indeed was a man, he wasn't very big. He wore all black and Xander still couldn't make out any features. Then Viktor flipped on a small flashlight, and when he ripped off his goggles, Xander found that it wasn't a man at all. Long red hair fell down around her shoulders and a her thick Russian accent hissed at Viktor to shut off the light.

Zhanna.

The light shut off, Xander bridged his hips, throwing Zhanna off balance, and swept her onto her back. He pressed an elbow down across her chest and leaned all of his weight on her as he whisper-shouted, "What is going on? Why would you do that?"

Zhanna squirmed beneath him, but it was no use; she couldn't move. She whisper-shouted back, "We have no time for this, more men are coming."

"Why the hell should I trust you, you betrayed us in Tuscany! Give me one reason I shouldn't kill you!"

Zhanna looked to her left at the same time Xander heard footsteps coming their way. Viktor hit the flashlight. Zhanna's

216

pistol popped and echoed through the trees. The man running their way flew off of his feet and landed on his back.

"Viktor think that is good reason to trust her, boss."

Xander looked down into Zhanna's eyes, and that spark of sincerity that he noticed in Tuscany remained.

"Xander, we must move. I am not your enemy."

In the distance they could hear more men coming. Xander rose to his feet, paused for a moment as he stared at Zhanna. His mind was fraught with confusion. His instincts were jumbled, but there was that sincerity he saw, and she had just saved his life. Guarded, he puffed out a hot breath of air in a cottony cloud and then finally held out his hand. She grabbed it with force, and as soon as she made it to her feet she turned toward Viktor. He thought she was helping him up, but before he could protest, she took his flashlight and cracked it over her knee, plunging them once again into the darkness.

Viktor said, "Hey! That was Viktor's torch!"

Zhanna covered his mouth. "Who the hell is this, Xander?"

"He saved my life and he didn't run when shit got a little tough." They both knew he was referring to Tuscany when Zhanna disappeared.

"I just saved your life, but now we must run, together. Now!" she whisper-shouted one last time as the footfalls drew closer around them. Leaves rustled and fallen branches cracked. Zhanna grabbed Xander by the hand and pulled him off to the right. As he and Viktor followed behind her, he couldn't reconcile why she would save his life. Especially after bailing on them in Tuscany, and then it hit him: how was she here and Kyle wasn't?

Xander stopped running and yanked Zhanna back toward him. "Where's Kyle?"

"Xander, we do not have time for this. I will explain, but right now we must get to tunnel! These men may know nothing about tunnel. Either way, it will be only way into mansion. We can still have element of surprise."

Xander wanted answers, but he knew she was right. He would have to wait, and for the moment, he would have to trust that she wasn't leading him into a trap. Quite a few yards and several twists and turns later, Zhanna pulled Xander to the ground with her.

"Help me," she said as Xander heard rustling all around him.

"Zhanna, I can't see."

He then felt her grab his hand with her freezing-cold hand, and she guided him down to what felt like a metal handle. "Just help me pull. It will be heavy."

Xander heard her grunt, and he began to pull with her. Whatever it was they were yanking on, it was heavier than he expected, and he readjusted his position to add more leverage. Behind them, the thudding of feet against earth was getting closer. Xander looked to his left and the flashlights were on now, and they were close.

"We must hurry! If they see us get in here, they will know—Father will know—where the tunnel leads and we will be trapped!" Urgency spiked in Zhanna's plea. He could hear in her voice that she was not putting on. For whatever reason, Zhanna seemed to be truly trying to help.

Xander wrapped his other hand around the metal handle, tightened every muscle in his body, and heaved with everything he had. Finally, he felt something give, and it slid a few inches toward them. The crack showed light coming from below. To their left, the flashlights drew closer and closer.

"Just little more, Xander. Pull!"

From off in the distance, they heard a man shout in their direction, "This way!"

Dragov's men were on top of them. They had only seconds before the oncoming flashlight beams made it to their position over this apparent secret tunnel. Xander clenched up one more time, closed his eyes, and pulled with as much force as he could muster. The veins in his arms jutted and the muscles under his skin filled up like a balloon. At the last second, he arched his back and the massive metal cover slid far enough back for them to fit through. Zhanna let go of the handle and practically stuffed Viktor down through the hole. Xander motioned for Zhanna to go next, and as she slid down inside he took one last look over his shoulder. The flashlights couldn't have been more than twenty yards away.

They hadn't moved the cover in time.

There was just no way they could not see him.

Hot Blooded, Cold Hearted

Dragov sat behind his desk; the yellow illumination of the lamp beside him was the only light in the room. He loaded a nine-millimeter magazine of hollow point bullets as smoke floated toward the ceiling from his cigar that rested in a fancy golden ashtray. A crystal glass full of scotch whisky reflected a rainbow of colors from the lamplight and gave the liquor a sparkling caramel color. The award-winning operatic baritone of Dmitri Hvorostovsky bellowed through the speakers in the corner of the room. A scene from *The Godfather* wouldn't have been more cliché. Dragov laid down the now full magazine, sat back in his seat, and took a white Styrofoam cup in his hand. He inhaled a deep, satisfying breath, letting the music, with the help of the whisky and tobacco, soothe him into relaxation. As the door to his office opened and two of his men walked in, he slobbered a massive wad of tobacco juice into his spit cup, then set the cup back down on his desk.

"This better be good news," Dragov told them.

The man in front winced and cleared his throat. He clearly did not want to say what he had to say. Dragov must have sensed that it wouldn't be such great news and slid the magazine into his nine-millimeter pistol, pulled back the slide, and was now holding the gun in his lap, expectantly. The man in front of him gulped, then spoke with a shaky tone.

"Boss, a helicopter landed on the grounds. We believe it was Xander King," he stuttered.

"How you not know for sure?" Dragov took a drag from his cigar and thickened the air with smoke.

"Someone, we think, a woman, helped him . . ."

Dragov replaced the cigar on the ashtray. His face was stoic. "Helped him . . ."

"Escape."

Dragov said nothing. His facial expression did not change. He simply raised the gun and shot the stammering man in the head. He set the gun back down and once again picked up his cigar. He looked the second man in the eye. "Two things. You can handle two things?"

"Yes, boss. No problem." This man did not stammer. His nerves were solid. Dragov liked this.

"One, find Xander King and this woman. Two, bring me one of the hostages. Anyone but Sam. You know which one is Sam?"

"Yes, boss. Find Xander King and bring hostage other than Sam. Anything else, boss?"

"Yes. Can you handle more? Unlike your comrade?" Dragov nodded to the man he'd just shot lying on the floor, blood running from his half-missing face. The man didn't even look down to acknowledge him.

"Andre can handle anything needed, boss."

"Good, find out if we have intercepted CIA plane coming from America."

"Yes, boss."

The man turned and left the room. Dragov picked up the phone and dialed a number in Virginia. A man answered and started right in.

"Dragov, have you killed them yet? This can't get back to the US government. People are already getting suspicious here."

"Hello to you, Manning."

"Cut the shit, Dragov. Are they dead?"

"You only need worry about you. If I find out you are helping Americans, you—caput."

"You know I wouldn't. I have too much to lose. Xander will find out about his father, if he hasn't already. I made a mistake bringing Jack in. He was loyal to the wrong people."

"A mistake only you will pay for."

"Listen, Dragov, your daughter—"

"My daughter is dead to me."

"Well, that might be true, but she's not dead. But that is what she wants you to be. I think she's been helping Xander and his team."

Dragov sat forward in his chair. The words made his blood run cold. He could hear the words of the man he'd just shot echoing in his mind—*we think a woman helped him*—and a vision of Zhanna flashed in his mind. He hadn't meant for her to see what he had done to her mother. He didn't care, but it wasn't meant for her to see. His mind remembered the coldness with which she greeted him thereafter, until the day she turned on him. That was the last day he had ever seen her, the day she put the knife to his throat.

"Dragov?" Manning interrupted the silence.

"Impossible."

"Whatever you say, but consider yourself warned."

Dragov did not speak. The door once again opened, and Andre brought in the hostage that he had requested. Dragov ended the call with Manning, picked up his gun, and got to his feet. Someone had to pay with their life for the mess being made on Dragov's own soil.

The old cowboy now standing in front of him would do just fine.

Tunnel Vision

Xander had been wrong: it wasn't too late. The flashlights had not found them in time. As quietly as he could, he had moved the cover back over the hole, sealing them in. The three of them heard faint voices of men above them. Xander and Zhanna caught their breath as Viktor stood with his back to them, staring down a narrow, dimly lit tunnel that stretched out in front of them.

Viktor turned toward them and looked up as he heard the voices overhead. He whispered, "Boss, it's good thing you have big muscles." Viktor made an ape like motion "Or those guys would have killed us. You and pretty lady make good team."

Zhanna glanced at Xander's still bulging arms. Xander noticed, straightened up, and gave her a quick flex.

Ever the showman.

Zhanna couldn't help but smile, then gathered herself and walked past Viktor. "Come, we have no time. Your friends were taken. They are in great danger. Father is not known for his mercy. And Xander . . ."

Zhanna paused, her face as serious as he had ever seen it. Xander rolled his hands forward, motioning for her to come out with it already.

"Xander, there is something you must know. Something I didn't know until recently, but . . . you're not going to like it."

"Are you going to tell me? Or are you just going to stand there until we are all dead?"

"It's your—"

The oversized, manhole-like cover shook above their heads, stopping Zhanna from relaying her secret.

"Xander, we must go now."

"You can't stop there. What were you going to say? Make it quick—"

The massive cover rattled again.

Time was up.

"You'll know soon. Let's go, your friends are in danger!"

That brought reality back to Xander, and his stomach tightened at the thought of his friends under Dragov's scrutiny. He glared past Zhanna, down the tunnel. He began to wonder if all bad guys had secret underground lairs. It seemed a little *Scooby-Doo* of them. He thought for a second that when he got hold of Dragov, that he might try and rip off his mask. Maybe he would find Manning's face underneath.

"Xander?" Zhanna broke his ridiculous train of thought. "We must go now!"

Dragov spit out what was left of his chewing tobacco into a paper cup, washed his mouth out with scotch, and motioned for one of his men to remove the gag from Jack Bronson's mouth. Dragov eyed the man up and down, from his red leather cowboy boots to his bushy gray eyebrows that wired out from under his cognac-colored cowboy hat.

"You look like clown. Like should be in old western movie with John Wayne."

Jack cleared his throat and extra countrified his twang just for Dragov. "Yeah? Well, you look like forty pounds of shit in a ten-pound sack, you fat son of a bitch."

If he hurt Dragov's feelings, Dragov didn't show it. Jack figured it wasn't the first time someone had made a crack about the man's girth. However, he was certain that whoever had done so before him surely didn't say much else after that. Dragov stared into the wily old cowboy's eyes as he fingered his pistol on his desk.

Jack couldn't help himself. "You get the trigger guard on that pistol modified?"

Dragov didn't respond.

"You know, so's you could fit your fat finger in there? I'll teach you how to shoot it if you untie these ropes."

"You have big mouth, Jack."

"Yep, and you have a big waistline." Jack knew he was pushing the envelope, but he didn't care. He wasn't going to give Dragov the satisfaction of seeing him scared. He knew that that is exactly what men like Dragov lived for.

"Where is this . . . Xander?" Dragov got straight to the point.

"Who?" Jack played coy.

Dragov wobbled over to Jack and struck him across the face with the butt of his pistol. Jack's jaw lit up in pain and quite possibly cracked under the blow. Jack raised back up, spit a wad of blood onto Dragov's crocodile-leather shoe, and looked him in the eye.

"Where is Xander?" Dragov asked again.

"You want the truth?" Jack spoke as blood ran from his mouth, down his chin.

"That would be good place to start."

"I really don't know. But I reckon after your bitch dog—Pavlovich—took him and Sam, he got away after murdering the incompetent son of a bitch. Probably just about here now to foil your plans of eatin' another pastrami sandwich. Hell, knowin' Xander, he might have even taken a minute to stick his pecker in your daughter's mouth. She seemed to like him when she was tellin' him all about her sicko daddy."

Dragov put a little extra oomph behind the next pistol to the head. Jack dropped to his knees under the blow but managed to keep his wit.

"What? Somethin' I said?"

Dragov kicked Jack in the crotch, and just as he put the pistol to his head, an alarm sounded and an intense buzzing sound filled the room.

Zhanna looked back at Xander as soon as she opened the door. "Shit, Father must have rigged this door since last time I am here."

"Gee, whatever gave you that impression?" Xander sarcastically remarked over the blaring buzz of the alarm.

"I think because of the alarm, boss." Viktor tried to help.

"Thanks, Captain Obvious."

Viktor didn't get it; he just stared back blankly.

If they had an element of surprise, it was now gone. The alarm continued as Zhanna motioned Viktor and Xander to follow. She led them down a hospital-like hallway: white tile floors below their feet, white walls, and white ceiling tile above. Zhanna moved quickly in front of them.

"Where are we going?" Xander called ahead.

"I know a secret way up, but we have to hurry. Father's men will be on us in seconds. Don't bother with any of the other doors."

"Do you know where they are keeping Kyle and Sam?"

"They will be one level up. There are holding cells there," she said, as if holding cells in someone's house were perfectly normal.

Xander followed as she moved them down the hall. It was lit with a dim florescent light. Up in front of them was a door on the left wall. The only door in the middle portion of the hallway. Zhanna and Viktor moved right past it without a glance, but as Xander did the same, he saw something out of the corner of his eye that made him stop dead in his tracks. Every muscle in his body seized. Zhanna looked back over her shoulder and noticed Xander not moving.

"Xander! Xander, we must hurry!"

Xander saw her lips moving but heard nothing. Xander didn't know it, but his body had temporarily gone into a state of shock. It had done so because his mind couldn't process what it had just seen. Or thought it had seen. The walls around Xander began to vibrate as a darkness crept up his spine and began to fill in the corners of his eyes. He was passing out.

You would too if you'd just seen your long dead father sitting alone in a room.

Alive.

Back to Life, Back to Reality

"Change of plan." Dragov took the pistol from Jack's head. With the sound of that alarm, Dragov knew his assumed impenetrable fortress had just been breached. And the way his men had been performing so far on this day, he wasn't about to chance the fact that they would be able to keep Xander from getting to him. He had underestimated the American up until this point. Dragov wasn't a man who made the same mistakes twice. Martin King was not going to be happy about this. If Zhanna really was with Xander, helping him, they would have come in through the tunnel. The tunnel that led to the door that tripped the alarm, and the door that led to the hallway that led to the room where Martin was trying to stay safe, and hidden from his own son. Xander may already have found him.

"Melania!" Dragov croaked, the first bit of fear trembling his voice.

"Yes, boss?"

"You and Andre stay with me, we go to car. Send everyone else to bottom floor. Radio men outside to go in through tunnel opening. Xander will be trapped. Mr. King wants him alive, but if he must die, then he must die."

Melania radioed her instructions to her men. Then the three of them exited toward the car park, leaving Jack where he sat on his knees, on the floor. His mouth was agape and his mind in shock at the words Dragov just spoke. Not only because his once thought long dead friend was apparently alive, but from the way Dragov's voice trembled when he mentioned Martin King, he was also afraid of him. That could only mean one thing.

"Dad!" Xander pounded on the door with both fists. His mind was racing, his heart was pounding, and his body ached with astonishment. "DAD!"

His father, far more weathered and far more gray than the last time he'd seen him, dead on the ground almost eleven years ago, was staring off into space, as if he couldn't hear Xander pounding and screaming.

"Xander! We must go! If we do not move now, we will be trapped! Your friends will be dead!" Zhanna shouted to him.

This time, the mention of his friends in trouble didn't snap Xander out of anything. No words could have. He continued to pound on the door in front of him, then a front kick, then more pounding. It was as if he were a little child pounding on his bedroom door. It wasn't making a dent, and his father was now on his feet. From Xander's adrenaline blurred vision, he didn't even process that his father—his father!—didn't look like a prisoner at all. The finely combed hair, the crisp navy-blue suit, the cigar in his hand as he stood from the comfortable brown leather couch—none of it registered. What did register, just as his father turned and looked him in the eye, was the fact that someone from the end of the hall where they had entered from was shooting at him. And if it wasn't for Viktor tackling Xander to the ground and Zhanna returning fire behind him, Xander would have been shot.

"Boss!" Viktor shouted as he shook Xander. "Boss!"

Xander wasn't responding, so Viktor reared back and punched Xander in the face. Zhanna continued to shoot to keep men from flooding the hallway. Xander finally snapped back to reality, and his rage-filled eyes met Viktor's.

Viktor mistook Xander's rage for being mad at him for hitting him, so he held up his hands as if to say sorry, then looked down the hall behind Xander. Xander pulled his pistol but didn't look in the direction Viktor was peering. Instead, he shot the man who walked into the hallway behind Zhanna.

They were trapped.

Dad?

Xander shucked Viktor aside and bounced to his feet. He grabbed the handle to the door once more, but this time when he looked in, his father was gone.

Had he really seen him?

He was sure that he had, but how could it be? As he processed, or tried to process, his father being in that room alive, he shot the man again at the end of the hall as he raised his gun toward Zhanna from his spot on the ground. They could hear shouts of Russian from both ends of the hall. Xander pushed the thought of his father out of his mind, pulled Viktor to his feet, and motioned for Zhanna to join them. The air around them was thick with the smell of gunpowder and metal. The shouts from either end of the hall had ceased. Xander knew they were ready to strike. He pulled his second pistol, Viktor racked the slide on his shotgun, and Zhanna readied her nine-millimeter.

"Anybody got any miracles?" Xander asked.

Zhanna peered into her magazine to check her bullet count before she shoved it back into her pistol. "Nyet, but have nine chances."

Just as she pulled back the slide, men came pouring into the hallway from both ends. There was no place to take cover and nowhere to run. Just bullets. And as they rang out inside that hallway, it was deafening. Two men shot first from the secret tunnel entrance, but both missed. Viktor and Xander did not. The man on the left was taken off his feet by the blast of Viktor's shotgun, and the man on the right lost the top of his head to Xander's bullet. Zhanna hit the two men who came in from the other side, and as two more entered, Viktor turned and blasted them as well. Xander sprinted back toward the tunnel-side hallway, leaving Zhanna and Viktor to defend the other side. As he approached the door, two more men filled the small space, and two more men lost their heads. Xander's aim did not falter as he ran. When another man entered, he jump-kicked him, knocked him onto his back, and slammed a bullet through his neck. Blood shot up like a geyser and Xander walked right through it, turned down the tunnel, shot the two men who were standing there waiting, and nailed one more man in the leg who was climbing down from the secret entrance they had come through only moments ago. The man pulled himself back up out of the hole, and the next thing Xander heard was the distinct sound of bouncing metal on concrete.

A grenade.

Xander dove backward through the door into the main hallway, and when he cleared the doorway, he kicked the door to the tunnel shut. Two bullets grazed his body from behind Zhanna and Viktor as they were sprinting toward him. He rolled toward them, shouted, "Get down," and simultaneously the grenade blew and the door to the hallway flew off its hinges, followed by a searing flame that ran up Xander's back. He rolled, sure he was on fire, his ears hearing nothing but a loud ring. Everything turned into slow motion. He was lying in front of the blown-off door to the hallway now. Two men jumped down from the manhole. His pistols lay on the floor of the tunnel in front of him, incinerated from the grenade blast, and when he looked to his left, Zhanna and Viktor lay weaponless on the floor. No doubt, they had run out of ammo. When he looked past them, a man in full army fatigues walked toward them with a pistol extended in front of him, just like the two men who had just dropped into the tunnel, guns coming at them from both sides. Their mouths were moving, but Xander could only hear the loud, high-pitched ring that filled his ears. They could have been shouting at him. They could have been shouting at each other, Xander had no idea. He looked back at Zhanna, and her face had gone pale.

The realization of certain death had a way of doing that to you.

The man walking toward them was almost upon them. Xander reached for Rambo but didn't pull him out of his sheath, in a last-ditch attempt to avoid provoking the three gunmen. The thought of bringing a knife to a gunfight inexplicably crossed Xander's mind, and either that or the madness of imminent death brought a smirk to his face. He rolled mindlessly out of the open doorway as the two men were about to come to the end of the tunnel. He looked back over Zhanna and Viktor down the hallway at the man with the gun walking toward them. That wiped the smirk right off his face. And just as the thought that they were finished finally crossed his mind, the man's face blew apart, bursting into a pink mist of brain and blood. A bullet had come through the small window in the door where he saw his father. Immediately following the gunshot there was a loud thud and the door itself flew inward and banged against the wall in the hallway. As the two men rounded the corner from the tunnel and pointed their guns at Xander's head, Sarah Gilbright walked through the kicked-in doorway and shot both of them dead before they ever had time to notice she was there.

And Now...I'm Going to Kill *Him!*

"Xander, are you okay?"

"Sarah." It was all he could manage.

Xander got to his feet, and they walked toward each other with purpose. Xander wrapped his arms around her and squeezed her against his chest.

"Sarah, I'm sorry about Tuscany—"

"Don't." She pulled back and looked into his eyes. "You've been through a lot, Xander, and—"

"It's no excuse. I should have been certain before I accused you of anything."

Xander's emotions were swirling. He felt such affection for her in that moment. It could have been all that was happening around him—his father, his friends in danger, death, even embarrassment for the way he had treated her. The fact that she had once again saved his ass. It could have been any of those things causing him to swell with emotion at the sight of her, the touch of her. But it also could be that he'd managed to develop feelings for her.

"How did you get here?" he asked.

Sarah pulled out her cell phone. "I'll explain later." Then she spoke into the phone. "Marv? Yes, Xander is okay . . . Sam?" Sarah looked to Xander.

Sam. Kyle. Shit!

Xander turned to Zhanna. "Can you take me to where they might be?"

Zhanna nodded and started down the hallway. Viktor followed her like a little puppy.

Sarah went back to the phone. "We aren't sure, but we're looking. Marv. . ." Sarah paused and gave Xander a weary look. "Dragov fled by car. Martin King was with him."

Xander felt like Mike Tyson had just punched him in the gut.

"I was able to put a tracker on three of the cars. You should be able to monitor them. We will find Sam and company while you find out where they are going. I have a feeling Xander is going to want to know exactly where they are headed."

Sarah clicked off the phone. "I'm sorry."

"You knew my father was alive?" A rush of anger flooded his face.

"No! No. Not until we landed here in Moscow. Xander, Mary Hartsfield is now the acting director of the CIA. They took Manning into custody just a little while ago. They promised to go easy if he gave up Dragov. But . . ."

"But what, Sarah?"

"But it was your father he flipped on. Dragov hasn't been in charge for a long time now. I'm so sorry."

A man's voice startled them all from the end of the hallway. "Jesus H. Christ. If y'all ain't a sight for sore eyes."

Sarah turned on a dime, whipping her gun in the direction of the voice. "Jack?"

"I'll be dammed. Xander King, in the flesh. Last I heard, you dropped backward out of a cargo plane. Oh, to be young again."

Xander dropped the thoughts of his father. It was all too much to comprehend at the moment. He needed to focus on what he did understand: getting his friends to safety and getting Dragov. In that order. "Sam and Kyle?"

"Last I saw 'em, they was okay. Your pilot is here too. Brave son of a bitch. Thought that was where I was goin', but this place is like a friggin' hotel."

"Were they in a cell?" Zhanna asked.

"Yep."

"Then they are up one floor. We must hurry before my father gets away. If he leaves Moscow, we'll never find him."

"He won't make it out of Moscow," Xander assured her. She gave him an unsure look.

Viktor noticed her doubting him and couldn't help himself. "Viktor doesn't know much, but I believe boss when he say Dragov won't make it."

"Thanks, Viktor." Xander put his arm around Sarah's waist and nudged her in Zhanna, Jack, and Viktor's direction.

"Follow me," Zhanna said, turning toward the hallway exit, stepping over a mini pile of dead Russian thugs as she went.

Jack was right, Dragov's compound was very much like a hotel. They took what resembled an emergency stairwell up to the floor above them. When the five of them walked into the hall, it was more like the Overlook Hotel in the movie *The Shining*. It seemed just as empty too. Zhanna walked ahead out into the hallway that was filled with crown molding and tacky hotel carpeting. Xander half expected to see the twin ghost girls waiting for them at the other end. To the right of the hall there looked to be a large ballroom. Zhanna walked right past it and all the way to a single closed door at the end of the hallway.

"Jack Torrance isn't going to be in there, is he?" Xander asked Zhanna. She didn't get the movie reference.

"I LOVED that movie." Sarah got it.

Zhanna tried the door, but of course it was locked.

"Viktor will open," Viktor said, puffing out his chest.

"You sure about that, Viktor? That looks like a heavy door." Xander smirked.

"Xander King not only one with muscles."

Viktor took three steps back and one to the side. He reminded Xander of a field goal kicker getting ready to kick an extra point. He was built like one too. Viktor swung his arms a couple of times in preparation, lowered his shoulder, and sprinted for the door.

Xander took a couple steps forward and leaned down over Viktor sprawled out on the floor. "I think you almost had it, buddy." Of course, he'd barely even shook the door. "You want me to finish it off for you?"

Viktor groaned. "If you get it, it's because Viktor loosened for you."

Sarah hid her smile, and Xander gave her a wink.

238

Without stepping back, Xander spun in place, whipping his leg around behind him and struck the door just above the lock. Not surprising to him, the door flew open under the power of his kick. What did surprise him was the blur that came through the door and knocked him flat on his back. Almost before anyone could stop her, Sam had her fist pulled back ready to strike.

"I'm happy to see you too, Sam, but this is a little embarrassing." Xander smiled from underneath her.

"Xander! You made it. I knew it!"

Xander had never seen such a happy look on Sam's face. The closest to it was the one he saw when he woke up from his coma a few days ago. Sam threw herself down and gave him a hug.

"You scared the shit out of me when you fell backward out of that plane. You really are one crazy bloke."

As she lifted herself up from on top of him, Kyle walked up, head shaking in wonder, hand extended. Xander took it with force, and Kyle helped him to his feet. They shared their customary handshake, then embraced in a massive man hug.

"Fuck you for scaring us."

"You mean for getting you out of that cell?"

"Yeah, that too."

Xander was holding a smile, but seeing his friends made him think of his father. He needed a minute with Sam and Kyle, alone. Bob walked out of the holding cell, and Xander gave him a "glad you're okay" nod.

"Was anyone around Dragov before he took off? Maybe heard where he was going?" Sarah asked the group.

Jack answered, "Well, if havin' the man hold his gun to your head after a couple of wallops to the jaw counts as being around him, I guess I was. Didn't say where they was goin', but as soon as that alarm went off, they left in a big ol' hurry."

"I'm glad you're okay, Jack," Sarah told him with the most sincere of looks.

Something triggered in Xander, and he moved toward Sarah and took her cheek in his hand after moving a strand of her blonde hair behind her right ear. "Thank you, Sarah. You saved our asses back there. You've been doing a lot of that lately."

She nestled his hand against her cheek with hers as they shared a long stare.

Kyle and Sam exchanged a glance, Sam raising her brow, and Kyle giving a shoulder-shrugging smirk. Xander let his hand fall to caress Sarah's arm as he looked over to Zhanna. "Can you do a quick sweep of the place? Make sure no one is left that can give us some clues where they may have gone?"

"Of course."

"Will you take Sarah, Bob, and Viktor with you? We'll meet you out front in ten."

Zhanna nodded. Xander looked back at Sarah. "Will you see if Marv knows where they are headed yet? I need a minute with Kyle and Sam."

Sarah knew he wanted to tell them about his father. She didn't need him to say it. He could feel that she knew. She smiled. "See you soon?"

"You're in good hands with Zhanna. Not that you can't take care of yourself."

Sarah glanced at his lips, then back to his eyes. Her desire to kiss him was apparent to everyone. Xander's desire to do the same surprised him in that moment. For the first time since he met Natalie Rockwell, another woman had caught his attention in a way that was entirely more than sexual.

240

"Xander King like pretty blonde-haired savior," Viktor blurted.

Sarah blushed, Xander dropped his grip from her arm, and everyone had a laugh.

Zhanna mercifully broke the embarrassing moment. "We had better get moving. We will meet you outside in ten minutes. Better have good plan by then." She smiled and began walking away from them.

Sarah mouthed the words "be careful" to Xander, and the four of them were off.

Sam got right to it. "Where could Dragov be going?"

"I don't know, but he isn't here." Xander made a face that neither one of them could read. "My dad isn't either."

No sense beating around the bush.

Kyle's face scrunched in confusion. "What? Your dad? I don't get it."

"I saw him. Here."

Kyle's face went from confusion to bewilderment. Sam's followed the same arc.

"Are you okay, man? Did you hit your head?" Kyle continued. Sam couldn't speak.

"My dad is alive. I saw him in a room, right below this one. He wouldn't even acknowledge me. I was beating on the door and screaming at him, but he ignored me. Come to think of it, he seemed perfectly relaxed . . ." Xander's wheels were turning. Sam and Kyle let them turn. "He was . . . he was smoking a cigar and wearing a suit. Like he wanted to be there. Like he wasn't being held against his will . . ." Xander trailed off. Lost in his own thoughts. Trying to make sense of what he'd seen. What seemed like some sort of dream. He remembered Sarah saying that Manning flipped on his father and that Dragov hadn't been in charge for a while now, but Xander was having trouble pulling it all together. Mostly because he didn't want to.

"Xander." Sam placed her hand on his shoulder. "Let's just go help them clear the house. Back them up if they need it and then we will go find Dragov."

"I know it sounds like I'm losing it, Sam." Xander looked back and forth between her and Kyle. "But Sarah confirmed it. She said they took Manning apart back at Langley and he confirmed my father was alive . . . maybe even in charge. We didn't have time to get into it, but I'm telling you, I saw him downstairs, and then Sarah saw him leave with Dragov."

"What the fuck, X? I mean, what the shit?" Kyle began to pace the room, freaking out. "This can't be. There has to be some sort of explanation. He must be drugged, or hypnotized, or—"

"Or not who I thought he was," Xander broke in.

Heartache dominated his face. That hung in the air for a moment. No one knew what to say. Kyle just grabbed his friend and gave him a hug.

"We'll figure this out, Xander. I promise."

Xander pulled back. "What is there to figure out?"

The air seemed to change in the hallway. Things suddenly began to become clear for Xander. Crystal clear.

"He lied to me my entire life. My mother too. That is probably why she slept with Jack. She was living with a liar. He wasn't who he said he was. He wasn't just in the CIA, he was helping to run an illegal underground empire."

Xander's face drained of its color and he staggered backward. Sam and Kyle both caught him and held him up.

"He faked his death and murdered my mother."

Xander's breathing became heavy as he hung in their arms.

"He left me and my sister to live alone."

Tears welled up in Xander's eyes.

"He's . . . he's been trying to kill *me*!"

And just like that, the hurt on his face made a visible turn to rage. Just as quickly as the tears had appeared, they were gone. Xander broke loose of Sam and Kyle's grip and his posture went stiff. The muscles clinched in his jaw. His hands balled into fists.

"And now . . . I'm going to kill *him*."

SEAL'd With a Kiss

"Xander, stop! Just wait a second!" Kyle shouted as they walked—stalked—into the grandiose foyer of the mafia boss's mansion. It had the same setup of Xander's foyer in Lexington, only with an overlay of gaudy marble, hideous gold, and loads of tacky. The massively oversized gold-and-crystal chandelier showered the three of them with a deep yellow glow. "Xander, you don't even know where you're going. Stop!"

Kyle grabbed him by the arm, and the face he saw when Xander wheeled around wasn't the Xander he knew at all. It was blank with ferocious intensity. Sarah and company, minus Viktor, were descending the stairs at that very moment.

"Is everything okay?" she called from the top of the stairs. Sarah had seen this look on Xander's face in Tuscany not long ago when he thought she had betrayed him. She shuddered. She immediately knew something was wrong.

Xander held Kyle's stare for a moment and then looked up at Sarah. "Where's Dragov? Where's my father?"

"That's why we came down." They all followed Sarah the rest of the way down the stairs. "Marv called, they stopped at an unknown location, now it appears they are on their way to Domodedovo Airport."

Bob chimed in. "That's the same airport where your jet is, Xander."

Xander nodded. "Where's Viktor?"

Just then the front door jangled and everyone turned and pulled their weapons. Viktor walked in, threw his hands up in the air, and pinned himself against the door. "It's just Viktor! It's just Viktor!"

They lowered their weapons.

"I had him go and check on the helicopter," said Sarah.

Xander looked back to Viktor expectantly.

"It wouldn't start, boss."

Everyone in the foyer let out a groan.

"You not let Viktor finish. Stupid old bird always does this. Viktor can fix. Just need five—maybe thirty minutes."

"That's a hell of a wide range, son," Jack noted.

"It's tricky. But just need little bit of time." Viktor held up his hand and pinched his index finger and thumb together until they were almost touching.

"I don't have time. Sarah, were there any other vehicles in the garage?" Xander asked.

"They took all of the cars."

"That wasn't my question."

"There—there was a motorcycle, but obviously that won't help us," she said, defensively.

"No, but it will help me."

Sam began to shake her head. "Xander . . ."

Xander ignored Sam and spoke once again to Sarah. "Pull up directions to the airport on your phone. I'll take it with me."

Before Sarah could answer, Sam spoke up again. "Xander, this is not the time for your X-Man solo routine."

Xander turned to face Sam. "Take the chopper to the airport when Viktor gets it going."

"Xander—"

"Sam!" he shouted. Then he managed to ease his tone. "Sam, this is not a debate. Like Zhanna said, if Dragov makes it out of Moscow, we may never find him. That means my dad too. I have to hit them before they have time to regroup."

"You're not going without me. You can't do this alone."

Xander took a step toward Sam, almost nose to nose now. "Do I have to remind you of what I can do alone? Have you forgotten how I found you in London? How I got you out of there *alone*, carrying you on my back?"

Sam's face hardened. "You know damn well I haven't forgotten about London. And I know exactly what you are capable of. More than anyone. And you know damn well what I am capable of. You don't think they will be watching for you? You plan on shooting back at them while you're maneuvering a bloody motorbike? No, Xander. You will not be going alone. You have had my back when I've needed you most, and I don't plan on leaving you now."

Sam looked to Sarah and Zhanna, then gave a sweeping look to the rest of the group, and finally settled on Viktor. "You get that chopper going and get everyone to the airport." She swept her look back over the rest of them. "Whatever your motivations for being here, for fighting this fight, whether it be personal, or for the love of country, revel in that motivation now. Let it fill you up as it has filled Xander. Let it bring out the best in all of your abilities, because we are going to need every ounce of it tonight. We are either leaving Moscow with our mission accomplished . . ." Sam turned her head, eyes focused solely on Xander's now. "Or we will die trying."

The last of her words echoed in the open foyer. The weight of her statement settled over them like a lead vest before an X-ray. They all looked around the room, not sure who should speak next or what should be said. Except for Viktor, he apparently wasn't so good with awkward silence.

"Oh, Viktor like her. She is badass bitch, boss. Don't know about rest of you, but Viktor is ready to kick fat Russian dick in!"

It didn't take long for everyone else to make up their minds. Jack spoke up first. "Fuck it, I'm in."

"I know a thing or two about helicopters," said Bob.

"Brother, you know I'm down," Kyle joined.

Zhanna stepped forward. "This ends tonight."

Everyone had spoken but Sarah. All eyes turned to her. She finished typing on her phone and walked up to Xander.

"Make sure you save some for us." Sarah handed him her phone, the GPS route to the airport already plugged in.

Xander's rage faltered momentarily; their selflessness overwhelmed him.

Jack came forward and handed Xander two pistols, and Sam a pistol and an AK-47. "Found these on the way downstairs. Fully loaded. Might come in handy."

They took the weapons from Jack, and as Xander tucked his away, Sarah took his face in her hands and gave him a long, meaningful look.

"Sam isn't the only one that has your back."

Then she kissed him.

Xander didn't need that kiss to know that Sarah meant what she said. She had proven herself through her actions far more than once in the short time he'd known her. She was a lot like him. She *understood* him.

She was also a *really* good kisser.

Sarah pulled away after running her hand through Xander's hair.

Sam checked the magazine on the AK-47, satisfied herself that it indeed was full, and snapped it back into place.

"Time to go and do what we all came here to do."

Life Is a Highway

Ten minutes later, Xander twisted back the accelerator with his right hand, pulling up the nose of the Yamaha R1 and sped down MKAD, the outer loop highway that ran around Moscow, toward Domodedovo Airport. It was dark now, and Xander easily weaved in and out of the small amount of traffic that rolled along the highway. The accelerometer registered 143 miles per hour. A metaphor for the last couple of weeks, he thought. Life in the fast lane. A life Xander supposed he had chosen when he was just a teenager. A teenager who had just lost both of his parents.

So he'd thought.

His life had been a whirlwind of violence and chaos since that day. And until today, he had directed his anger at an unknown bad guy. A mythical figure with fangs and talons. A murderous stranger who, seemingly without reason, took his parents from him and his sister. But there was no evil man with horns. No, the evil mythical creature that Xander had conjured all these years was nothing more than his very own father. All that Xander had put himself through over the last decade was because of him. The things, good or bad, that made Xander who he is today.

A trained killer.

A smattering of red taillights sporadically danced back and forth in front of him on the otherwise dark highway. What was he doing? Why was he still so hell-bent on pursuing this now that he knew the road ended at his father's feet? Could he really kill his own father?

A rolling chill prickled down Xander's spine. His lungs were on fire and he wasn't even exerting himself. He sat up on the bike and backed off of the throttle. The motorcycle groaned as its rpm wound their way down. He lifted the clear shield on his helmet to let some cold but much needed fresh air in, then downshifted and steered to the far right lane, slowing to around forty-five miles per hour.

Sam squeezed his waist, and over the wind rushing past them and the hum of the motorcycle, she shouted to him, "Xander, are you all right?"

Xander continued to steer and hold the throttle steady as he turned on the motorcycle as much as he could to face her.

"Xander?" Sam leaned around to meet his eyes.

Shifting his head back and forth between her and the road in front of him, he spoke with an uneven voice. "Sam, what are we doing?"

"Pull over."

Ignoring her request, he continued riding along in the right hand lane. "Shouldn't I just let this go? It's my father?"

Sam was quiet for a moment, deciding between what should be done and what must be done.

"Sam?" he shouted back to her.

She once again raised her voice over the noise of the road. "If you don't see this through, will you ever have peace?"

"Will I ever have peace if I do?"

It was a good question but one Sam was ready for. From the moment this entire crusade for vengeance had begun, Sam's biggest worry wasn't if Xander would achieve revenge. Her concern was that Xander would always be left hollow after he finally did.

She shouted, "Honestly? I don't know. But I do know that if you don't have a chat with your father about it, no matter what closure that chat may or may not yield, you will always wonder. I'm not saying you shouldn't kill the man, I'm not saying you should. What I am saying is that you must confront him, or the questions of why he did what he did to your mother—your entire family—will never let you rest."

Xander turned his body back toward the road. Sam let him be. She knew he was trying to process. A moment later he turned back to her.

"What would you do?"

Sam now had a decision to make. She never had much of a relationship with her family, even before they were all dead. The decision was easy for her. She thought for a moment, trying to put herself in Xander's shoes. She pictured the scene that Xander had so vividly described when he witnessed his beloved mother gunned down in front of him. In her mind she could see Xander's young face, staring at the blood that leaked out of his poor mother's back. Xander glanced back at her, the question in his eyes. Then, she swallowed hard and answered Xander as she always had, holding nothing back.

"I'd kill the motherfucker."

Xander didn't answer. He didn't need to. He slammed his windshield closed on his helmet, leaned forward, and spiked the throttle. The motorcycle leapt forward, and in a matter of seconds they were doing 150 miles an hour, a blur in the night. They were speeding toward Vitalii Dragov, Martin King, and a large group of Russia's most notorious mafia thugs.

Xander had agreed with Sam.

Slow Motion, Art, and a Fireworks Display

Xander and Sam were like a lightning bolt as they took the off-ramp from the MKAD and continued onto A-105. They were only minutes from the airport now. For what it was worth, they hadn't seen a plane's lights fill up the night's sky. Maybe they would make it in time. Maybe Dragov and Xander's father never really planned on leaving. They could very well be riding right into a trap. It only took twenty-four seconds on A-105 before it was apparent that the trap notion was at least partially true as a blacked-out Cadillac Escalade EXT swerved over in front of Sam and Xander's surging rocket.

Xander tapped down on the front and back brakes at the same time, applying even pressure so as not to go into a stoppie, where the bike's back end pitched upward and they rode solely on the front tire. The applying of that even pressure, however, still didn't keep the back end from sliding out to the left on him as they skidded. The sound of the tires screeching against pavement and the roar of the SUV's engine filled the air around them. Xander was ready for this sideways skid as well, and like moving his hands on a guitar to play the perfect note, he played the brakes in harmony to straighten the motorcycle and maintain their balance. It was the second Escalade that dropped back on their right side with a gun out the window that threatened the key of the dangerous tune he was playing. But this wasn't Sam's first rodeo on the back of a motorcycle with Xander. Four years ago they had found themselves in Rome in a similar situation.

Just as normal friends would.

Sam had already pulled the AK-47, and just as Xander hit the throttle and swerved to roar past the left side of the Caddy in front of them, she squeezed off a short burst of three bullets, the second of which punched right through the hand of the man holding the gun. It was a good thing too because this was a well-coordinated attack. A third Escalade—Russians aren't known for their creativity—swerved into the lane in front of them, and Xander was forced once again to lay on the brakes, sending them back into what would have been the line of fire. Thanks to Sam, a bloody hand was all that greeted them. Until, of course, the tailgate lifted on the Escalade in the middle. The three Escalades pulled even in front of them, closing off all three lanes of the highway. Xander checked his left rearview mirror and, no surprise to him, three more Escalades took up the lanes behind them.

At least one of those was white.

They were in a bad spot. The other two tailgates rose on the Escalades in front of them, and they were now staring down the barrels of three semiautomatic assault rifles. The interior of the truck's lights illuminated the three men behind the guns. All three were dressed in all black, down to their matching ski masks. Beyond the trucks in front of them they could see the lights of the airport reaching up into the black sky.

So close, yet so far away.

Xander had no choice but to act fast; his only hope was that Sam would be ready. From the center of the middle lane, Xander drifted to his left, until he was perfectly aligned with the white dotted line that separated the lanes. Xander found that as with most moments of surged adrenaline, everything around him, including his breathing, slowed to a crawl. His senses heightened. He could smell the burnt rubber, the gasoline fumes from the Escalade's massive engines, and he swore he even saw Sam nod in the side mirror, as if to say, *we are in this slow-motion world together.* And just like that, the slow motion ended as he squeezed the hand brake on the right handle bar, clamping the brakes down on the front tire. As the back end of the bike came up, Sam had a clear line of sight, and as she gripped the back of Xander's T-shirt with her left hand, she sprayed the AK from left to right, dropping every single one of the three men holding guns in front of them. Because he'd hit the brakes, the three Escalades behind them roared past and there couldn't have been more than two inches on either side of the motorcycle as they did. Xander moving onto the dotted line so they wouldn't hit the bike when he suddenly hit the brakes was a stroke of genius. Just as soon as the Escalades flew by, Xander let go of the front brake, and the back tire slammed down as he simultaneously pulled his pistol with his left hand and shot out the back tire of the Caddy on the left, sending it careening off the road, leaving a space for him to pull away.

But just as he gave the bike gas, swerved around the back two Escalades, and then swerved back to go in between the left two Escalades in front of him, the drivers swerved together, cutting him off. He immediately steered left to go around on the strip they had left when they came together in front of him, but the driver quickly cut him off by swerving to his left.

They were still trapped.

The sides of the road would be too risky. They were all gravel, and if you've never been on a motorcycle, gravel and motorcycles don't mix. But as two more men began to steady their guns on them from the backseats of the two Escalades in front of them, he was left with no other choice. Sensing that this was the only option, Sam squeezed both arms around Xander. Just as the men fired their guns, Xander swerved wildly to the left, avoiding the bullets, and plunging into the gravel. At first, when he turned back to the right, paralleling them to the road, the back end searched for grip in the loose rocks as it slid wildly out to the left. To keep from toppling over sideways, Xander was forced to jerk the steering column back to the left, entering into a deadly game of one-hundred-mile-per-hour motorbike balance.

Sam had the wherewithal to leave the steering worry to Xander, and if she hadn't, they would have been dead. As Xander desperately fought to regain control of the death machine, Sam became one herself. She brought the AK up to shoulder height and held the trigger down for as long as it would shoot. The bullets arched left, right, up, and down as they followed the tilt and lean of the wobbling motorcycle. The result was like one of those artists—if you can call them artists—who fling paint all over a canvas by swinging a brush wildly through the air. The result, a come-what-may smattering of paint wherever it might fall. Sam's bullets painted the Escalade in much the same way. They sprayed up, down, left and right, taking out the man holding his gun through the rear window. The blood from his forehead was a masterpiece of its own. And just as Xander decided that gunning the throttle would finally straighten out the motorcycle, the last bullet in the AK-47's magazine found its way to the cheekbone of the driver in the SUV. The motorcycle surged forward, up onto the smooth blacktop now, and Xander heard what Sam was able to turn and see. The dead man in the driver's seat fell forward onto the right side of the steering wheel and turned the Escalade right in front of the other two SUVs. In a spectacular crash, the Escalade flipped up in the air, and the sound of the twisted metal, like a tornado demolishing an aluminum barn, reached all the way to the motorcycle. Tires scorched the blacktop and the rest of the SUVs came together in an automobile fireworks display, worthy of the greatest of Fourth of July celebrations. It all ended in a fiery blast—the grand finale—and Xander leaned forward as he spiked the throttle and the bike sped away toward the airport.

Let's Make a Deal

The engine of the motorcycle wound down as Xander slowed, pulling into the eerily quiet parking lot. That didn't lower Xander's heightened senses. He and Sam were well aware that all eyes were on them. If Vitalii Dragov and Martin King were smart, they would level them with an RPG missile right now. So far, no screaming missiles were headed their way, and just an empty parking lot that overlooked three private aircraft hangars loomed in front of them. Xander pulled the bike into the first parking space inside the lot, behind a van, which just so happened to be the lone vehicle there. It provided at least a small amount of cover. They were around a hundred yards from the nearest hangar.

Xander waited for Sam to get off from behind him before he peeled himself off the bike. As he stood, his legs maintained a comically bowlegged frame. Sam couldn't help herself.

"Okay, cowboy." She nodded toward his still separated legs. "What now?"

Xander looked down and couldn't help but smile as he removed his helmet. A streetlight shined down over them, almost in a spotlight.

"Nice moves back there, Samantha."

"We make a hell of a team."

"No sign of the helicopter full of our cavalry yet. It looks like we're on our own."

"Wouldn't have it any other way." As Sam removed her helmet, her dark hair fell around her face and her smile curled into a confident smirk.

"What now?" Xander asked.

Before Sam could answer, they heard a cell phone ring. They both looked around like it would be on some invisible man standing beside them; then Xander felt a buzz in his pants. Sarah's phone. He pulled the phone from his pocket; the number was blocked. Xander answered without speaking, placing the call on speakerphone.

"Xander, turn the motorcycle around and get the hell out of here now. I don't want you to end up like your mother."

Hearing his father's voice on the other end of the cell phone did a lot of things to Xander all at once. The first feeling was a pang of nostalgia, remembering the goofy sayings and all the lessons that voice had taught him. The second feeling was disbelief, that after all these years of supposedly being dead, it could actually be him. If Xander hadn't heard Sarah tell him about Manning flipping on his dad, and if he hadn't seen him

259

with his own eyes just a bit ago, he would have believed that someone was playing a sick and twisted joke on him. The third feeling, the feeling that stomped on the other two feelings, was one of sheer, unadulterated, blood-boiling, skin-roasting anger.

"Fuck you. Come out here like a man and talk about it."

"Aah, I see we are very much alike, you and I, son."

"You and I are nothing alike."

"So, you think because you were a Navy SEAL, Black Ops, and all those other meaningless titles that you are better than your old man, huh? You have no idea what I've been through in my life."

"You're right, I don't even know who the fuck you are. But step out into this parking lot and you'll find out exactly who I am and what I'm made of."

Sam swore she could see steam wafting into the cool air off Xander's head. Then she realized she actually could; it was from him being in that motorcycle helmet for so long. She wanted to help, but there was nothing for her to say. This is the moment that her partner—her friend—had been waiting for since he was just a teenager. All she could do was be there for him in the aftermath. If either of them were around for the aftermath.

"Xander, I've lived a long and mostly brutal life. That hardens a man. Thickens his skin in a way that you couldn't imagine. You think I would be afraid of you? I'm not saying I'm not proud of you, son, 'cause you are a hell of a soldier. But your tools have yet to be sharpened enough to take a man like me."

"Try me."

The man on the other end of the phone was no longer his father in Xander's mind. He was now only known as the man

260

who killed his mother, the man who stole the last decade of Xander's life, and Xander didn't want to bear that burden any longer. No matter what that meant.

"I'll tell you what, son, you leave your weapons where you stand, walk into that middle hangar there in front of you with your pretty *unarmed* girlfriend, and I'll make you a deal."

"I'm listening."

"I'll let you have your shot at me. I know more about fighting than you will ever learn, but *if* you win, I'll instruct everyone here that you will be free to go. You and your girlfriend there and the rest of your friends that I captured so easily earlier today."

"And if you win?"

"They're all dead. Everyone but you."

"What happens to me?"

"You come to work for me. I think we'd make a pretty damn good team. You and I together could run the whole damn world."

Xander looked up at Sam.

"Xander, you know it's a trap. We both know you can't win. Even if you win, you lose. He will never let you go."

Xander didn't respond. He removed both pistols from the back of the waistline of his pants and tossed them on the ground.

"Sam stays out here and you've got a deal."

"Deal," Martin King said without hesitation.

Xander ended the call.

"Xander, you can't—"

Xander interrupted, "I have put you and Kyle in danger far too many times already during my search for revenge. I won't do it anymore. This ends now, and it ends with me. If you are truly my friend, Sam, you will get on that motorcycle and get the hell out of here. Get on your phone and tell everyone else the same thing."

"Xander, I can't leave. I won't leave."

She spoke those last words to Xander's back. He had already started the short walk toward the end of his long journey. And this time, for the first time, Sam didn't follow.

Vanquish

A small glass door in the middle of the massive white airplane hangar had been propped open, awaiting his arrival. Xander knew that Sam was probably right. There was no way they were going to let him out of there alive, win or lose. But just because someone doesn't let you do something doesn't mean you can't do it. Stupid of him to think this way, but he knew Sam wouldn't leave. He knew she wouldn't be calling Kyle and the helicopter full of his allies, telling them to turn back. All he could hope for is that they could bail him out one last time after he put an end to this chapter of his life. He would have plenty of time to make it up to them later. And if he didn't make it, he had left enough of his fortune to Kyle and Sam to be able to take care of everyone without him. Come what may, this would be the end of his lifelong quest.

Xander walked through the open glass door and into what was an empty office. More like a reception area. Generic gray carpet covered the floors, the walls all painted white, and pictures of different types of aircrafts, old and new, sporadically filled the voids. The only person in there with him was at the far end of the room; it was Melanie—or Melania. Just one of the many painful betrayals of the last couple of days. She wore a sarcastic smile and opened a door for him. The door that led to the area where all the planes were stored. The area where he would finally face his demons.

Well . . . demon.

He wasn't exactly sure what awaited him in the next room. His father made it seem as though he wanted to actually fight Xander to put an end to this. Something Xander found absolutely absurd. The only chance the old man had at beating Xander would be to shoot him as he was unarmed. And maybe that was the plan. Maybe all he wanted to do was get Xander unarmed so he could show the people who worked for him just how ruthless he could be. Mercilessly gunning down his own son, proving that no one could cross him and live to tell about it. Or maybe the son of a bitch was crazy and thought he could *actually* take Xander in a fight. One could only be so lucky.

Xander walked through the door, not giving Melania a second look. Once through, the ceiling vaulted to over forty feet. Massive florescent light fixtures hung down in rows, illuminating a wide-open space that could fit at least six or seven of Xander's G650-sized aircrafts inside it. As it were, there was one such plane—not his—on the far left end of the hangar; the rest was empty except for a circle of rare collectible cars that had been parked in the middle. In the center of the circle of cars—old Mustangs, Lamborghinis, Rolls-Royces, and such—was an open circle about the size of a UFC Octagon. Seems that Martin King has a flare for the dramatic. All around the cars were what looked like extras from the set of the movie

The Expendables. Half of the Russian thugs were even wearing those stupid beret hats. All of them in their militant-style combat clothing, all of them armed.

Xander was screwed.

In the middle of the circle and the cars, surrounded by the ridiculous-looking spectators, stood a man about the same height as Xander, in a navy-blue suit, who had white hair and a white beard. As the goons parted and Xander entered the ring-sized circle, he could see that his father's face was tan and leathery. He must not spend much time in Russia. He had already removed his suit jacket and rolled the sleeves of his white button-down shirt up to his elbows, two buttons undone at the top. The air in the hangar stank of jet fuel and arrogance; the warmth in it enabled the foul body odor around him to linger as well. Leaning against the hood of a black vintage Porsche 911 Turbo, sinking the nose of it almost all the way to the floor, was a fat, ugly son of a bitch with a pockmarked face and terribly dyed black hair, sucking on a cigar. Elvis, if he'd survived and ate pierogies six times a day for the last thirty-nine years.

Dragov.

Amazingly, with danger all around him, his father, once thought dead, and the looming threat of death possibly just moments away, Xander found himself completely calm. He was ready for this. He stopped twenty feet from his father and just looked him solemnly in the eye. Xander's face held no emotion. Mostly because he felt nothing. The time for all of that had passed.

"You look good, son."

Xander didn't speak, his face still void of emotion. Over his father's broad shoulders, through the open hangar door, the sun was just beginning its trek across the sky. It cast a light shadow over his father's face, hooding his eyes, making him seem even more sinister than his deep and gravelly voice could manage alone.

"I must admit, you've got balls. Maybe not so heavy in the brain department, but you've got balls."

Xander stood stoic.

"You've got nothing to say to your old man after all this time?"

Xander held his posture, his arms down by his side. "I don't have a father. He died ten years ago. You know, the CIA operative."

Martin King made a face.

"You've been talking to Jack, I see. He also tell you he slept with your mother?"

"He did. He also told me you were about to take down that fat son of a bitch." Xander pointed at Dragov.

"It's true, I was."

"Let me guess, he made you an offer you couldn't refuse?"

"Xander, one last lesson if I may. Life is all about change, that's the only constant really. Now, it's not the change that makes a man, it's how he adapts to it. I adapted to change when I saw the opportunity. I want to watch you put that into practice, right now. You think you can do that?"

Xander just glared into his eyes.

"I know you're used to doing things your own way, I was too. Now, I'm not telling you it will be easy, but I think if you and I came together, we could make a lot of money. We could run shit, me and you. Maybe even change the world."

"And what would that world look like exactly?" Xander placated him.

"That's the beauty of it. It would look like whatever the hell we want. With what Dragov and I have built here, and with your connections and reputation in the US, we could do some great things."

"So, that would be the team? The World Dominators starting lineup would be you, me, and Dom Deluise over there? No thanks."

"I don't understand you, boy. You left the military 'cause they were doing things you didn't agree with, right? So what's the problem? We do things much differently here."

"Two wrongs don't make a right."

"You think you know it all, don't you?"

Xander kept a calm voice. "I know that you are a liar, a traitor, and you could really use a new tailor."

"I am not a traitor!" His father slammed his fist down on the hood of the Lamborghini behind him, losing his cool for the first time. The men around him shifted their guns to Xander. Martin King held up his hand, gesturing for them to stand down. What a sweetheart.

"No reason to take out your frustrations on such an innocent Italian classic," Xander prodded.

His father took a few steps toward him. "Would you rather I take them out on you?"

"You see me running?" Xander held stance. He hoped that no one could see his heart pounding in his chest. His muscles were begging him to do what he does best. His instincts screamed at him to end it, and end it quick. But Xander had to hold his cool while his father goaded him, giving him time to scan the hangar, piecing together a plan to escape after this— whatever *this* ended up being—was over. There was nothing jumping out at him at the moment. He had to remain calm. Suppress the dragon.

"No, I don't see you running. You may not be the sharpest tool in the shed, but at least you aren't a coward."

"See, I told you, you and I are nothing alike."

"You think I'm a coward? You think a coward could build what I've built here?"

"No, I think a coward murders an innocent woman and leaves his children all alone."

Martin King took a couple more steps forward. He was within arm's length now. His face morphed from a scowl to an arrogant smirk. "Boo-fucking-hoo."

Xander held his judging gaze.

"Never thought you'd turn out to be a fucking baby. I knew your mommy coddled you too much when you were a kid."

Xander's body temperature shot up several degrees with the mention of his mother coming from his father's—her murderer's—lips. He called her mommy.

"What's wrong, you gonna cry?"

Then he shoved Xander. Xander's expression didn't falter. He swallowed his rage and stepped back where he was, never losing his father's stare. He couldn't react. Not until he—

It was then that he noticed, off in the distance, through the open door of the hangar, almost like a boat a mile off the coast in the ocean, what looked like a helicopter. Xander blinked for the first time, making sure he wasn't seeing things.

"Awe, poor baby boy doesn't like being pushed around?"

His father pushed him again, a little more force this time. Xander was moved back a couple of feet; he shuffled his legs to maintain his balance. He looked back toward his father's eyes, but his focus was over his shoulder, where it was now clear that it indeed was a helicopter. They were coming to get him. A wave of emotion came over him as he thought of his friends risking their lives for him. A wave of emotion that was abruptly cut off.

"Your mommy didn't like when I pushed her around either."

His last thought about the helicopter, before Xander's eyes glazed over with rage at his father's statement, was that everyone else would notice the helicopter at any moment. It was almost time to make his move.

Thirty seconds.

His internal clock started ticking.

"She definitely didn't like these—"

Martin King brought his left arm up and jabbed at Xander's face. But Xander's face moved in a fluid motion to dodge it, and it moved in the same fluid motion back to the other side to dodge his father's oncoming right hand, and did the same to dodge the left hook that followed.

"Zero for three, old man." Xander had channeled his rage into pure, laser-like focus.

Twenty seconds.

Martin threw three more punches, which Xander easily parried, then with his forearm blocked a head kick that quickly followed. The old man had speed for his age, but it might as well have been slow motion for Xander.

Xander couldn't help but smile.

"Zero for six. That must be hard on the ego."

His father's face turned from aggression to frustrated rage.

Ten seconds.

The helicopter was within earshot now. If everyone wasn't so entirely enthralled with seeing Martin King—their fearless leader—looking like a fool, they would have already heard it. They also would have seen Samantha Harrison poke her head around the corner of the open hangar door. Martin took a couple more swipes at Xander, missing wildly. Then, in a last-ditch and spineless effort, he attempted to kick Xander in the pills. Xander caught his father's shoe, lifted, and pushed forward all in the same short, powerful burst, and sent his father flying several feet backward, landing with a thud on his ass. His overly tanned face flashed red, all the way down his neck. First in embarrassment, then in rage.

Three.

Sam had managed to duck inside the hangar and hit the button that lowers the massive, tri-folding vertical door. It lurched, making an awful cranking noise, and as it began to lower toward the concrete below, everyone's attention was instantly divided.

Two.

Xander's father looked back from seeing Sam rush out the doorway, his eyes burning into Xander's.

"Looks like your girlfriend is as dumb as your mommy was, just doesn't know when to leave. She'll be dead just like her too."

One.

Xander stalked toward his father. Toward his mother's murderer. Toward the man who had been trying to kill his own son. All he could see was red. Martin King rose to his feet. Frozen in shock that Xander was finally coming for him. Outside the hangar door, which was now only a few feet from being shut, Sam let off a few rounds from her AK-47, and it drew exactly the attention she was hoping for. Everyone in the hangar looked out toward the gunfire in surprise.

270

Everyone but Xander and his father.

Xander turned his stalk into two short bursts and leapt into the air, in what looked like the technique of a superman punch. But Xander, in midair—when his father had assumed he was pulling his arm back for a punch—instead had unsheathed his knife. As he carried it forward, backed with the power of over ten years of built-up rage, he plunged its six-inch serrated blade straight into the right side of his father's neck.

Cut and Run

Before the blood had a chance to shoot from the hole in his father's neck, and long before his lifeless body hit the ground, Xander was gone. As soon as Xander's feet hit the concrete, he went into a hurricane-like spin and stabbed Vitalii Dragov in the left side of his fat neck. Blood spewed from Dragov's open jugular like an open fire hydrant. But Xander didn't stick around to see that either. He had already taken two steps onto the vintage Lamborghini's hood, long-jumped over the back end, and was halfway to the hangar door. The hangar door, which was just a little over a foot from being completely closed. Sam hadn't expected Xander to carry out the two assassinations before he bolted for the door when she went to shut it. In hindsight, she should've known. Otherwise, she would have never hit the close button. Now she was frantically waving her arm like a third base coach waving a runner home, as he raced for the closing door. The speed with which Xander was able to kill both his father and Dragov was so astonishing, so blindingly fast, that the hired guns hadn't yet recovered. But as Xander reached max speed and the door rolled relentlessly toward the floor, he knew their reaction was coming.

A clamorous orchestra of bullets rang out just as Xander slid feetfirst for the bottom of the door. As he slid underneath it, it was so close that his nose grazed the bottom of the gate as his head made it through. As the smooth, poured concrete floor of the hangar floor turned to the blacktop of the tarmac, tiny rocks and uneven pavement burned a rash up his back at the last of his slide. Like a symphony of firecrackers, the bullets that were meant for him smacked against the now closed metal door, a literal hair behind his head. The first thing he saw from his back was a helicopter hovering above him. Kyle, Sarah, and Zhanna were already on their way down a rope ladder, and he could see a cowboy hat peeking up behind the chain gun above them.

Jack.

It was a comical sight. Even in that moment of battle. It was like a terrible version of *The A-Team*. The B-Team, if you will. Sam reached down and lifted Xander to his feet.

"You're bloody crazy, Xander King," she shouted over the deafening thwap of the helicopter's rotors as she handed him the pistols he'd left behind in the parking lot just moments before.

Just then Kyle came running over and threw his arms around Xander. "You made it! Let's get out of here, Bob spotted your G6 over there." Kyle pointed to the beautiful bird just as Sarah caught up and wrapped her arms around him. A hug had never felt so good. The plane was sitting off to the right of the hangar, about a football field and a half away. The sight of the silver crown on the tail of that plane sparked a pang of longing in Xander's core. He was beyond ready to be done with this chapter of his life. And it was right here, in his grasp.

They turned toward the jet together. Zhanna and Bob were in front of them, halfway to the plane.

Sam shouted at Kyle, "Why wouldn't you answer your phone, damn it?

Kyle looked at Sam, then smiled at Xander and said, "I was busy."

Sam made a face.

Xander pulled Sarah's phone from his pocket, as Kyle showed his phone. Both cell phones were on a call. Sam didn't have to ask; she already knew it was a call to each other.

"You beautiful wankers, that's how you knew not to come in too early!"

"We could hear everything," said Kyle. "We had been circling around for ten minutes!"

Xander's face went from smile to serious. They weren't in the clear yet. "What about Jack?"

Still running, Kyle shouted, "I tried to get him to let me stay behind and cover you. But he insisted. He's gonna man the chain gun until we're clear, then he's going to go back to the Ukraine with Viktor, and wait for you to send a plane. Oh . . . here."

While Kyle was explaining, he had been doing something on his phone. The chain gun began to spit its venom above them, in the direction of the hangar. Jack was already pushing the Russian thugs back. Kyle handed Xander his phone. He had been dialing Jack.

Xander heard the phone ring once. "Cowboy's phone, this is Viktor!"

"Viktor, get that helicopter out of here!" Xander screamed over the rolling thunder of the massive machine gun and the swoop of the helicopter. The four of them were at Xander's jet now, and Bob had already begun firing up the engines.

"Boss? Boss, you made it! Cowboy and Viktor are busy saving your ass, but will call you from Ukraine and tell you where to send big check!"

Xander hustled onto his jet after everyone else was in and shut the plane's door. "Okay Viktor, nice work! I'll make sure the check is delivered by a couple of knockouts, just for you."

"Viktor like knockouts, boss. But Zhanna can deliver, okay? Sorry boss, time to go. Man have rocket launcher." Viktor stated that last line with the casualness of a man watching a movie screen. Crazy bastard.

The call ended. Xander looked out the window, back toward the hangar. Gunmen were crawling out from the side door like bees from a shaken hive. Some were firing at the helicopter, some were being ripped to pieces by Jack Bronson and his chain gun. Xander felt helpless as the jet began to move.

Bob shouted from the cockpit, "Buckle up back there! This could be rough!"

Sam noticed Xander eyeing the release button for the door.

"Xander, step away from that door. You've cheated death enough today. You stepping out that door and firing the last ten bullets in those pistols will do Viktor and Jack no good . . . Xander . . ."

Xander looked at Sam, then back to the door.

Sarah leaned forward and placed her hand on his arm. "Xander, please don't. You'll just be unnecessarily putting us in danger too."

Xander knew she was right. He knew that Viktor and Jack were capable, and he knew there was nothing he could do to help.

For once, he let that be enough.

Peyton Manning's Got Nothing on Xander King

As the jet backed away, Zhanna stepped in between Sarah and Xander, taking Xander's attention with a worried look.

"My father?"

"He's dead."

Her face held no expression. "You're certain?"

"By my hands. I don't leave doubt."

Zhanna nodded. Her face slumped into concern.

"Your father?" she asked.

Kyle stood and looked at Xander, full of worry and concern. The plane jerked and started forward. Xander rebalanced and looked at Kyle.

"Dead."

Unlike Zhanna, Kyle didn't need Xander to reconfirm. He knew it was over. His heart broke for his friend. Never in a thousand lifetimes when they started this journey of searching for the person who killed Xander's parents had either of them ever fathomed it would end this way. Kyle didn't say anything, for he knew words could never suffice. He just wanted to be there for his friend.

"Uh, Xander! We've got company!" Bob shouted from the cockpit.

"Get us out of here, Bob. Let me worry about them."

"Roger!"

The plane lurched forward and the engines screamed. Xander regained his balance, and as if the captain had come over the loud speaker and announced the Grand Canyon could be seen out your right side windows during a flight over Arizona, everyone in the G6 rushed to get a look at what was coming. In the distance, as Xander peered over Sarah's shoulder, the rising sun was shining on a topless Jeep Wrangler, military green, pulling out of the now wide-open hangar door. The fire was still coming from the chain gun in Viktor's helicopter, but Xander knew it couldn't possibly have much ammunition left. It was also distracted by the few soldiers who were left beside the hangar, leaving the Jeep an open run at their plane, free from fire.

"That fucking twat!" Sam shouted from her seat by the window. She was peering out at the oncoming Jeep; somehow she had found a pair of binoculars.

"What?" Kyle asked.

With a stone-cold killer look, Sam looked over to Xander. "Melanie. I never did like that bitch."

She wasn't joking. The two of them never seemed to mesh. Must have been some sort of primordial female instinct Sam had been tapping into.

"I'll kill her!" Sam launched herself from her chair. Kyle caught her.

Xander tried reasoning as the plane began picking up speed, not far from the runway now. "Sam, we can't stop this plane. What are you going to do? Jump out, shoot her, then jump back in? You're starting to act like me."

"I'll run from the plane and leave her a little present." Sam produced a hand grenade from her back belt loop. "A little souvenir I found in a bin outside the hangar."

"Then what, Sam? We go all *Star Trek* and beam you up to the jet? Bob is talented, but he's no Scotty, and this plane is fancy, but it doesn't have the technology of the Starship Enterprise . . . yet."

Sam looked defeated. Xander knew how badly she wanted to end Melanie for turning on them. Xander would just be happy with getting everyone he loved in the air safely. He thought for a moment about how that was very much unlike him. Playing it safe. Had things already begun to change?

The Jeep was gaining on them. Close enough now to where Xander could see Melanie's short black hair blowing in the wind. Two men in the seat behind her.

"Bob?" Xander shouted, glancing back between the window and the cockpit.

"I see them, Xander. Turning onto the runway now. Time to buckle up!"

Everyone heard Bob shout at them to buckle up, but no one listened. They all remained huddled around the windows, nervously watching as the Jeep grew closer. As the jet turned the corner onto the runway, the Jeep took an angle that if timed correctly, they would be within shooting distance around the middle of the runway.

"Bob!" Xander shouted once more.

Bob answered without words. The engines went into full thrust, throwing everyone back into their seats and Xander to the floor.

"We're not gonna make it!" Kyle shouted.

Xander picked himself up off the floor. The plane shot forward like a rock out of a slingshot. As it approached the position of the Jeep, the Jeep turned parallel and drove ahead of them in the strip of grass that separated the tarmac from the runway.

"Xander, why is that man standing—what is that in his hands?"

Xander knew without looking. The last thing Viktor had said before their call ended a minute ago was something about a rocket launcher. Melanie must have picked up the man who was holding it before racing toward the plane.

"Xander! They've got an RPG! I'm gonna have to veer off—"

Xander cut him off. "Just get us in the air, Bob!" Then he turned to Sam. "Grenade."

While everyone else looked at Xander like he was on fire, Sam didn't hesitate. She tossed him the grenade.

"Xander!" Sarah was horrified. Kyle's face crinkled in the way it might if the devil himself were standing in front of him. Zhanna, like Sam, knew what Xander was doing.

Xander rushed past the first row of seats. "Get up!" he screamed at Kyle who was seated, unbeknownst to Kyle next to the emergency exit window. In a split second, Xander had decided on the emergency exit window instead of the door. Once they had taken off, there was a possibility that the hydraulic door would not shut, forcing them to land. Chancing the fact that someone could once again catch up to them. The emergency exit window, however, manually popped inward and could easily be shoved back into place once they were clear of the Jeep and rising to cruising altitude.

If they could get clear of the Jeep.

As Xander pulled the release, just above the window, and the window released slightly toward them, Xander could see the Jeep just on the side in front of the wing. The man in black was hoisting the rocket launcher onto his shoulder. There were a million things that could go wrong here, Xander knew it, and any mistake would end in all of them dying. Whether from the rocket or the very grenade he held in his hand. He also knew that if he didn't throw the grenade, they were certainly dead. The G6 was a big-ass plane. It would take a blind man to miss its back end with a rocket launcher from anywhere inside of fifty feet.

With the grenade dangling from his mouth by the pin held in his teeth, Xander took the now visible handles on the left and right side of the emergency exit window in his hands, jerked it out of place, and handed the removable window and attached panel to Kyle. Wind from the nearly one-hundred-mile-per-hour streak down the runway filled the cabin, and the roar of the engine just outside the open window screamed back at them—so loudly that when Xander pulled the grenade from his mouth, the pin still in his teeth, he couldn't hear Sarah scream in horror as Xander began to cook it off in his right hand. He glanced at Kyle. Kyle stared at the grenade like it was a bullet shot from a gun that had 40,000 knives and an evil witch attached to the end of it.

"Now, Xander!" Sam screamed from behind him.

As if someone had hit the slow-motion button again, seconds to Xander felt like minutes. He was at the count of three in his head. The jet had really picked up speed now, and the nose of the Jeep had disappeared from sight. He could no longer see the man holding the rocket launcher, but he could *feel* the man's finger wrapped around the trigger, getting ready to squeeze. The nose of the jet began to pull upward.

Now or never.

Xander reared back—Peyton Manning at his finest—and started his forward motion. The wingspan on a G6 is ninety-nine feet and seven inches. Subtracting the eight and a half feet for the cabin, each wing was around forty-five feet long. Under normal circumstances, if he gave it all he had, Xander could throw a grenade fifty yards or more.

These were *not* normal circumstances.

The suction of the Rolls-Royce engine, just to the right outside the open window, would be strong enough to suck in just about anything while running at full throttle as it was then. Couple that with the force of the wind blowing back toward it, even a fifty-yard throw might not make it around the engine. The fact that Xander would have to drop down and heave the grenade sidearm to get it out the window would take at least twenty yards off his maximum throw. He had no choice but to try.

With everything inside of him, an animalistic roar from his lungs, the tendons and muscles in his arm and shoulder bending to their furthest reach, Xander brought his arm forward and released the grenade, sending it through the window at fastball speed, exactly two seconds before Xander expected it to explode. Slow motion turned to fast-forward, and in one second the grenade skipped off the wing of the plane, out of suction range of the engine—*YES!*—and dropped quickly out of sight— *YES!*—less than one second later they heard an explosion, just as the back wheels of the plane lifted off the ground.

"YES!" Kyle shouted, hands raised, from the seat in front of Xander. "Yes! Yes! Yes! Yes!"

"Yes?" Sarah screamed in the form of a question as she white-knuckle-clutched the seat underneath her. Then she shouted, "Yes!" as the elated look on Zhanna's face said they were clear. Not to mention the obvious fact that their plane hadn't been blown to smithereens.

Two seconds later, as they all roared cheers of "we're alive!" excitement, they heard an explosion in the distance, off the left side of the plane. Surprised, they looked at each other for a split second, then rushed over and looked down out of the rear windows to see an explosion cloud of black smoke pluming toward the sky in the middle of an empty field. Jack would later explain to them just how close the rocket the man fired had come to clipping the rear end of the plane, and how the exploding grenade that Xander had thrown moved the line of fire just enough at the very last moment. He would go on to say that he and Viktor's view from the helicopter as they were pulling away was quite spectacular. "Down right amazin'," to quote him exactly. He also would mention that Viktor shouted Xander King's praises for the entire excruciating four-hour helicopter ride back to Ukraine.

While watching the black smoke fill the air for a few moments, they all let the fact that they had just completely cheated death wash over them. And as everyone hugged each other with the hugs that only survivors of a near-death experience could enjoy, Xander popped the emergency exit window back into place and collapsed into the adjacent white leather chair.

He didn't so much as fidget for well over six hours.

Cheers

Six hours later, it wasn't the rustling of movement around him, it wasn't the hum of the G6's engines, and it wasn't even turbulence that finally woke Xander. Instead, it was the sweetest scent in the entire world that roused him from the depths of exhaustion.

Pizza.

It took him a couple of attempts at opening his eyes before his lids lifted, and when they did, his stomach screamed and his mouth watered when he saw a mini pizza, a can of Coke—condensation still sliding down its side—and of course a magnificently beautiful bottle of his very own King's Ransom bourbon. He hadn't thought about food in a while, what with all the *little* distractions of the past two days, but now it was apparent that he had never been hungrier in his entire life. He glanced to his right, and the cabin of his plane was filled with the people whom he cared for most in the world. Short of his family, these people here were pretty much it for him. Sam glanced over and noticed Xander waking.

"Cheers, old boy, I thought you might fancy a little sustenance. I would have made you something else besides pizza, but I'm not sure you actually like anything else. Not to mention, the only thing you stock the freezer with is, well, pizza." She gave him a warm smile.

Xander ran his hands up and down his face and smiled back.

Before Xander could answer, Kyle popped his head over the back of Xander's chair, mussed Xander's hair, and handed him a Red Bull.

"Now it's the perfect meal." Kyle smiled.

Xander's heart was full in that moment. Sarah walked up and took a seat beside him. Her smile was as bright as a flash photograph in the darkest of caves.

"Dig in, sleepy head." She rubbed the back of his hand. "I managed to patch up your leg while you were sleeping. The bullet must have just grazed you, but it opened up the fresh scar tissue from the bullet you took on the yacht. That's why there was so much blood.

Xander glanced down at his bandaged leg, gave it a reassuring wiggle, and picked up his plate.

"Thanks. Wow, I was really out." He acknowledged everyone as he pulled the first slice from the individual sized pie. Even though it was just a frozen pizza, the first bite may as well have been the greatest bite he'd ever taken. They say your taste buds are muted at high altitude. In that moment, Xander couldn't find an ounce of truth in that statement. He knew the weight of what happened in Russia with his father would settle over him soon, but until it did, he was going to do his very best to enjoy what was in front of him.

"You guys get any sleep?" Xander asked with a mouthful of sauce, crust, and cheese. Sarah poured him a drink, and everyone gathered around him with a drink of their own.

Sarah answered, "We all dozed off for a bit. I think it was the showers that really helped us feel better."

"Shit, I bet I smell like a subway tunnel." Xander laughed as he wiped his mouth.

Kyle raised his glass, and Zhanna, Sarah, and Sam did the same.

"To Xander. Best friend," he said as he gestured from himself to Sam. "New friend," as he nodded toward Zhanna. "And lover friend," as he nodded toward Sarah. Sarah turned the shade of a fire truck and smiled the smile of a thirteen-year-old girl who just got passed a love note from her crush. Xander couldn't help but smile back at her beautiful aura. Kyle continued, "I know the last couple of weeks—hell, the last ten years—have been tough, but I just want you to know that we are here. Whatever comes next for any of us, we always know that you have our backs, and we just want you to know that it has meant the world to us to have your back too. We love you and we are excited to take the next steps of this crazy life together. Cheers, brother."

Kyle clinked Xander's glass, and everyone else followed suit, agreeing wholeheartedly with Kyle's words.

"Thanks, Kyle." Xander took a sip of his King's Ransom bourbon and Coke. The sweet mixture tickled his mouth and brought saliva to his jowls. "I can't thank all of you enough. I'm sorry that I made my personal vendetta everyone else's problem, but my life will forever be better because of your help.

Zhanna," he said, taking her eyes with his, "we don't know each other very well yet, but I thank you for getting me inside your father's compound so that we could do what we both set out to do. And I hope we can get to know each other better soon."

She gave him a nod. "I do as well, Xander. Believe me, it meant as much to me as it did you, what happened back there. Thank you."

Xander nodded, then looked at Sarah. "Sarah, you came out of nowhere. Next to Sam, you are just about the baddest woman I've ever met. The way you handle yourself in the heat of things is truly inspiring. Not to mention how miserably gorgeous you are." He winked.

"Me?" Sarah smiled at him. "Xander, I don't think there is a woman alive that has looked into those baby blues and ever been the same."

Xander really wanted to end the toast right then and take her to the bathroom to shower with him, but he forged ahead, taking his eyes from hers and moving them to Sam.

"Sammy." Xander's voice faltered a bit. "You continue to amaze me. There isn't another partner in crime I'd rather have. In battle and in life."

"Cheers, mate."

Samantha Harrison, the sentimental.

Xander smiled and moved on.

"Kyle, no words brother. I love you."

"Love you too, X."

Xander set his drink on the table in front of him and grabbed another slice of pizza.

"Let's all just enjoy the rest of this ride back to Kentucky, get a good night's sleep tonight, and after a massive breakfast, I say we plan a celebration worthy of royalty for tomorrow night. That sound okay with everyone?

Everyone was indeed okay with that plan. It was hard not to be.

Eight hours later they landed at the Bluegrass Airport in Lexington, Kentucky. A fleet of drivers chauffeured them to Xander's horse farm, and everyone settled into their beds. Xander had gotten a call on the flight from Marv, letting him know that he and Mary Hartsfield had made it safely back to Langley. He also informed Xander that Jack had checked in and they were safe in the Ukraine. He said Jack mentioned that Xander owed him big-time—not because of his help with the mission, but for having to stay the night in the company of "that crazy bastard" Viktor.

All in all it was a successful mission. No one who wasn't supposed to die ended up dying. That is always a success.

Xander told Kyle good night and led Sarah by the hand, down the hall to his bedroom.

"I can sleep in the other room if you need some time to yourself, Xander," Sarah whispered as they approached his door. Xander answered by pulling her inside his room, shutting the door behind them, and kissing her on the lips with a hunger saved for only those kisses that you *really* mean.

"You sent the text that night that saved my life here at the house. You knew all of those men were coming for me."

Sarah didn't speak. She just gave him a smile that turned every gear in his libido.

Words were spoken after that, not in conversation but in the throes of passion. They made love for hours. Her skin became his skin, intertwined in the timeless dance that lovers dance. Their minds above the clouds as their bodies became as one. A connection that enveloped the two of them so completely that neither one of them would ever be the same.

All-encompassing.

Sarah Gilbright had managed to steal Xander's heart somewhere along the way.

And Xander didn't mind, not one little bit.

King's Ransom

After Sarah and Xander finally collapsed in exhaustion, an hour passed and Xander was still staring up at the same strip of moonlight that streaked along the ceiling over his bed. His body still thrummed with pleasure from the intoxication of Sarah's body. He vibrated in relaxation, but his mind couldn't rest, mostly due to the surprise of how calm and clear everything seemed to him. The moment he had found out it was his father who was responsible for Xander's heartache, he thought for certain that it would haunt him for the rest of his life. He would never have guessed that taking his father's life would have lifted the burden. He would have sworn it would have had the opposite effect. But as he lay there, watching the blades of the ceiling fan twirl overhead, relief and excitement for the future played in his mind. For the first time in a long time, he was truly excited about life. Sure, there had been many moments over the years that he cherished. But no matter how great those were, they were always shrouded in anger and sadness. He had the feeling that he could finally let it all go. His mother's death was no longer the focus of his memory of her. Instead, it had already been replaced with the myriad good times they spent laughing and playing together during his childhood.

Xander put both hands behind his head and smiled. He didn't have a clue what was next, but he was excited. He knew that he wanted to continue to try to make a positive difference in the world. And who knows, now that Mary Hartsfield had taken over for Director Manning, maybe there was room to work together with the government again. Of course, he would make the rules, but it would be nice not to have to worry about doing things illegally. It could work.

Maybe.

His thoughts then drifted to Natalie Rockwell, as they inevitably seemed to do since she barged into his life. His feelings hadn't dampened for her. But something certainly was different now that Sarah was here. As much as his entire being wanted Natalie, he felt just as strongly for Sarah now. As he thought about it, things just made more sense with her too. Natalie could never understand Xander's life the way Sarah could. Xander just wanted Natalie to be happy. If that meant an existence without him bringing unwarranted trouble into her life, then that was the way it should be. He would always have a giant place in his heart for her.

Xander glanced over at Sarah beside him. So delicate. He wondered for a moment if it was the last couple of hours with Sarah that made him think of Natalie this way. He wondered if in the morning it would be Natalie he would think of first.

Sarah rustled beside him.

"Everything okay?" she asked, her voice wrapped in sleep.

Xander leaned over and kissed her forehead.

"I'm going to get some water." He brushed a strand of hair back behind her ear. "Can I get you anything?"

"A kiss."

Xander obliged, then rolled out of bed, pulled on a T-shirt and a pair of cotton pajama shorts, slipped his feet into a pair of slippers, and made his way downstairs. Moonlight poured into the kitchen window. Xander grabbed a bottle of water from the refrigerator and walked over to the window that looked out over the back of his property. In the distance he could see the moonlight sparkling off the top of the weathervane at the top of the stables.

King's Ransom.

He remembered a text that his head trainer, Gary, had sent earlier saying that his favorite racehorse would be leaving the stables early in the morning for Belmont Park in New York to get acclimated for the upcoming race. The finale of the Triple Crown. Xander hadn't seen Ransom in a while. He didn't even get to see him win The Preakness. An excitement came over Xander and he just couldn't wait any longer to pet his equine best friend on the nose. Xander went back to the refrigerator, grabbed a nice juicy red apple, and practically skipped out the back door and out onto the patio. As soon as he opened the door, the warm summer night fell over him like a warm blanket, fresh from the dryer. The smell of pine, grass, and a hint of honeysuckle flooded his senses as he walked down the steps, around the pool, and down the narrow drive toward the stables. The sliver of uncovered moon shed plenty of light on the path, and Xander tossed the apple in his hand as he listened to the vibrating chorus of the cicadas and the intermittent solos of a family of tree frogs. Crickets offered the treble and a couple of bullfrogs supplied the bass. Summer nights in the south were unbeatable.

As he approached the stables, the scents were swapped for hay and horse manure. Not in a bad way, though. Xander tugged on the massive sliding door that opened to the stable and stepped inside. The door on the other side had been left open, not an uncommon thing. It gave the horses some fresh air and kept it from being so stale inside. As he walked along the stalls, his other thoroughbreds-in-training stuck their curious heads out to see who might be visiting at that hour. Xander continued past them toward King's Ransom at the far right-hand corner of the barn. The moonlight was coming in the open door and shining directly on his stall. Xander couldn't see his head yet. You couldn't miss it if it was there. Ransom was a behemoth among giants. Xander figured the old boy was probably lying down for a nap.

The closer Xander got to his stall, the more a strange and foreign scent met his nose. A very metallic scent. Not a common smell at all for the stables, so it really stood out. He couldn't put his finger on what it was. Not until he peered over the stall door and looked down at the ground, then it became horrifyingly clear what the metallic smell was.

Blood.

The sight inside the stall nearly knocked Xander off his feet and the apple fell from his hand as he lost control of his ability to hold on to it. There on the hay-and-dirt-covered ground lay his beloved King's Ransom—his body completely separated from his head. The amount of blood in the stall could have been mistaken for an oil spill. It was everywhere. Xander was having a hard time processing what he was seeing. He opened the door to the stall and stepped inside. Blood pooled around his slippers. Ransom's head sat about a foot from his body, his eyes still open. Frozen in a look of shock. Xander's heart dropped and emotion flooded his being. His throat tightened and his stomach clinched as he dropped to his knees in the gap between body and head. One hand on Ransom's massive, but cold, front quarter, the other rested on his neck, just above the mess of torn muscle and bone. He was so caught off guard that the shock of the moment stole his air.

Xander was so overcome that he just continued to stare down at the lifeless body of his beloved friend. Images of him frolicking in the pasture came over him. The moment when Ransom crossed the finish line at the Kentucky Derby, laying the blanket of roses across his back in the winner's circle, and the day he first saw him at the yearling auction all played across his mind like an old home movie.

And just as soon as it appeared, suddenly it was gone. The beautiful movie playing in his mind's eye disappeared, and it was replaced by the most horrifying thing that Xander had ever seen. He was so distraught over seeing his horse dead on the floor of that stall that until that moment, he hadn't even noticed.

On the wood-planked back wall of the stall, directly in front of him, was something that scared him in a way that he had never been frightened before. In messy print handwriting, written in the blood of his dead racehorse, scrawled out in big bold letters were two simple and bone chilling words . . .

Natalie Rockwell.

Letter from the Author

Dear Reader,

I just wanted to take a moment to thank you for spending a few of your precious hours with my imagination. My only hope is that *Vanquish* was as much fun for you to read as it was for me to write.

Xander is in a real spot right now. And Natalie, as you now know, is in even worse shape. I am currently doing my best to help Xander get her out of trouble. Needless to say, Xander has been too busy to take my calls. You'll find out what happens as soon as I do when I release the third book in the series, *King's Ransom,* at the end of April.

The response to Xander and company has been amazing, and I have been humbled by the kind words that readers continue to share online and via e-mail. As long as you are willing to read, I will continue to write. Thank you again for helping to make my dreams come true.

As always, my favorite thing on earth is interacting with enthusiastic readers, so whether it is about Xander or about landing on the moon, let's have a chat about it. E-mail me any time at info@bradleywrightauthor.com or catch up with me on Facebook.

Thanks again for reading.

All the best,
Bradley Wright

Bradley Wright is the author of the Xander King series. He and his wife spend time in both sunny California and the great state of Kentucky. He does his very best to be charming, witty, and clever. When those attempts inevitably fail, he locks himself in a room and makes up characters who always seem to find him far more interesting than real people do. Funny how that works.

Bradley has been writing since he was a child. He started with songs and poems but finally gave in to writing stories when the voices in his head resorted to shouting. He is inspired by every author he reads, most notably, Stephen King and Carsten Stroud.

For more information visit www.bradleywrightauthor.com.

Cheers!

Made in the USA
Middletown, DE
23 October 2018